# Too Much Trouble

A Gritty Crime Thriller

Matthew Doggett

Five Brothers Publishing

# Contents

For my uncle Matt, who was the first to encourage me to write this story. And the first to read it.
And for my dad, who introduced me to Jack Reacher.

# Get Your Free Book

V ISIT **MATTHEWDOGGETTAUTHOR.COM/TROUBLE** FOR A

**free** action-packed novella featuring the character you're about to come to know and love.

# Prologue

N O ONE REALLY KNEW where the idea came from. It showed up in a briefing report as a footnote. Something to be mentioned if there was time. You could call it the product of institutional thinking. In much the same way that institutions have a memory, they can also, at times, come up with somewhat original ideas.

This particular idea didn't travel the normal idea train. It was sidelined early on. It was taken hostage and forced to zigzag around in the lower and eventually upper echelons of the United States government before landing on an implementer's desk. But not a normal implementer. And not really on his desk so much as in his ear.

As far as a paper trail for this jumble of words comprising a coherent thought, there was none. That trail ended on the first day of its inception—in a paper shredder.

It was mentioned—read off the paper—and then forgotten by almost everyone in the room. It was not uncommon for such an occurrence. It was, in fact, quite common for all types of both terrific and terrible ideas to be given life in the form of discussion in that particular room. Most were seen for what they were and quickly forgotten. This one, however, slept in hibernation for the better part of a year, in the back of a young man's mind.

Like most half-formed ideas, it wasn't much to look at. It took this young man—Stuart Vanguard, Jr.—to really bring it to life. To tinker and research and twist it around in his head to get it ready for implementation. It also needed to be done at the right time. A lot changes in the world in a year, and the need arose in that time for an idea such as this.

Six months after Stuart Vanguard, Jr. allowed this idea to take root in his mind, he got a promotion. After a psych evaluation, various hoops through which to jump, a thorough and invasive background check, and a favor called in by his father, Stuart Vanguard Sr., the young man was transferred to a different office, with a different boss, where a different set of skills was needed of him.

Vanguard Jr. had all but forgotten about it when he was reading a newspaper one morning. The front-page article about challenges faced by those states that, by popular vote, had recently made marijuana legal, jarred the hibernating idea loose. He then spent the better part of a week putting together a presentation for his boss. Of course, his presentation was nothing but a practiced speech, because of the sensitive nature of their work and the somewhat heinous nature of the idea that he was putting forth.

As it turned out, his boss was receptive to the idea. The older man called together those people whom he thought could organize such a project on a small scale. To test it.

It was a judgment call.

At that point Vanguard's role as incubator was complete. He was not privy to the meeting two days later that his boss organized. Three men sat in the large, solemnly lavish government office and discussed the idea for several hours. Rolling it around and making sure, above all, that if the implementation of the idea went sideways or blew up in their collective face, it wouldn't lead back to them. Or, in fact, anywhere near them.

In the end they decided that, with proper precaution, it could be done. Their cost-benefit analysis was complete to all three men's satisfaction. If it was successful, they could brag about it among certain company. If it failed, they would deny any knowledge of its existence. Either way, they would be kept out of the spotlight, and that was exactly where they preferred to be.

An encrypted call went out the next morning.

A week later, a specialist was flying to Colorado on a commercial flight, traveling under an assumed name.

# One

TROUBLE STARTED LIMBERING UP for a workout. He hadn't expected one, but he had learned a long time ago that you had to get your exercise in whenever it felt right. And this was feeling more right with every passing moment.

He looked around the convenience store, making sure no one else was around. Even if there was someone to witness his workout, he didn't think it would matter much. He wasn't going to be here for much longer. Just passing through on his way to a much-needed change of scenery.

He looked out at his motorcycle—his baby—at the pump. A small problem: he still needed to gas up. The whole reason for the stop here. Still, he was in the middle of nowhere. Even if the clerk called the police, Trouble would be long gone before they arrived.

Only a small problem.

Of course, if she did call the police and they happened to be close by, Trouble would be arrested. No doubt. And a search of his person would yield enough heroin to make sure he stayed away for a long time. He wouldn't get hit with a distribution charge; it wasn't that much. But still, it was enough to keep him in jail for the remainder of his thirties. It was a risk.

Trouble leaned slightly to the right, looking past the guy's shoulder at the young clerk. She was visibly shaking now, her eyes cast down.

She wouldn't call the police.

"This is such bullshit," the guy at the counter said, his voice rising, rife with indignation. "Just sell me the fucking beer you dumb bitch." Trouble watched as he pushed the case of piss-beer across the counter and into the girl's trembling hand resting there. She pulled it back as if the case was hot to the touch.

"I-I'm sorry, I can't sell you the beer, sir. Not without ID. I could get in trouble." She spoke haltingly, her eyes still cast down at the grimy plastic counter. *Don't you worry about trouble,* Trouble thought. *I've got your back.*

"I don't look old enough to buy beer?" The guy asked, near shouting now.

Trouble thought it could go either way. He was a big guy, but that didn't mean anything. Trouble figured the asshole could be anywhere from eighteen to twenty-five years old. Hard to say.

"Look at me, you cunt!" the guy yelled, leaning over the counter, reaching for either the beer or the girl—or both—Trouble couldn't tell. The clerk jumped back and bumped into a wall of cigarettes. Before the guy could reach either, Trouble yanked him back by the collar of his pastel shirt.

Let the workout begin.

Not wanting to mess up the store, Trouble spun the guy around and shoved him backward through the door, the electronic bell clanging indifferently as the guy toppled back and landed on a shiny oil stain on the concrete slab under the tall aluminum awning covering the pumps. Trouble stepped back to the clerk and laid a twenty on the counter. "Pump four, please," he said to the shocked girl before heading outside.

The asshole's face was brick red and twisted into a sneer as he collected himself off the ground.

"Fuck off," Trouble said, walking toward his motorcycle. The guy let him get past, as Trouble knew he would. The sound of shuffling feet gave him away as he stepped toward Trouble and swung a roundhouse, aiming to connect with the back of his head. It was a strange move, Trouble thought later. If it had connected, the guy likely would have broken his hand. Trouble may have been dazed, but it wouldn't have done much more to him.

Anger does strange things to people.

Trouble ducked and sidestepped, turned around, and swung an elbow into the guy's teeth. He felt the incisors fold back into the guy's mouth through his leather jacket sleeve. Amazingly, he stayed upright and came at Trouble again. He got a glancing blow off Trouble's shoulder and one good shot to the ribs before Trouble put him down with a punch to the kidney and a kick to the head. The guy collapsed back against an empty pump.

When Trouble finished filling his gas tank, the asshole was still unconscious. The clerk had watched the whole thing from inside the little gas station. She waved goodbye to Trouble as he rode out of the parking lot. She seemed like a sweet girl.

Trouble was right. She didn't call the police. But evidently, she had called someone. As he rode out of the gas station, a dusty pickup truck screeched into the lot. Two guys jumped out and walked up to the unconscious asshole. One was older and one was about the girl's age. Maybe father and brother or boyfriend. The girl pointed at Trouble as he rode away. The two men waved at him. Trouble put up a hand in reply.

Happy to help. He needed the exercise, anyway.

# Two

B RAD THOMPSON FELT LUCKY. As he walked through
the rear exit door of the small white building, he felt as
if things were finally coming together for him. His band had
booked a few gigs in the upcoming weeks at fairly decent venues
around Denver, and the lead singer/manager was working to
put together a tour in the surrounding states. They had an
album in the works—they had paid for the studio time themselves—and they were going to promote the shit out of it.

Sure, he and his girlfriend, Trina, had another big blowout
fight, but that was a couple of weeks ago now. Plus, the whole
fight was about Brad not bringing any money in, aside from
the occasional hundred bucks or so from a particularly good
show, which didn't happen very often. How many times had
he explained to her ("mansplained," she called it) that the world
just wasn't quite ready for a death-noise-synth-metal band of
*Burned Ego*'s talent?

She'd usually respond to this argument by asking why he
didn't go out and get a job until the world was ready. *As if.* She
knew what she was getting into when they got together three

years ago. Of course, back then he was still working at Best Buy. He got fired for missing a shift too many shortly after they had moved in together.

It wasn't like she couldn't afford it, with her grown-up job doing something or other for an insurance company. Trina had told him numerous times what it was she did, but he never seemed able to remember it for more than five minutes.

He really wasn't a bad boyfriend, which is why the constant arguments had troubled him. Their fights consisted of some passive-aggressive give and take, escalating after a few hours or a few days into full-blown shouting matches, usually in the cluttered living room of their one-bedroom apartment.

Brad had never laid hands on Trina, or any other woman for that matter, and he was always pretty quick to apologize when he knew he was in the wrong. He was fiercely loyal and never cheated. Plus, after a fight, Brad would always bring home sushi for Trina, and a little turtle carved out of soap from a cute mom n' pop boutique they had visited on one of their first dates. Trina had gushed over the sea turtles, which were her favorite animal, and Brad had remembered. He recalled it vividly, seeing her eyes crinkle and her mouth turn up at the sides, and hearing the barely audible sound of affection that she made. It was then that he knew he was crazy about her, that his heart jumped in his chest and his stomach did a somersault. He was hers.

Their very first fight had been about food, as it is with so many couples. So common it was, and so silly, that that very night Brad had seen the first of many memes on the internet about that very issue. In every meme he'd seen that the indecisive yet picky half of the partnership was the woman.

With Brad and Trina, the roles were reversed. On that night, just under three years ago, Trina had wanted to go out to eat and Brad had said okay, and that he didn't care where they went. So after a lot of suggestions put forth by Trina, and a lot of halfhearted "Sure babe, whatever you want," from Brad, Trina finally decided on a new sushi joint, to which Brad responded, "Oh babe, anything but sushi."

This had been too much for Trina, who, at the time, was incredibly hungry, stressed from a particularly hard day at work, and having doubts about the indecisive boy she found herself living with at twenty-four. When the short but emotionally draining fight, and ensuing make-up session, were over, they both laughed about it when Brad, casually strolling around the internet on his phone, stumbled across the meme and showed it to Trina in what they both agreed was an incredibly synchronis-tic happening. It was an illuminating moment not only in their relationship, but also in their young lives. They noted that they still had a lot to learn about each other and that they both had certain idiosyncrasies that would inevitably get on each other's nerves.

Since then, they had had other fights about trivial, and some not-so-trivial things, but their most recent rows felt different somehow. Brad wasn't sure if he was just overreacting to an unusually long run of disagreements and bad luck, or if there was really an insurmountable rift forming between them. It had seemed as if his world was falling apart around him. Like he was locked in a perpetual winter. Nothing growing and thriving, everything shriveling and dying.

That winter had lasted six months, up until about two weeks ago. Fights with Trina every other day (which was kind of okay when they had make-up sex, but even *that* hadn't been happening lately). Fights with his bandmates over the direction and marketing of *Burned Ego.* No employment prospects that didn't involve serving food. An increasing cost of living, barely any *Burned Ego* shows getting booked, and to top it all off, his parents had refused to loan him any more money.

*What's a twenty-eight-year-old musician supposed to do?* But then, out of the blue, from a friend of a friend, he got a line on a job. An easy, well-paying, not-going-to-interfere-with-his-band kind of job. *Uh, yes, please.*

Since then, he and Trina were having more sex and fighting less, and the rift seemed to have healed itself. He and the rest of his band had come to a consensus (albeit a tentative one) about the direction of the band, and his money problems seemed to be over.

He took a few steps away from the building and took a moment to pause and feel the sun on his face, the breeze through his hair, the sweet smell of a swiftly budding summer. *Yeah, life is good.*

Not for the first time he wondered how in the hell he got so lucky to get such a job. Most, if not all, of the other businesses like this one hired people with lots of experience and training, not to mention heavy equipment and serious protocols. He definitely wasn't going to bring it up to his boss, though. He didn't want to give her any ideas. Plus, he felt like thinking about it too much and too hard would surely jinx it, so he pushed these thoughts aside as he got into his old, sun-faded hatchback and started on his way.

He tried his best to take a different route every time—like he had been told when he started out—but there were only so many variations unless he went out of the way. He didn't want to turn a thirty-minute job into an hour. After all, he got paid the same either way.

If he had taken a long way, he probably could have escaped the fate that awaited him. At least for that day.

But he didn't.

He kept one eye on the road ahead and another on his mirrors, looking to see if he was being followed. He didn't recognize any of the cars, all looked normal. He didn't have any bad feelings, so he decided to take a route he had taken the day before yesterday. He was sure he'd be fine. As he took a right on 40th, he turned the radio up, started singing along to some watered-down-bubble-gum-pop song that he didn't know the words to. Top 40, opiate-of-the-masses pop was a guilty pleasure of his. He would surely be kicked out of the band if his fellow musicians ever learned of this heinous inclination. He was in the zone and once again noted how things were looking up.

Then, as he pulled up to a stop sign, he was rear-ended, his head jerking back against the headrest with the minor impact.

"Shit!" he said as he glared into the rear-view mirror. He put the car in park and got out, rubbing his neck. It was nothing more than a love tap, and Brad was fine, but he figured it best to play the injured card until he saw what he was working with. Sure, his finances were finally looking good, but he was always looking for opportunities to score some easy money. A fender bender could be a lucrative accident. It was the American way.

It was a P.T. Cruiser that hit him, the kind of vehicle that, in Brad's mind, was driven exclusively by young women or old women who wished they were still young. There was no visible damage to either car.

A middle-aged, clean-cut Hispanic man got out of the driver's seat and approached Brad, looking apologetic. Brad noticed a scar at the top of the guy's forehead, abutting his hairline, but paid it no mind. If he'd had a better memory, he would have remembered that a man fitting this description was a suspect in a triple homicide. Brad had seen a police sketch of the man in front of him not two nights previously. According to the news report, which went in one ear and out the other, the guy was associated with an up-and-coming Mexican cartel believed to be operating in Denver.

Brad noticed a young and just as clean-cut Caucasian guy getting out of the passenger side, looking serious. The guy looked younger than Brad and was a head taller. He wore a short-sleeve collared shirt and khaki shorts. He approached the passenger side of Brad's hatchback. There was one more man in the back seat of the Cruiser, sitting there, staring.

"I'm so sorry. You okay, man?" the driver asked. The scar bounced on his forehead as he raised his eyebrows with the question.

"I don't know," Brad said, still rubbing his neck, selling it. "You knocked my head back pretty good."

The driver smiled at him.

"What do you have in here?" the passenger asked. Brad turned around and saw him at the front passenger side of his hatchback, pointing through the window at the bag on the seat. Suddenly Brad felt very nervous. He took his hand away from his neck.

"Oh, oh, that's nothing. Just some work stuff. I'm actually feeling fine now, guys. No need for insurance," he said, backing up to get in his car.

"Looks like a bank bag to me. And a big one at that. Looks stuffed to the brim. What do you say, Mr. G? Does that look like a full bank bag to you?" the passenger asked, addressing the Hispanic man with the scar.

"Yeah, Mason. It sure does," Mr. G said, without moving to look at the bag. Brad looked at Mason, who brought his gaze slowly up from the bag to rest on Brad's eyes, over the roof of the car. Brad couldn't hold his gaze and looked back to the driver, who still stood at the back of the hatchback, smiling at him. A car drove slowly by. None of the men said anything. When the passing car was gone, they were alone on the street.

"Well, I should be go—"

"Say, you look familiar. You don't work for Lori, do you?" the passenger—Mason—asked, cutting him off. Relief flowed over Brad like the summer wind, warm and welcoming. They were friends with his boss. He was freaking out for nothing. He turned his head back to the passenger, smiling with relief.

"Yeah, actually I do. Small worl—" Brad was cut off again, but not by a voice. This time it was a loud crack and a bullet entering his abdomen, just below the solar plexus, punching the wind out of him.

He sat down hard on the asphalt, not meaning to. His legs had stopped working. He looked up in disbelief at the driver with the scar. Mr. G, he'd been called. There was a gun in his hand below his smiling mouth. A smile that hadn't changed since his first exchange with Brad, who suddenly remembered the news report he'd seen. His mind was grappling with the situation, with the blood pouring out of his abdomen, and with the pain only just starting to make itself known.

The smile remained unchanged as Mr. G walked up to Brad, who was coming to terms with the fact that he had actually been shot. The man with the scar kept his eyes on Brad's as he walked up and put another bullet in him. This time the bullet entered Brad's skull, leaving quite the mess of blood and brains on the asphalt next to the front of the hatchback.

When the police arrived several minutes later, the P.T. Cruiser was gone, along with all its passengers and the bag of money that had been on Brad's passenger seat.

# Three

TIM WATCHED IN DISMAY as the sedan pulled up to the curb, the kid driving bright-eyed and wide-mouthed. Tim looked at Joseph, standing beside him, and the look he saw on his co-worker's face told him everything. Joseph's bushy eyebrows came together, his plain features twisting into a grimace that was more subdued than angry. He was about a head shorter than Tim, ten years older, and putting on a little of that fat that starts to gather with force right around thirty-five, an age which Joe was on the wrong side of. Still, he was a professional, Tim knew. They'd been working together long enough. It wasn't Joe's style to get all bent out of shape at the first sign of trouble. No, he saved that for later. But even then, it was a constructive sort of bent, and he got things done.

Tim shrugged and swiveled his head over his shoulder to look at Ray, who was squatting against the side of the brick building, smoking. Tim watched as realization dawned on Ray's face, his countenance darkening as the kid stepped out of the sedan like a used car salesman about to start his bullshit spiel.

Ray's name wasn't Ray at all. Tim didn't know what it was, but it sure as hell wasn't Ray. Someone had told him once that it was an ironic nickname because the guy was such a fucking ray of sunshine. Tim's guess was the guy was of Middle Eastern descent, but he didn't know for sure. Like Tim himself, Ray was a person of color. What color exactly, he didn't know. Not that it mattered, really. All he knew was that the guy dressed well and didn't fuck around.

Ray looked briefly back at Tim before standing up and putting his dark attention on the kid whose name Tim couldn't remember.

It was the edge of summer and the weather couldn't have been better in the Mile High City. The morning sun bent softly off the four-year-old sedan, the gold-khaki paint reflecting for a moment Tim's face as he stepped off the curb and around the hood to the driver's side. The kid passed him, smiling. Tim shook his head solemnly. He knew what was coming. He paused at the door, a smattering of traffic passing behind him, and looked over the car.

Joseph knew that there was nothing to be done about the car at this late juncture, of this Tim had no doubt. They had developed a sort of working communication that required few words, so Tim wasn't surprised when Joe stepped around the kid and opened the front passenger door. He, too, stopped and looked back at Ray.

Apparently, the kid was as dumb as he was happy because the smile was still on his face. A smile that said "Gee, didn't I do

good? Now, gimme a treat and let me play with the big boys."
Tim watched with a sense of foreboding as Ray stepped up and
stared at the kid, who was probably twenty or so. The car was
a sort of audition, and the three who had been waiting on the
sidewalk were the ones to impress. They weren't. Not in the
least.

To Tim's surprise, Ray didn't do anything rash. He stepped
away from the kid, who was just starting to sense that something
was wrong. If he would've kept his mouth shut, he would have
been fine, but his fish-mouth opened up and words spilled out,
assaulting Ray as he stepped to the back door of the car.

"What? No 'thank you'? You guys run some crew. A guy
steals a car for you and all he gets is the stink-eye." Ray stopped
suddenly, as if he'd been hit in the back by the kid. He turned
slowly and stepped back up on the curb. Damn, but the kid had
some balls. He didn't even flinch, just stood there with his big
teeth sprouting out of his half-open mouth. Tim sighed.

Ray opened his mouth to say something but thought better
of it. Instead, he elbowed the kid in the nose. Hard. The kid
went down on the stained and spotted sidewalk with a gasp of
air and wide eyes.

"This look like a fucking truck to you?" Ray asked, gesturing
at the sedan idling three feet away.

"Truck. Car. What's the difference?" the kid said in a nasal
whine. Ray blew his stack. He started kicking the kid with his
sharp Derby shoes. He got a couple of good hits as the kid

scrambled away on the sidewalk, blood pouring out of his nose, staining the concrete.

"Ray!" Tim said, tapping his wrist to indicate it was time to go.

Ray spewed some virulent curses at the kid, who had made it to his feet and was stumbling down the sidewalk, and walked back to the car.

The mood in the car wasn't much different than it had been on the sidewalk. Tim wasn't sure about the others, but he had a strange feeling about this job. It wasn't something he necessarily wanted to do, but he understood that it had to be done. This was the way things worked. If they didn't do this job, then they would lose all credibility and would soon be out of well-paying work. Tim, for one, didn't want to go back to robbing gas stations and dealing dope. He'd done enough of that shit.

As they drove past a man and a woman walking into a high-fashion boutique, Joe mentioned something about the woman's ass. Ray laughed a booming, raspy laugh. Tim chuckled, too. But he hadn't been looking at her. He'd been looking at the man who, in his own right, had a great ass. Tim had no interest in women, but his co-workers didn't know this.

In all honesty, it probably would have been nothing more than a little awkward and uncomfortable for a few weeks if he just came out and told his co-workers, but he decided not to take the chance.

One of the downsides of Tim's line of work was not just a lack of health and dental insurance, but a general lack of understanding when it came to the whole men-being-sexual-ly-attracted-to-other-men thing. He thought of his co-workers as being stuck in the 1950s when it came to sexual orientation. Tim loved his job and didn't want to lose it over something easily kept to himself. He liked the freedom and the adrenaline and the pay—at least currently.

Unfortunately, keeping a hetero facade meant that he had to take part in macho and degrading behavior toward women from time to time, but he always felt bad about it. He said a silent sorry to the victims of catcalls and lewd remarks. He was surprised that Ray hadn't rolled down the window to call out to the woman. He supposed it was too early, and they were all concerned about the sedan. Any other time, though, Ray would have made his attraction known to the woman—and would've jumped at the chance to scare the living shit out of her boyfriend.

It was strange, but Tim willingly engaged in the same behavior towards men in the gay clubs he frequented during his off time, mostly towards the more effeminate guys that happened by. In Tim's experience, the men seemed to like it. Something about the culture and the club environment, he supposed. In fact, he had been laid several times as a direct result of the lewd and promiscuous remarks he'd made at men. He had never heard of a single man who had been laid doing the same at women. Of course, it wasn't the norm in the clubs, but it worked for him. Maybe it was the sheer confidence he exuded.

It took them fifteen minutes to get to their destination, where they parked the car and sat, waiting and watching and hoping that having the sedan wouldn't end up being an issue. What little idle chatter there was had died down. Chatter that had mostly consisted of bitching about the various untested recruits, the recent change of tactics, and whether it was wise to try to do what they were doing, especially the way they were doing it. None of it was serious conversation. It was simply the kind of complaining that people do about their jobs the world over, usually without even realizing that they're doing it at all.

As the time grew near, they stopped talking and started preparing for action, checking weapons and extra clips, looking around for police, making sure the line of sight was good. Double and triple checking, like good soldiers always do.

Then, at the back of a brown building down and across the street, a service door opened. All three men in the sedan held their breath and looked hard at the man who walked out. It didn't take long to see that he was headed for a big American truck parked in the alley behind the building. *Fuck*. You could almost hear it, although none of the men said a word. *Fuck. A goddamn pickup.*

It wasn't just the big truck. It was the man driving the big truck that posed a new problem. Something in the way he held himself made it clear that they were dealing with a professional. He was a big man, six-foot-three or taller, though it was hard to tell from a distance. He looked around carefully as he exited the building, scanning his sectors. He almost certainly had a gun on him.

Problems.

They were going to have to get creative, and quick. The plan had been to take the courier within three blocks of the building. After that, the odds became tilted. A chase was no good, and they didn't know his route either, but they knew that he took the same three-block exit out of the area every time, then split his route up from there, not taking the same exact path two times in a week.

Ramming the target—their original plan—was no good, for obvious reasons. Joseph, Ray, and Tim still hadn't said a word since the man had exited the building. They all knew that they had to think and think fast. Tim put the sedan in drive and headed off to follow the truck, trusting that he would come up with something, and if he didn't, Joe or Ray would before it was too late.

Within two blocks they had a new plan. Though they wouldn't be able to move inside the three blocks they originally hoped for, they could still minimize exposure. Hopefully, the guy in the truck wouldn't get clever and go around in a circle.

They raced down an alley parallel to the street and got ahead of the truck quickly. The morning rush hour was over, so traffic was on their side. Tim stopped the car, jumped out, and ran to the corner of the street. Joe jumped in the driver's seat as Tim headed away. Tim slowed to a walk just before he came into view at the intersection. As he reached the corner, the truck pulled up to the stoplight. If the light had been green, it would've been out of his hands and resting on Joe and Ray's capable shoulders. But the light was red. The big guy in the truck glanced to his left, directly at Tim, the one pedestrian on the visible street.

He looked Tim up and down with practiced ease and then back to the light, waiting for it to change. No threat assumed, apparently. Tim smiled to himself. He was twenty-five and dressed like every millennial: skinny jeans, tight shirt, trendy leather jacket, bright-colored, high-top shoes. He looked like a hipster.

What his clothes hid were his not inconsiderable weapons. He had an M9 Beretta tucked into his waistband at the back, hidden by the light leather jacket. Although he looked thin at a glance, he was incredibly toned, the body of a gymnast, and much stronger than he appeared. Finally, he carried a small but sharp knife in an ankle holster, hidden by the bunching of his skinny jeans just above his right shoe.

Behind him, Tim heard the sedan with Joseph and Ray in it cross the street into the next alley over. They would be waiting at the next intersection. Tim passed in front of the idling truck and turned down its flank. Just a normal guy out for a walk.

Once he knew he was in the guy's blind spot, he pulled out his pistol and turned in one quick move, rushing the passenger-side door. He simultaneously slammed the butt of his gun into the window and tried the door handle on the off chance it was unlocked.

Doing both at once was the smart play. It would save him a precious second or two if the door happened to be unlocked and trying the door first could alert the driver who could hit the gas and take off. Plus, a lot of modern cars locked automatically when the vehicle got up to a certain speed or went a certain distance—or a combination of both. Tim wasn't exactly sure on that front.

As it turned out, the door was locked. The window shattered and Tim got his right arm and gun hooked into the cab, and his feet planted firmly on the footrail of the lifted truck, just as the guy hit the gas. He fired a warning shot and the driver's side window shattered.

"Stop the fucking car."

Keeping his eyes on the road, the guy did as he was told, pulling over to the side and into a row of empty parallel parking spots. Tim noted that the guy looked more angry than scared, which told him that he shouldn't mess around with this one.

The driver's arm muscles bulged and flexed as he gripped the steering wheel with both hands, tense with anger and adrenaline. He looked ex-military. He had a buzz cut and some sort of skull and knife tattoo on his left forearm that Tim guessed was probably Army, but didn't know for sure. He wore a short-sleeved plaid collared shirt, blue jeans, and shit kickers. A cowboy.

"Put it in park," Tim commanded.

Cowboy did as he was told. Tim kept his gun on the guy as he opened the door from the inside with his left hand. He stepped off the truck's footrail and onto the sidewalk, swinging the door open as he did so. A few cars passed on the street, but no one was stopping or slowing, and he heard no sirens. Tim had to make this quick. Firing a gun in the city wouldn't go unnoticed. Luckily, they were in an area where most of the businesses were mechanics, machine shops, recycling centers, or pawn shops. Little foot traffic, and all kinds of noise going on. They had a little time.

"Okay," Tim said, settling into the passenger seat, sitting on the broken glass. "Put it in drive and very slowly take us past the next light. You see that ugly, tan sedan parked up on the right?"

The guy nodded, still looking ahead, still pissed.

"Park behind it."

They were about a hundred yards from the sedan with Joseph and Ray inside. Tim could see Joseph looking in the rear-view mirror and Ray twisting around in the back seat, staring at the truck.

Tim held his gun on Cowboy with his right hand and started rifling around in the truck with his left. He looked in the glove box, under his seat, in the center console, but didn't find what he was looking for.

"Where's the money?"

"What money?"

"Don't fuck with me, man. I watched you carry it out of the shop. It was under your left arm in one of those red bank bags. Now, where is it? Or I shoot you and find it myself." Cowboy hesitated, a look of determination on his face.

"Look," Tim sighed. "This isn't about you. It's payback for something your boss's boss did. It's about evening the score. See, they killed a courier. It doesn't have to go that way. You don't have to die. But I'm under orders to get the money. So, *where. The fuck. Is it*?"

They had pulled up behind the sedan. Joseph and Ray started to get out of the car, guns in hand. They stopped when they saw a woman walking down the sidewalk toward them. Cowboy started reaching down with his left hand, between the seat and the door.

"Ah ah ah," Tim warned. "Tell me. Don't move your hands off the steering wheel."

Cowboy opened his mouth to say something, but then he stopped. He'd noticed the woman on the sidewalk. Tim saw movement from the same direction out of the corner of his eye and turned slightly to see what it was.

The woman had stopped on the sidewalk near the front right corner of the truck, staring at the two men. Or, rather, she was staring at the gun Tim was holding. She looked surprised and unsure.

Tim thought maybe she worked at a bail bond shop or one of the pawn shops in the area. Her clothes looked old and worn, as did her face and slumped shoulders, but her eyes were hard, tense, now darting between Tim's face and the gun in his hand.

They stared at each other for what seemed like a long time, then Tim sensed movement from Cowboy and turned back to see a .38 Special coming up in his right hand, almost level with

Tim's head. The lady on the sidewalk decided to run just before Cowboy took a shot at Tim, who ducked his head left a few inches. The gun fired next to him, the bullet traveling through the glassless window and narrowly missing the woman's head as she ran past the truck.

Tim took a shot at Cowboy a second later. He was deaf and his eyes were wrenched shut, so his shot went a little wide, hitting Cowboy high in his left arm. When Tim opened his eyes, he had hold of Cowboy's right wrist with his left hand, fighting to keep the gun out of his face.

Joe and Ray got out of the sedan and were making their way to the truck, but Tim yelled at them, still struggling with Cowboy.

"She saw my face. She saw us all. I got this. Go!"

Joe and Ray ran off after the woman.

Turning his full attention back to the injured cowboy, Tim pushed down, angling his gun barrel directly onto the man's right forearm. He pulled the trigger. Cowboy dropped the gun and screamed, unable to hold it with his forearm shattered, his tendons severed. Tim immediately put his pistol to Cowboy's head. He turned away just before he fired two shots in quick succession. Blood splattered the right side of his face.

Stepping out of the truck, Tim heard gunshots and looked down the sidewalk. He saw the woman's body hit the sidewalk some fifty yards away. The way she hit told him she was dead before she met the concrete. Joe and Ray were running back toward him, their arms pumping and eyes wide. Tim ran around to the driver's side of the truck, yanked the door open, and let Cowboy fall out onto the pavement, the top half of his head gone.

He searched the storage space of the door and found the bank bag, wiped some of the blood off of the bag and onto Cowboy's plaid shirt, then said, "Let's get the fuck out of here," as Joe and Ray came running up.

The three men took a step toward the sedan and then stopped. People were poking their heads out of shop doors, cell phones held tensely to their ears. There were no cars on the road. Whether a coincidence or a result of the gunfire, they didn't know. For a mostly industrial part of town, it was way too silent, too still. There was a heaviness in the air, and everyone around sensed it.

For a moment, Tim thought it was the deaths that did it. That on some level, deep down past the subconscious, people could sense when someone was killed close by. Maybe it didn't even have to be close by, maybe that was just where it was strongest.

He had felt similar things before, but this time was a little different somehow—a little clearer, a little heavier. Like all the negative energy he caused in his life—all the murders and beatings and the times he didn't tip the wait staff—were about to come full circle and land right on his head.

He didn't know how or when. After all, it was just a feeling and a fleeting one at that. He snapped out of it when Ray yelled for him to get in the car. He hadn't noticed that they were ready to go, waiting for him.

As they sped away in the stolen sedan, Tim just couldn't shake the feeling taking hold in his gut.

It was the feeling that trouble was coming for him.

# Four

D ETECTIVE GIBNEY STARED AT the drying blood on the sidewalk, seeing it but not really seeing it. Three dead bodies in two weeks. From two separate incidents. Within a couple miles of each other. Around the same time of day.

Denver was no stranger to homicide. In fact, the murder rate had been climbing, but so had the population. To be expected to a certain point. But these two felt different, somehow. Daylight murders weren't very commonplace, outside of domestic violence homicides, and so it was worrying. Like there were new operators in town.

There had been talk of cartels operating around Denver, trying to get in on the legal marijuana trade any way they could. The massive influx of cash into the state had been attracting all types.

Just because it was now legal didn't mean the cartels were going to throw their hands up in the air and say, "*Well, there's nothing we can do. We'll just have to give up on selling weed in legalized states. We had a good run, but oh well.*" Not likely at all, Gibney thought.

They were always making drug arrests around the city, but they had not been able to link any of those arrests to cartels. Which didn't really mean anything. It was a losing fight, in his opinion. They mostly got street-level dealers and maybe a lieutenant or two. But the bigger the fish you arrest in any criminal organization worth its weight, the harder it gets to pry information from them. It was a matter of who they're more scared of: the police or their own bosses. The police would lock them up and give them three hots and a cot, whereas their bosses would have them and their family brutally murdered if they found out they had talked. No choice at all, really. Plus, there was the monetary incentive. Most of the guys they arrested made as much or more in a month than Gibney himself did in a year, easy.

Where one was arrested, there were two waiting to take his place. A losing battle. *War on drugs my hairy ball bag*, he thought. What it is is a money-making venture, for both sides. Federal funding and tons of jobs for the American economy: jail builders, prison guards, police, parole officers, border patrol officers, judges, lawyers, and rehab programs, just to name a few. A multi-billion dollar industry. He shuddered to think about how many people would be out of a job if drugs were to vanish or become legal. Plus, there was massive demand. America the beautiful and the really fucking high.

Of course, none of this was even touching on the problem of prescribed opiates like hydrocodone, OxyContin, and morphine. Or other synthetic opiates like fentanyl or carfentanyl, which is an elephant tranquilizer, for fuck's sake. This line of thinking brought up thoughts of big pharma, overprescribing doctors and their poor pain management practices, and ill-conceived drug treatment programs (the biggest of which was prison itself) that did nothing to address the underlying issues.

It gave him a headache, and he decided to focus on his breathing to calm down a little bit, something his ex-wife had taught him during their divorce. It worked better if he closed his eyes, but he was at a crime scene, so he did it with his eyes open. Last thing he needed was to have people giving him shit for meditating on the job.

It was his second case as a detective, and the whole reason he'd taken the detective's exam was because he felt like he wasn't doing enough good patrolling the streets and risking his life to do what amounted to, in his mind, taking out the garbage. Get a couple of bags of garbage off the street and into the system until the next day or the next week when more garbage showed up. It was never ending. At least as a detective he could go after murderers and people that were more than just errand boys for higher-ups.

He thought things would be different in Denver and as a detective, but so far, they felt the same as Cleveland, where he'd started his police career. But he was a fresh detective, so maybe it would be different once he got used to it. The money was better, anyway.

He was still concentrating on his breathing when Detective Wane came up behind him and jabbed him in a kidney with a stiff index finger. Gibney jumped a little and spun around, knowing full well who he would see. Wane stood behind him, grinning her stupid big grin. She was a monster of a woman, and next to Gibney she looked even bigger, because he was barely five-five and had a slight build. She was six-three and probably two-twenty. She worked out harder than any man he'd ever met and had even done some amateur bodybuilding in her youth. Now she was pushing fifty but could still bench three hundred.

Her black hair was cut short, which accentuated her prominent cheekbones, and was slowly going gray. She wore a pantsuit today, like every other day. This one was dark gray and certainly had to be custom made. Gibney didn't think they made clothes that big for women. He wore a khaki suit and jacket, a black shirt with no tie, and black boots that were polished to a shine, which, he thought, looked as nice as any of his dress shoes, and were much more comfortable. He was fifteen years Wane's junior, and she treated him like he was just out of the academy, even though his official detective's training was over.

"Wane," he said, rolling his eyes. Her smile didn't falter.

"What's wrong, little buddy?" she said, putting a giant hand on his shoulder in mock sympathy. "You feeling a little wheezy? Want to lie down? This police work isn't for everyone, you know."

"Can we just get to work, please?"

Gibney had been dealing with this kind of shit his whole life. First in high school, then the marines, and then as a police officer. He tried his best not to develop a Napoleon complex, but sometimes resistance is futile. He wasn't *that* short, after all. It would pass. It was a hazing thing, and it didn't matter what job you had, there were always going to be people you worked with who felt the need to give you a little bit of shit until you proved you could take it. So be it.

"You're the one who's been here for half an hour already. What do you think?" Wane asked as she turned to the crime scene, realizing that Gibney wasn't going to return fire today.

"Looks similar to the one in Globeville last week. Glass on the road back there, coupled with reports of shots fired, tells me that someone smashed his window and jumped in, then fired a warning shot, busting the other window. Made him pull over up here. Then I'm guessing the suspect got distracted by the woman walking by. Driver went for a gun and got a single shot off. Suspect shot the driver four times, got what he was looking for, and took off."

"So, who killed the woman?"

"He had friends. Reports of a tan sedan parked in front of the truck. Two guys ran after her when she realized what was going on. They didn't want witnesses, apparently. Shot her in the back."

"Jesus," Wane said. "Did we get descriptions of the three?"

"Yeah, but they're not worth a shit. These guys are either black, brown, white, or all of the above. I'm thinking this is the same crew from the one last week. Probably drug related. So, we've got to figure out what this guy was moving that got him killed."

# Five

*I* HAVEN'T BEEN WORKING *this job for two weeks yet, and already the shit is about to hit the fan,* Trouble thought as the feeling took hold in his stomach. He wasn't sure exactly what was about to go down, but Trouble's nose for trouble was almost never wrong. It was a distinct feeling. Like his stomach was simultaneously growing and shrinking, jumping and dropping.

Somewhere in the back of his brain, he tried to recall the last time his gut had cried wolf. He knew it had happened once or twice, but couldn't remember when. *Too much dope today,* he thought. *Too much fucking dope every day.* But even that thought was quickly overshadowed by the hold that dope had on him. The way he felt after shooting up. The sweet warm numbness. The promise of not giving a shit about anything for at least fifteen minutes. Destructive as it was—as the logical part of him knew it was—he still craved it with a ferocity that frightened him.

The sight of an SUV on the side street up ahead snapped him out of his heroin daydream. It was nosing forward; the driver seeming to hesitate. He had seen the SUV before. Too many times before to be just a coincidence. Or maybe it wasn't the SUV that he'd seen, but the two men in the front seats. He wasn't sure. He didn't have a good look at them. They were too far away, and the sun glinted off the windshield. Whether it was the vehicle or the people in it or some combination of the two didn't matter. What mattered was that feeling in Trouble's gut, telling him something was about to go sideways.

Trouble was about three blocks into the sixteen-block trip, on a residential street, motorcycle in low gear. Denver, Colorado. Just cruising along like he had done every other day for the thirteen days he'd had the job. Not fast, not slow. Staying just above the speed limit. Changing his route every day. Staying as alert as he could while operating on a daily dose of heroin that would kill anyone without his stellar tolerance.

He slowed to a stop in the road and stared at the SUV. Two men in the front. Tinted windows in the back blocked Trouble's view, but his gut told him there was at least one more there. The guys in the front were staring right back at him. He could only make out the shape of their heads. He couldn't see their eyes, but he knew they were staring at him. Clearly, they realized they had been spotted. Cars started to pile up behind Trouble, honking at first and then going around when there was room, hurling obscenities, and shaking heads as they drove by. Trouble ignored them.

He sat there and thought, his synapses firing dully and at half-speed, thanks to the dope that was currently fogging his brain. The last thing he wanted was a gunfight in the middle of this bustling little neighborhood. It was a beautiful summer day. Mid-morning. Saturday in Colorado. People were out walking their dogs, mowing their lawns. Kids were out riding bikes and skateboards. People out living their lives, certainly not expecting a hail of gunfire.

*What to do?*

The easiest answer was to pull a U-turn and outrun the bastards. No way they could keep up with Trouble on his bike, not in a big, unwieldy thing like an SUV. But that meant that they would still be around tomorrow. Probably in a different car. Harder to spot. Today, Trouble knew what they were driving and where they were. He had an edge of sorts.

*What to do?*

As was his usual response to any question that had to be answered quickly, he opted for his favorite answer: *fuck it.* Trouble pulled back the throttle and yanked his handlebars to the left, his back tire spinning so fast it whipped around behind him while he pivoted on his left foot, then he got both feet on the bike, but he didn't quite get it under control. He was going too fast. Too much power.

He fishtailed and then spilled onto the asphalt. Recovering, he hefted the bike up onto its wheels quickly. He looked behind him as he sat down, seeing the SUV closing the distance. He faced forward and took off down the street again, fighting the urge to smile. The SUV was following him. *I should take up acting,* Trouble thought to himself, knowing he had sold the little spill perfectly.

He watched the SUV recede in his side mirrors, thinking, hoping that this was some half-assed attempt at a robbery. The seldom used—and therefore weak—optimistic part of Trouble tried to assure him that these guys weren't willing to kill him for the money he was moving. No. No way. These guys were just out for some easy cash. Not ready to pull the trigger and turn the chase nasty.

Unfortunately, Trouble's gut disagreed. It was really no choice at all once he realized that. Go with the gut. Easy. *It has kept me alive for this long,* he thought, and then*, holy shit!* as a parked car decided to join the traffic flow, pulling out in front of him. He grabbed the brakes and went into a controlled skid, stopping just a few feet from the car and the startled woman in it. He sat for a second, checking his side mirrors until he saw what his gut already told him was true. A guy emerged from the front passenger window of the SUV, hauling himself half out the window, holding onto the car with one hand and a pistol with the other.

Then he fired.

But Trouble was already moving, pulling back on the throttle while yelling, "Get down!" at the woman in the car just before her window exploded. He didn't think she'd been hit, but couldn't be sure as he powered down the street, hoping the SUV would keep following. It did. He kept enough distance that they could see any moves he made, but weren't close enough to shoot at him. The guy was still hanging out the window, waiting to get close.

Being new to the city, Trouble didn't really know of any spots he could take them where there wouldn't be people. So he looked down every side street, at every parking lot, at every house, hoping for a break. Finally, after the longest mile of his life, he caught one.

He turned down a street on his right. Not a street really, but a short road between two apartment buildings that stopped at a dead end. A dark green dumpster sat right in the middle, backed by a guardrail with yellow reflectors attached and a chain-link fence behind it. Beyond that, a swath of green Colorado grass and trees in full summer splendor. Just enough room between the back of the dumpster and the guardrail to fit a motorcycle. Perfect.

Trouble parked and had just enough time to dig into his saddlebag and get his backup .45 and to pull his regular .45 out from his inside jacket pocket. Peeking from behind the dumpster, he watched as they squealed around the corner. He waited for them to get close enough for reasonable accuracy and walked out and opened up with both guns. Not really wanting to kill anyone, he aimed mostly at the bottom center of the windshield, thinking that the bullets would have to pass through lots of SUV before exiting to the somewhat busy street beyond. Plus, if there was only one guy in the back, he might not hit any of them. Shock and awe. Make them turn around and live to fight another day. Let them know that as long as he was the courier on this route, they would have to work hard for the money.

The driver slammed on the brakes as soon as the gunfire started, but the guy hanging out the window didn't have a firm enough grip. He was flung forward and almost onto the hood, but the back of his legs hit the inside of the door, twisting and pulling him back and down. Bodyweight and momentum pulled him awkwardly out onto the blacktop head-first, his head landing just behind the wheel. This happened so fast Trouble barely registered it. He kept firing.

The driver jammed the SUV into reverse and hit the gas. The front passenger's side of the vehicle bumped up as he backed over his guy's head and k-turned to take off. Trouble saw the guy's head turn the wrong way and knew that, at the very least, his neck had been broken. He stopped firing and watched the SUV peel around the corner, back onto the road they had come down. A guy in a little red sedan had to brake hard to keep from hitting them. He glanced toward Trouble briefly as he started driving away. He didn't seem to notice the man on the ground.

From when Trouble opened fire on the SUV, to the guy in the little red sedan skidding to a stop, less than ten seconds had passed. Trouble estimated that he still had two or three rounds in each gun, each with a nine-round capacity.

Trouble walked up to the guy on the ground and saw that he was clean cut, of Hispanic descent, had an old scar along his forehead—and was still alive. "Ahh, shit man," Trouble said softly as he looked into the guy's eyes. The pain there was immense and, for Trouble, unimaginable. He took out his phone to call 911 and then stopped himself. His guns weren't exactly legal, and he really didn't want to spend time in jail again. He decided to search the guy for a cell phone and call with that. Nothing to trace back to Trouble. But as he knelt to begin, he noticed that the labored breathing had stopped. He looked back at the guy's eyes to see that the life had left them, pain and all.

Shell casings were the only evidence that could conceivably incriminate Trouble in the unfortunate incident. But, as a matter of habit, Trouble always loaded bullets into his clips with gloves on. The way he saw it, if you were ever in a position where you had to load a clip too quickly to bother with gloves, you were as good as dead anyway. Stopping to load bullets into a clip in the middle of a firefight is the last thing you want to be doing. Not that Trouble was getting into gunfights on a regular basis, but he had long since accepted that he had shit luck. And being prepared to head off even shittier luck consumed a significant amount of his brainpower.

So the shell casings on the ground were nothing to worry about. Trembling slightly from adrenaline, Trouble mounted his motorcycle and the distant but growing sounds of sirens were drowned out by engine noise as he started his bike and rode off. Just cruising along. Not fast, not slow. Staying just above the speed limit.

***

"You aren't paying me enough for this shit," Trouble said. "I want hazard pay."

He had made the cash drop like he was supposed to, going a roundabout way to avoid scrutiny by the police, who had no doubt found the dead guy near the dumpster. Now he was back at the dispensary, confronting his boss, a graying but severe-looking woman in her middle fifties. Trouble thought she looked more like a lawyer than a weed dealer, but marijuana is big business, after all, and since its legal status changed, it had been attracting all kinds.

Still on edge from the shootout, Trouble stood too close to her and a head taller, essentially looking straight down at her. He gave her credit for standing her ground, looking right back up at him, not giving an inch. They stayed like that for a long moment in her cramped little office, staring at each other, not speaking. Finally, she broke the silence.

"Why don't you tell me what happened, and we'll discuss it."

To be fair, Trouble hadn't begun with any sort of preamble. He had just walked in through the front door, past the customers and the employees helping them, and into the back office. When she saw him come in, she stood up to greet him and he went around her desk and damn near stepped on her toes.

He realized that he was a little too amped up from the whole ordeal. After all, how could she have known that someone would try to steal the money from Trouble? He stepped away from her. His shoulders slumped as he made his way back around her desk to sit in a padded folding chair, breathing out and trying to relieve the tension that had built up in his body. His thoughts turned to the relief heroin would bring.

There were old, dented filing cabinets in the far corners of the office, behind the desk. They had stacks of notebooks, manila folders, and loose paperwork on top of them. As did her desk, which, underneath the loose mail and paperwork, looked like it would be at home in a thrift store, for sale cheap yet unable to sell because of its poor condition. There were stacks of what looked like law books and more paperwork placed haphazardly around the office on the floor. In the corner behind her desk sat a squat, immensely heavy-looking safe, out of which she gave him the money for transport every day. Trouble sat down in the folding chair as his boss sat down in the only other chair in the tiny room, a threadbare, high-backed, imitation leather chair whose condition matched that of the desk.

"Dark blue SUV was tailing me. I think they got lost or something waiting for me to come out today because I saw them right off and they just froze. So I turned around and made like I lost control of my bike. I let them get close enough to follow. I wanted to see what they would do. Then I actually almost got in a crash and they took a shot at me. So I shot back."

"Oh my god," she said. "That's terrible. Are you hurt?"

Something seemed off about her reaction. Trouble thought it was almost a little too much. Then again, he didn't really know the woman at all. He'd only been working for her for two weeks.

"No, I'm fine. They just took off when I fired a few warning shots at them," he lied.

"Well, that's good. You made the drop, I take it?" she asked.

"Yes, I did." Trouble pulled a receipt out of a jacket pocket and handed it across the desk. "So, how about that hazard pay? I'm guessing there's a reason you aren't hiring teams in armored cars to transport this cash for you, right?"

She just looked at him.

"Listen," he said with a sigh. "I don't really care. I'm not sure what the law is here, but I know that this is a cash business right now. I know you're in some sort of gray area with the banks because weed is illegal at the federal level. So I do know that you need to transport your cash. So I'll keep doing it, and I'll mind my own business about it, as long as you pay me what I think is fair. Deal?"

"How much?"

"Fifty percent more. Starting with the run I just did."

She leaned forward and put her elbows on her second-hand desk, linked her fingers together in front of her mouth. She kept looking at him.

He looked back.

"Fine," she said. "But that's it. I'm not paying you any more than that, even if you get shot at every day, twice a day. If I'm paying you that much, you deal with it however you see fit, as long as you keep me out of it and protect my money. Got it?"

"My thoughts exactly," Trouble said, smiling.

# Six

"Oh, fuck me. What just happened?"

Mason twitched his eyes from the road to the rear-view mirror. He hadn't said a word since it had happened. Since that fucking motorcycle courier had killed Mr. G. But Leroy, in the back seat, kept saying the same thing over and over again. Mason was trying to think, and Leroy wouldn't shut the fuck up.

He gripped the steering wheel hard, the skin on his knuckles going a pink-tinged white as he looked at the bullet holes in the windshield. It dawned on him that he could have easily been shot. The biker was accurate with his pistols and—for whatever reason—had decided to only scare them off. It was a lapse in judgment that would cost the biker his life, Mason decided as he drove.

The more he thought about it, the more he knew that it was inevitable. The plan that had come into his head in the last five miles suddenly seemed like it had been there all his life, just waiting for this moment. There was no other way.

"Oh, fucking goddamn. We're so fucked, man. What are we gonna do, Mason?"

Leroy was five years older than Mason and had been with Mr. G for a long time. But the younger man couldn't understand why. He certainly wasn't acting his age. If this was the way he reacted when things went to shit, how could he have survived this long in the game? *But, then again,* Mason thought, *probably nothing like this has ever happened to him before.* Probably if it had, Leroy would be decomposing in a barrel somewhere. Or else his head would've been severed and shoved into his chest cavity.

Mason pulled his pale green eyes from the road again and looked into the rear-view mirror, meeting Leroy's deep brown eyes. He wondered momentarily if Leroy had somehow seen into his mind as they looked at each other; the moment becoming longer than it should've been. He pushed such a silly thought from his mind and realized that Leroy was waiting for him to say something. To tell him what they were going to do. But Mason couldn't tell him that. Not the truth, anyway. Not yet.

Mason went over the encounter in his mind again. The truth was, he hadn't really even registered it when Mr. G had fallen out the window. He was only paying attention to the bullets that he felt punching into the windshield and passing him not a foot away. Only paying attention to the guns that were firing those bullets, and how the biker had kept walking toward them as he fired. Long, confident strides.

Mason had never been one to shy away from a fight. Not since he was a teenager. If he had kept going straight—gunned it—he probably would have crunched over the biker's body instead of Mr. G's. So why hadn't he? Panic had overtaken him. Why then, at that moment? Something about the biker. He hadn't liked the way the guy looked from the get-go. But he hadn't said anything. He couldn't have, really.

He had let Mr. G talk him into chasing the guy when they could have just come back another day and got him as he was walking out of the dispensary. But really, he couldn't have refused the boss. Not him. Not Mr. G. Not the old fucking idiot cartel lord who had grown bored and wanted to relive his glory days. Hanging out the goddamn window like it was fucking Juarez. He had been asking for trouble. It was Mr. G's own fault, really.

Mason thought about the way the right side of the car bumped up and how the motion brought with it the realization that Mr. G had fallen out the window. And that it was, without a doubt, Mr. G who he had just run over. He still had the feeling that nearly paralyzed him when he realized. It was a fear worse than that of the biker's bullets smashing through his skin and muscle and bone. It was the sure prospect of a slow, gruesome, torturous death. A death he knew was coming. Leroy would have to tell what had happened. He had no allegiance to Mason. Not really. They had barely been working together a year, and even then, they didn't do much talking. Mason despised him for being Mr. G's pet. His yes man.

Now Leroy was going to get him killed. Mr. Z wouldn't like what had happened at all. Those types of people didn't like it when one of their own was killed. Accident or not, it had happened on Leroy and Mason's watch. But mostly Mason's. It was his city. He was the tour guide, taking the two around, having a little fun. Leroy would surely tell what had happened if for no other reason than to avoid being murdered himself.

Unless there was something Mason could do about it.

*But first thing's first,* Mason thought. They were riding around in a stolen SUV with bullet holes in the windshield. He had to ditch the car, and quickly. He kept his eyes open for an opportunity, knowing Leroy wasn't going to be any help. Mason's glances in the rear-view mirror told him so. Leroy's brows were furrowed, and he glanced worryingly out the windows on both sides, as if retribution would come down upon him at any moment. He had stopped speaking out loud to Mason, but he was still muttering. Mason couldn't hear what he was saying, but he thought it was more of the same.

Leroy looked at the mirror and caught Mason staring at him. Mason looked away, still afraid that somehow Leroy could see what he was thinking, the gears turning. Gears that Leroy would soon be thrown into if Mason had his way.

There was a Safeway up ahead. It would have to do. He didn't have time to finesse a grand theft auto at the moment. It would take too long. He would simply smash and grab some soccer mom's ride. Mason directed the car smoothly into a spot near the back of the parking lot. He saw three people going into the store and four coming out. Way too many people to be doing this. He thought for a moment and pulled out his phone. He texted his best friend and longtime business partner, Colton. *911. Meet me at 741 in fifteen minutes.*

"What are we doing here?" Leroy asked, suddenly realizing that they weren't moving anymore.

"We gotta switch cars. This one has bullet holes in it. You gonna help me?"

"Why don't we just go back? We need to get back and explain to them what happened. We—"

"Because we're driving a fucking stolen car with bullet holes in it. We'll never get there at all if the cops arrest us. So, we get a new car from one of these nice old ladies here, and *then* we go back and explain what happened. Got it?"

Mason was surprised to see anger in Leroy's eyes in the mirror.

"Fuck you, *Mason*. This shit's your fucking fault, anyway. Why didn't you just keep driving and run the guy over? He wouldn't have hit you. I bet he would have run away, anyway. He was a bad fucking shot. He wasn't even close to hitting any of us."

"He *meant* to shoot the middle of the windshield, you fucking idiot. The guy's a better fucking shot than you are. He would've shot me and Mr. G if I didn't do anything. Probably you, too. Mr. G's the one who wanted to hang out the window like a... a..." he couldn't finish the thought. The look in Leroy's eyes told him to stop. "Look," Mason continued, pointing through the windshield at a hunched lady pushing a shopping cart slowly to a Buick. "There's our ride."

Without waiting for a response, Mason put the car in drive and maneuvered to the spot directly behind the Buick in the next parking column over. The old lady had the trunk open and was putting her bags inside, about ten yards in front of them.

"Let's go," Mason said, looking around quickly to make sure it was as clear as it could be. He stepped out of the car before Leroy could voice an objection, which he surely would have. Or maybe not. Maybe Mason had unwittingly jarred him from his daze by arguing with him about the whole incident. It was as if Leroy suddenly realized who he was and where he was. He'd gone from badass gangster to whiny little bitch and back to badass gangster in a matter of minutes.

Mason regretted starting the argument as he walked across the cracked blacktop. The old lady noticed as his shadow fell across her shopping cart. She looked up with a ready smile, maybe expecting help from the nice, clean-cut young man who stood before her. Mason smiled back. He expected no less. He had one of those faces that people seemed to trust. It was something he used to his advantage whenever he could. Leroy approached the lady from the other side.

"We need your car, ma'am," Mason said.

"Oh?" the lady said, then cackled. It immediately put Mason on edge.

"Yes. If you'll just hand me the keys, we'll leave you here to do what you will. But I don't have time to fuck around with your old ass right now." The conversation had gotten away from him. It was the look on her face that did it. And that fucking cackle. He started it off trying to be polite, but it quickly degraded as his temper flared. It was a regular occurrence for him.

The lady looked from Mason to Leroy and back again, no longer smiling. Mason put a hand on the gun tucked in the back of his waistband.

"Fuck you," she spit, reaching inside her purse for who-knows-what. Mason yanked out his weapon and swung it. He felt her brittle skull give way under the butt of his gun. She fell to the ground like a sack of old, dusty potatoes. If she wasn't dead, she would wake up with several broken bones, just from the fall. Mason didn't think she would ever wake up, though.

"Jesus Christ, man," Leroy whispered, staring at the crumpled figure on the ground behind the car. Mason yanked the keys out of the trunk lid, shut it, and headed to the driver's seat. Leroy barely got in the front passenger's seat before Mason pulled through the empty spot ahead of the car and proceeded to cruise out of the parking lot and into the flow of Saturday traffic. They made a left and then a right. Mason rolled down the windows with the old-school electric panel on his left. Leroy just shook his head and looked out the window.

The Buick pulled into a neighborhood ten minutes later. Mason checked his mirrors before pulling the car over to the side of the road and putting it in park. He looked at Leroy, who was still looking out the window.

"What the hell are we doing here?" Leroy asked, exasperated.

"Meeting Colton."

"In this shitty neighborhood? What, does he live here or something?"

Mason ignored him. He looked at his watch.

"This is taking too fucking long. The longer we wait to tell Mr. Z, the worse it's gonna be," Leroy said, pulling out his phone. Mason heard fear in his voice.

"Don't," Mason said. He was losing patience. He wanted to get this done already, but was hesitant to do it without Colton. Something in his tone made Leroy turn to him, a strange look on his face. Mason realized he had to say something, and quick, or things were going to get out of control.

"They have the ability to listen to those things," Mason said, gesturing at the phone in Leroy's hand. "It's the first thing they do when someone gets killed. They listen for chatter. This isn't Mexico, Leroy. You can't just call people and talk about stuff like this. It isn't done."

Leroy looked back at him, disbelieving at first. Mason said nothing. He didn't want to lay it on too thick.

"Fine. But we've got to do it soon. Believe me, Mr. Z will understand that it was an accident. I mean, if anything, it's the biker's fault. For all we know, Mr. G got shot, and that's why he fell out of the window."

Leroy was lying through his teeth, and Mason knew it.

"We're just meeting Colton and he's going to drive us. I don't want to drive this thing any longer than I have to. In fact, let's go wait in this trap house. We use it all the time." Mason got out of the car and walked across the street to stand in front of a worn-down and clearly abandoned house. Leroy looked at the faded numbers on the facade. 741. He sighed and got out of the car to follow Mason into the house.

"How long until he gets here?" Leroy said as they stepped through the front door of the dilapidated house. They were the last words he ever spoke.

Mason closed the front door behind Leroy. The door didn't latch or lock, but it stayed flush with the frame. There was a living room to the left, which Leroy stepped into, looking around curiously. It was dark in the house—the windows were boarded up. He struggled to see into the corners of the room after being in the sun outside.

Leroy walked further into the living room, waiting for his eyes to adjust, and stepped on some sort of plastic. He looked down to see that he was standing on the edge of a tarp. It took his mind too long to put it together. The tarp. The abandoned house. Mason's excuses. What really sealed it was the sound of someone else stepping on the tarp.

Leroy spun toward the sound. Colton emerged out of a dark corner of the living room. He had a knife in one hand and a determined look on his face. Leroy didn't have time to go for his gun. Instinct kicked in and he put up his hands to try and protect himself from the incoming blade. Colton's first powerful swing hit bone in Leroy's right hand and bounced back. Leroy screamed in pain. The second swing brought the knife into Leroy's forearm. It missed bone and pushed out the other side. Colton yanked it down, using the sharp blade to pull the knife out of Leroy's flesh, tearing a six-inch gash through muscle, veins, and tendons.

As Leroy's mind was processing the fact that his arm had been sliced open, he felt a breathtaking pain in his back. Mason had buried his own knife in Leroy's back, puncturing a kidney. Colton pushed his blade in at the base of Leroy's neck, just under his chin. Mason stabbed him in the back twice more before he fell to the floor. Mason and Colton kept stabbing Leroy as he lay on the ground.

They kept stabbing long after he was dead.

When their fun had been had—because that was, indeed, how both men saw the murder—and they finally stopped stabbing Leroy's body, Mason stood up to catch his breath. "You got this? I've got to get over to Mr. Z before too much time passes. Otherwise, I'm a dead man. I'll tell you the whole story later, but for now, I want everyone on the lookout for a big biker guy. Dark hair, jeans, leather jacket, maybe thirty. Rides a motorcycle like in Sons of Chaos or whatever that show is. No one moves on him until I say so. Got it?"

Colton, who had always been good at following orders, nodded.

"Don't you need to change? You're covered in blood."

Mason looked down at himself. He was splashed in Leroy's blood. "No," he said. "It'll make my story about Leroy and Mr. G getting shot that much more believable. I'll tell them I tried to save both men." He smiled at the thought of it. It was a good one, if he did say so himself.

# Seven

S HARON BAILEY CAUGHT THE case and arrived at the scene alert but distracted, which was rare for her. She had other things on her mind. Pressing matters. She was young for a detective, but she had her sights set on a goal, and she wouldn't back down. She had been like this since she could remember. It was a family trait, instilled in her by her father at a very young age.

She dressed better than anyone in the department, and she knew that many thought she was the best looking, too. She was half Hispanic but looked more Middle Eastern or Mediterranean. People called her "exotic." It was a problem.

Her last partner had been a man. Just like her first. And the one in between them. It seemed like they couldn't just do the job working with her. Eventually, they all wanted to fuck her—even the ones with wives and kids. And no matter how hard she tried to dissuade them of that notion—how she tried to give them signals from the very beginning that she was not, under any circumstances, going to sleep with her partner—or any cop for that matter—it still always ended badly.

To be fair, she'd never tried all that hard to be gentle with the three partners she'd had since becoming a detective. She was a blunt woman. But something about that bluntness apparently made her irresistible to the male detectives. She didn't quite understand it.

Her carefully maintained outward appearance was indicative of the way she thought. No one ever saw her joking around or, really, doing anything but working. Her perfectly manicured eyebrows always had a faintly furrowed look, like she was thinking hard.

Some of the uniformed men, and even a woman or two, called it "resting bitch-face." Her no-frills demeanor did nothing to dissuade the impression around the station that she was, in fact, a bitch. She heard the talk, and she didn't care. She hadn't become a cop to make friends. She'd done it to make a difference.

Outside of work was a different story, but only fractionally so, and only around her close friends and family. She had goals to meet and a timeline in which to do it. She would let herself relax when those goals were met and her life was the way she wanted it.

She took the whole scene in. The shell casings on the quiet little road leading to the dumpster, and the body about halfway between the dumpster and the main street. She looked at the small apartment buildings separated by the little road. Four units each, eight in total. Probably run by the same management company. She doubted that there were security cameras anywhere. She headed over toward the body to get a better look, but was sidelined when a uniform came up to her.

"Detective," the young man said, meeting her eyes for only a moment. She was used to it. "We have a witness over here. We took his statement, but I just wanted to see if you were interested in talking to him." Bailey looked the way the uniform had gestured to see a middle-aged man leaning against a little red sedan, looking bored and a little peeved.

"Did he see anything?" she asked the young man whose name tag read Simon.

"He almost ran into a blue SUV speeding away. Didn't get the license plate. Looked over this way and saw a big guy in a leather jacket and jeans, he thinks. Caucasian."

"Any vehicle near the big guy?"

Simon shook his head. "Not that he saw."

"Did he see the dead man?"

"No. Not at first, anyway. He said he only saw the big guy. 'A biker' were the words he used. Then he drove off. Didn't put it together until he saw the police racing that way. Then, he said that he started to think that maybe there was someone on the ground. So, he turned around and followed the police, to see. That's it."

"Okay, Officer. You can let him go now."

Bailey took a last look at the witness and then walked up to the dead body and knelt, looking at the faint tire marks left on the man's head. It looked clear what the cause of death was. She looked at the guy's open eyes, the scar on his head, and something clicked. *What the hell? No way. Holy shit, no way.* She pulled out her phone, logged into the DPD website, and entered a name, all the while hoping that she was wrong. Hoping that it wasn't him. Hoping that it was just someone who looked like him.

The file pulled up, and she tapped on a picture of the man with her thumb, making it fill the entire phone screen. She held it next to the man's head and compared the two. It was him. "Oh man," she whispered to herself, unsure exactly what this man's death meant.

"You okay, Detective? You look a little sick," Simon asked, after signaling his partner to let the witness go.

Bailey tore her eyes from the dead man's face and looked up at the uniform. She managed a weak smile.

"I'm fine, thanks. Been feeling a little sick today, is all." She stood up. *Damn. We're about to have a war on our hands. Goddamn.*

# Eight

S OMETHING WASN'T RIGHT, AND Trouble knew it. He decided, as he got off the phone with his dealer, that he would do a little research to gain a better understanding of what exactly was going on in the marijuana industry in Colorado. Lori's reaction to the news of the attempted robbery was one clue, and the fact that she was willing to pay him what he asked was another. The very fact that he had the job at all, and not some armored security company, spoke volumes. But he was new to Colorado, and he didn't want to jump to conclusions.

Hell, recreational marijuana was new to the country. There were bound to be kinks to iron out. Maybe he was witnessing history. If that were the case, he was going to take advantage of it. The job was a cash cow, and it would do nicely to support his nasty little habit.

But people trying to kill him. That was a problem. One he would deal with in due time. He currently had more pressing matters to tend to. It wasn't a first for him, to say the least. He was a sort of criminal, after all. People generally wanted to harm criminals, in his experience. Especially other criminals.

But just because he was a criminal didn't mean that he was for sale. He had his limits and his rules, and things he just wouldn't do. He had, once or twice before, found himself in the employ of people that didn't share his affinity for moral fortitude, and didn't take no for an answer.

Those people were the types that would hire him to do a specific job, and then suddenly change that job to include something wholly unacceptable to Trouble. Something that, had they asked him to do it during initial negotiations, he would have told them to shove somewhere unpleasant. In those situations, Trouble had little choice but to make his opinion known, in whatever way the situation called for.

Sometimes it called for drastic violence. Like when the terms of the job were "do it or we'll kill you." So Trouble found himself in a gray area of the criminal underworld, much like how the legal marijuana industry was in a gray area in American law.

He had to be fairly picky about the jobs that he took. And on top of all that, he had terrible luck. Like the universe was trying to kill him. Like he was a mistake. Like he should have died years ago, but due to some fluke, some glitch in the matrix, he hadn't. Ever since, the balance had been just a little off, and his luck was the universe's way of trying to set things back to normal. But it hadn't worked yet. He'd be damned if he was going to go down without a fight, universal imbalance or not.

Trouble looked around him as he stood next to his bike outside the dispensary. He looked across the street at the gas station and the strip mall next to that. He looked at the Jiffy Lube garage catty-corner from him. Nothing out of the ordinary. No shady guys waiting in an SUV. He stepped up to his bike, swung his right leg over, fired up the engine, and sat down.

His leather jacket flapped around his back as he rode away from the dispensary. It was early summer, and warm out, but Trouble always wore his leather. Not only as protection against road-rash, a good place to store his gun, and a fashionable way to cover the track marks up and down his arms, but also because he'd had it for years, through thick and thin. It was his good luck charm, and he felt sure that if one day he lost it, that would be the end of him. His shit luck would finally get him. All would be right with the universe.

Even if the manner of his death didn't have anything to do with the jacket, like slipping on a banana peel in a subway station and then subsequently getting robbed and murdered by a pack of bloodthirsty, nunchuck-wielding girl scouts, he was sure that losing the jacket meant losing his life. It was a silly thought, but he wasn't about to test its validity. He wore a plain black t-shirt under the jacket, bluejeans, and Doc Martens high-top boots. None of his other apparel held the same superstitions as his jacket. He could take 'em or leave 'em.

He had much of the day before the last cash run. He did two every day. One mid-morning and one just before close. Heading down the road, he had a brief moment of enjoyment smelling the crisp, thin Colorado air, feeling the nice cooling wind blow past him. Then his thoughts returned to the fact that he didn't have any dope left and it had been several hours since he'd fixed.

Even with his addiction, several hours wasn't enough to start the withdrawal process, but he started feeling that familiar, uncomfortable tingling up his spine. He knew logically that if he had some dope in his pocket at this moment, he wouldn't be feeling the way he was. But not having any dope brought up all those little voices that were so insistent, telling him that he was going to get sick. That he was going to feel like shit soon. That his dealer was out or busted. Any little thing that could go wrong to keep him from getting high would go wrong.

He suddenly felt cold sweat all over his skin. His addiction easily overpowered his logic and sent him down a spiral of worry and physical discomfort that would continue until he fixed. Then, whenever he ran out again, it would start all over. Rinse and repeat. Over and over. Until he got clean. *If* he ever got clean.

Sixteen minutes later, Trouble pulled into the now-familiar neighborhood, that little seed of excitement in his belly. He found it funny, but buying dope got him about as nervous as participating in a gunfight. *A therapist would love me*, he thought, not for the first time.

His dealer's house was a one-story structure that looked small from the outside, only because it was deeper than it was wide. It was in a nice middle-class neighborhood just north of Sloan's Lake. Most of the houses looked the same, with little variations.

Like the floor plan was flipped on every other house, or the shingles were different colors, or some of them had stucco facades.

It looked like a new development. Less than ten years old, Trouble thought. Green lawns and flower beds and neatly trimmed bushes. There were a few people out and about. One guy doing yard work. A couple of kids playing basketball on one of those transportable hoops, the ones where you fill the base with sand or water, so it doesn't tip over.

A slight breeze stirred the air, carrying a faint pine scent. Small, snow-white clouds skated slowly by overhead. Trouble rode through the neighborhood, going the speed limit, nodding to people who looked at him. Just a normal guy riding around on a beautiful Saturday. Absolutely *not* going to buy drugs.

A man in a shiny white SUV passed him going the opposite direction. Trouble glanced at him and nodded his head. The guy just stared at him as they drove past each other, doing the obligatory twenty-five mph. Trouble didn't recognize the guy. He was sure he'd never seen him before. He thought maybe he was an undercover cop for a second, but dismissed that idea as he got a better look at the guy. He saw the sparkle of a thick gold chain at the guy's neck and the look in his eye before they passed out of easy viewing sight. No, the guy was no cop. Trouble didn't know what he was, but he didn't like him.

Trouble shook it off after the moment passed. He always thought that people could somehow tell that he was a junkie. If they got a look at the track marks on his arms, they could, but all other outward appearances were normal. Still, paranoia was one of the side effects of his lifelong shit luck. So, he went out of his way to seem normal. If that meant smiling or nodding or waving to other normal people, people he would usually ignore, so be it. Anything to keep from getting rolled by the cops. Trouble glanced into a side mirror before making the turn into his dealer's driveway. The white SUV was gone.

Trouble always called ahead because his guy, Sam, wouldn't have it any other way. He told Trouble the first time they'd met that if he ever showed up there without calling ahead, he would be treated as a hostile. Trouble had no reason to doubt him, even though the speech sounded a little practiced. Trouble had dealt with addicts regularly for almost all his life, and he knew how they could get when they were sick. He knew how he himself could get occasionally. It wasn't pretty.

Every time Trouble showed up, Sam was in his garage with the door up, waiting. Trouble had never been inside the house but to use the bathroom, and even then, Sam seemed reluctant to let him and had been waiting to escort him back to the garage when he was finished. Trouble didn't blame him. He knew from the setup in the bathroom that the guy had a wife: potpourri in a little basket and soap carved to look like flowers. Floral shower curtain, matching towels embroidered with little roses. Definitely not the work of Sam, who, according to the mutual friend they had, used to be the baddest of badass bikers.

He had been the president of a little M.C. in Phoenix for a decade but got out of the game after spending a few years in prison. Or, at least, semi-out. They hadn't known each other for long. Sure, their mutual friend had vouched for him, but Sam was careful. Trouble had the feeling that he would warm up to him a little bit, but it would take time.

He had liked Sam right away and was glad they could do business. He hadn't been about to take a job in a place where he couldn't get dope, so it worked out well. Trouble was not a big fan of wandering around in seedy parts of town asking people for drugs. He'd known people to do that and had done it himself in desperate times, but it was asking to get robbed, killed, or thrown in jail.

Sam walked out of his garage as Trouble approached and greeted him with a hearty slap on the back and a "Hey, buddy" when Trouble was off his bike in the driveway. Trouble knew the jovial greeting was probably more a show for any neighbors watching than genuine emotion. It didn't bother him.

Sam was a good four inches taller, forty pounds heavier, and ten years older than Trouble. It wasn't hard for him to believe that the guy had been, and still was, one badass dude. He had black hair cut short and sprinkled with little specks of gray. His beard was full and about eight inches long. It had a gray stripe the full length down, just off-center. He was wearing a black A-shirt, black pants, and was walking around barefoot. He had random tattoos all up and down his arms and poking out from under the shirt.

Trouble figured him for maybe thirty pounds of fat and two-hundred and ten pounds of muscle. He had a gruff voice and could be extremely intimidating, but only when he wanted to be. He would greet his neighbors whenever he saw them out and chat with passersby. From what Trouble had seen, everyone in the neighborhood seemed to know and like him.

Sam put his arm around Trouble's shoulders and led him into the garage.

"Lemme show you this bike I'm working on," he said as they walked to one of the three bikes that were currently being rebuilt or repaired in the space. They talked about motorcycles and the weather and current events. All small talk, although they both genuinely enjoyed talking about motorcycles. It was another reason Trouble liked the guy. This was their process. At some point during the conversation, Sam would open a tool chest and say something like, "Did you leave this here last time?" Only it wouldn't be a tool. It would be the dope. Already weighed out and in a little plastic baggie, ready to go. Trouble would have the agreed-upon amount of money folded up in his pocket. He would exchange the money for the dope.

They would then chat for another few minutes and Trouble would say goodbye. Sometimes he was there for fifteen minutes, other times an hour. He didn't mind it. He liked being careful, and it wasn't like he had any other friends in Denver. Sam was it. Kind of sad, really.

This time Sam grabbed a little plastic container that once held fuses and said, "Oh man, I almost forgot, I found those fuses for you."

"Oh yeah, thanks. I totally spaced it," Trouble replied, opening the case and glancing at the little baggie inside. "How much do I owe you?"

"Just give me ten and buy me a beer next week."

"You got it." Trouble handed him the hundred dollars that he retrieved from a pocket. He put the dope in his jacket.

Five minutes later, Trouble was on his way again, excited to get high. Driving home from Sam's house was like what Trouble imagined waiting for Christmas morning would've been like if he had ever experienced a normal Christmas. He couldn't get there soon enough.

His apartment building was rundown and seedy. It wasn't really an apartment at all, but an old extended-stay, off-brand motel. In the living room, which also doubled for the entryway, den, and dining room, there was a tattered leather couch that was probably older than Trouble, a small wood framed coffee table with a single piece of glass in the middle, and a small flat screen TV bolted to the wall across from the couch. There was a little kitchenette complete with microwave, hot plate, and miniature fridge. To the left of the kitchenette, there was a small bathroom with a small shower and no bathtub. Beyond that, a bedroom with a queen bed and a small nightstand.

It wasn't great by any means, but it was the first place Trouble had found that would accept cash without a credit card for backup. Just a hefty deposit. He hated signing leases, and he didn't carry credit or debit cards, so his options were limited.

Plus, it was within his budget, if you could call the quick and dirty calculations he did in his head a budget.

He threw his jacket onto a couch arm as he sat down and reached under the coffee table for a small paper bag that contained syringes. Looking through, he couldn't find one that hadn't been used at least once. He didn't even think about going out to get fresh ones. He just found one that looked fairly clean and sharp and set it aside on top of the coffee table.

They were disposable, one-use needles, but heroin is a hell of a drug, and little errands like buying new syringes felt, in an addict's mind, like a whole big ordeal. Never mind the fact that there was a pharmacy not two blocks away where he could get them over the counter. If he had been sharing needles with someone, it would have been a different story. Different risks involved. As it was, he did his dope alone and preferred it that way. The needles went dull after a few uses and made shooting more difficult, but he was sure that there were several in the bag that he had only used once.

In the middle of the table was a black hand towel folded over itself. He unfolded it to reveal a wad of cotton and a spoon bent so if placed on a flat surface, the liquid in it wouldn't spill out. He pulled the towel to the edge of the table and lined it up in front of him. He leaned over and got the dope out of his jacket pocket and set it next to the spoon on the towel. He dug a plastic lighter out of his pants pocket and then sat down on the floor in front of the coffee table, his back to the couch. He opened the little bag and dumped out the single chunk of heroin that was inside.

Back in California, he had been doing some much better dope, but out here he stuck to the black tar that he got from Sam, because it did the trick. He just had to up the dose a bit to get the same effect as the powder he was used to. He cut off a chunk of the sticky, dark-brown substance with his pocketknife and placed it into the spoon. He looked around for the plastic bottle of water that he had somewhere, finding it after a moment. He unscrewed the blue plastic cap and poured it full from the bottle before setting it on the table. He picked up his chosen syringe and took off the orange protective cap, exposing the tiny needle. He stuck the tip of the needle in the cap of water and pulled the plunger, filling it about a third of the way up. Then he pushed the water back out on top of the little black rock that sat in the spoon.

He lifted the spoon up, lit the lighter, and placed the flame under the spoon, just touching and blackening the underside until the water started bubbling, which didn't take long. Moving the lighter around underneath the spoon, he made sure to evenly cook all the water and dope together. When he was satisfied, he set the spoon down on the towel and the lighter on the glass of the coffee table.

He used the little orange protective cap to mix up the heroin that hadn't fully dissolved. Then he pinched off a small bit of cotton from the ball and rolled that bit into a tiny sphere. He dropped it into the brown water in the spoon, watching as the cotton went from dry and white to pale brown and wet. He picked up the syringe, stuck the needle in the middle of the little ball of cotton, and pulled the plunger back, sucking the brown water into the syringe through the little bit of cotton, which acted as a filter, leaving the impurities behind, collected around the cotton. Trouble held up the syringe, tapped it with his finger, and pushed the plunger just enough to get rid of the air bubbles that ended up inside. It was ready.

After a year of daily use, Trouble could rarely find a usable vein in either of his arms to hit. He would poke around for fifteen or twenty minutes, trying to find one. Sometimes, he got lucky. But lately he had just been going directly for his legs, despite the comparative pain and discomfort it caused.

He stood up, took off his belt, and pulled his jeans down, leaving his boxers on. Then he sat down on the couch and bent at the waist to inspect his legs, passing over the little bruises that indicated a spot where he'd recently hit or tried to hit. Sometimes the veins in the legs were deceptive. He could see them, greenish-blue and faint, but sometimes he couldn't reach them. They would be too far under the skin for the little needle to puncture. It got easier around the calves or the shins, but it was also more awkward to try and shoot there. So he stuck with the thighs.

He found one that looked promising about halfway down the inside of his right thigh. He wrapped his belt over the area and inspected the spot further, hoping that slowing the circulation to his leg would help the vein pop a little, making it easier to hit. It still looked promising, so he grabbed the loaded syringe from the coffee table in front of him and brought it to the spot, concentrating hard, the tip of his tongue sticking out the side of his mouth, his heart beating a little faster with excitement and anticipation. He slid the needle into his skin, keeping it pointed toward him, toward his heart. Once he thought he was in the vein, he pulled the plunger back a little while watching the tip of the syringe. Through the clear plastic, he saw blood flow in and mix with the dark-brown liquid. He was in. First try. *Yes.*

He pulled the plunger back more and watched more blood flow in, then he slowly depressed the plunger and watched the mixture of blood and heroin disappear into his body. When the syringe was empty, he pulled the needle out of his skin, set it down on the coffee table, and then unwrapped the belt from his upper thigh, setting it aside on the couch.

He sank back into the couch and waited. It didn't take long. It started at the back of his head, where the spine meets the skull. A warm, welcoming rush swept up the back of his head and then seemed to pour through his whole body. Euphoria. He felt it swarm his stomach. Like a mixture of being excited and slightly nervous about something you want to do but have never tried, and the way you feel just before you drift off to sleep, not thinking about anything. Multiplied by a hundred. Like floating in a hot tub filled with silk, cotton, and clouds. Feeling simultaneously heavy and light, extremely alive and yet somehow not there at all. His eyelids grew heavy, and he felt as if he were sinking further into the couch. A couch that was old and lumpy and not comfortable, but that now felt like the best couch in the world.

No place he'd rather be. Nothing he'd rather be doing. No better feeling to have.

A smile crept across his face, and a contented sigh escaped his mouth. Sitting there on the couch, his pants still around his ankles, he wallowed in his addiction and successfully escaped the memories and thoughts that had been following him for the last year. Memories that had driven him to seek solace in the arms of what had become his best friend, his full-time job, his lover, and his only family: heroin.

# Nine

Trouble's next run—the closing run—went off without a hitch. He'd nodded off for a while, enjoying the semi-consciousness of a nice big shot of dope. He had awakened two hours before he had to be there for the second and final run of the day. Two hours was just enough time to do another shot, enjoy the high for a while, then head off to work.

When he had started the job, he'd had the foresight to set a couple of standing alarms, one for the morning and one for the evening, to make sure he was up in time to do his runs. There was no telling when he would nod off. He found he could sleep all the way through his high and wake up feeling sick, occasionally. Other times, he slept for an hour or so, only to wake up and do more dope. This was one of the reasons why his habit was so expensive and his tolerance so high.

Upon waking on Sunday morning, he still had enough dope for one more big shot before he went to do the first run of the day, and a little leftover for after. He did the run, keeping alert and taking a long, out-of-the-way route to get the bank bag to its destination. For the first time, he took it to a different location. He thought that was strange.

For the two weeks that he'd had the job, he'd been taking the bank bags to a closed restaurant and handing it off to the same big, mean-looking guy in a suit, as other big, mean-looking guys in suits stared at him from around the restaurant. The place was under construction, and apparently would be for a long time. Trouble never saw anyone working on the place. Just guys standing around, looking mean. He was sure they had guns under their suit jackets.

It made a kind of sense to him, at first. He knew that banks all had ties to the federal government, although he didn't know the details of those ties. Any money going through those banks had to be legit. Again, he didn't know why, but guessed it had something to do with money laundering laws. The way he figured it, anyone had the right to protect their money, and if they couldn't go to the banks, then they had to get creative. Maybe this was some kind of pop-up banking operation. A place to put all the cash that came through the dispensary, to keep it safe. What happened from there, he had no idea.

Today, instead of taking the money to the restaurant, he brought the money to a house in an upper-middle-class neighborhood. His boss had given him the address, and he'd put it into his old generic smartphone, purposely taking random detours as he went, allowing the driving app to suggest new routes. The guys protecting the place were the same. Trouble handed the bag off to the same guy, signed the same clipboard, and got the same little receipt.

Since being shot at the day before, Trouble had been looking at things a little differently. Trying to figure out what this operation was. But he just didn't have enough information to come to a conclusion that made any sort of sense to him. He decided that, instead of just scoring, getting high, and nodding off, he would score, get high, and do some research. Then he would nod off.

His hope had been that he could make the dope he got yesterday last for two days, but he did it all in less than twenty-four hours. It was a common occurrence. If he had it, he would do it just about as quickly as he could. Presently, he only had enough for one shot left.

He took the receipt back to his boss, got his cash for the run, and called Sam, who picked up on the second ring.

"Hey, man," Trouble said. "I was hoping to swing by in about fifteen. You available?" There was a beat and Trouble thought that maybe the call had been dropped.

Then Sam spoke. "No, I'm not," he said. "I won't be available for another twenty-four hours or so."

Trouble's heart dropped. His mind started racing. Panic gripped him. He was going to get sick. The little bit he had left wouldn't get him through twenty-four hours. No way. He was going to be sweating and shaking and vomiting. He would barely be able to do the second run of the day. The run in the morning would be out of the question. No more work until he scored again. Which meant he would probably lose the job. Lori didn't strike him as the understanding type. She'd find someone else. Someone cheaper.

Twenty-four hours was an eternity without dope. The whole reason he'd saved a little bit was so he wouldn't start to worry, but it wasn't helping. The bit he had wouldn't even get him high. It would only prolong detox for a few hours, at most. All of this raced through his mind in the time it took Sam to take another long beat—like he was distracted or thinking hard about something.

"But I knew you'd be calling today, so I talked to a friend of mine, and he said he could help you out with something." And as quickly as that, Trouble's heart stopped racing, and he stopped feeling premature sickness all through his body. Sweet relief. He wouldn't be sick after all.

"With the same thing?" Trouble asked, hope in his voice.

"Not exactly, but almost as good. Some say better, actually. You've heard of F, right?"

Fentanyl. He knew the statistics. Something like 60,000 overdose deaths in the last year in the U.S. alone, and although there weren't any specific numbers for fentanyl, a hefty portion of those deaths were said to have been caused by the deadly synthetic opioid. People had actually been sent into overdose by just touching the stuff in powder form, or so the stories went. Granted, those people had zero tolerance, but even for someone like Trouble, it was rolling the dice. Like playing Russian Roulette.

"Yes. That'll do it. How's this going to work?" Despite the dangers, he was kind of excited to try fentanyl for the first time. The logical, sane part of him once again screaming to be heard was drowned out by the sweet, insistent voice of his addiction.

Sam told him where to go, who to talk to, and to be careful.

Thirty minutes later, Trouble showed up at a house on the northeast side of Denver. The polar opposite of Sam's house and neighborhood, the place looked like a drug den. Faded white paint was coming up off the walls of the house. Part of the roof was sagging in, the front yard was littered with trash and old car parts, and the windows were boarded up. The surrounding houses weren't faring much better.

Trouble noted the numbers on the facade. 741.

It was exactly the kind of house that he liked to avoid. It was a cop magnet. He fully expected to see an unmarked car sitting down the street, the plainclothes cop inside trying to blend in and hide at the same time. Trouble rode down the street and back, checking side streets and alleys, looking for police. He didn't see any, unmarked or otherwise. If it hadn't been the middle of the day—if it had been nighttime—he probably wouldn't have risked it. At least, that's what he told himself. But it's amazing the risks a sick addict will take.

He didn't think Sam would set him up, but he didn't know the guy all that well. Best to be careful. He stopped down the street from the house and shut off his engine. He pulled his cash payment for the morning's run out of his pants pocket, selected a few bills, and put them in his left jacket pocket. He stuffed the rest of his money down inside his boot. Not the best hiding place, but he wasn't about to leave it in his bike on the street. He pulled his .45 out of his inside jacket pocket and checked that he had a full clip and one in the chamber. He had reloaded both his guns the day before, but always liked to be sure. He clicked the safety off, put the gun in his outside jacket pocket, and kept his hand on it, index finger just outside the trigger guard.

He knocked on the door with his left hand and heard scuffling inside. It sounded like a few people moving around, but only one guy opened the door. He looked completely out of place in the dingy house. He was a clean-cut Caucasian guy, looking profoundly serious, even as he smiled the kind of polite smile that people do when they're trying to make strangers feel comfortable. Trouble thought that he looked vaguely familiar but couldn't place where he'd seen him before.

"You must be Trouble," the guy said, pulling the door wide, sticking out his right hand for Trouble to shake. Trouble looked at the guy's hand as he stepped around it, never taking his own hand off the gun concealed in his pocket. Inside the house was worse than outside. It looked like a true drug house. Holes in the drywall, trash all over the floor and piled up against the walls, spray paint tags and crude sexual drawings on every flat surface. The ceiling was sagging in some places and missing in others, giving a direct line of sight into the darkness of the A-frame attic.

On Trouble's left as he walked in was what used to be a living room, devoid of all furniture save a stained twin mattress.

There were beer cans, syringes, and broken crack pipes mingling with all the random fast-food and junk food wrappers. There was a stain on the floor by the wall that might have been dried blood, but it was too dark inside to tell for sure. To Trouble's right, there was a bathroom, but the toilet was missing and the porcelain sink was broken. He stopped by the bathroom with his back to the wall to wait for the guy to either sell him the drugs or lead him to where they would do the deal.

"You're Mason?" Trouble asked the guy as he closed the door.

"You got it," Mason said. "So how much are you looking for?"

"What do you have? Pills? Powder?"

"I've got powder. I sell it a gram for eighty, or ten for a tenth. So you're better off buying in grams." *Damn,* Trouble thought, *that's cheaper than dope. No wonder this shit is so popular.* It made him suspicious. He started worrying about getting ripped off, but there wasn't much he could do. He didn't have a rig on him to shoot with, and he didn't really want to spend more time in the shitty little house than he needed to.

"Okay, I'll take a gram," Trouble said, handing the guy eighty in twenties with his left hand. His right hand hadn't left the gun in his pocket.

"Alright. Wait here," Mason said as he walked down the hallway to where Trouble assumed the kitchen and bedrooms were. Soon after Mason was out of sight, Trouble heard voices talking low. There were more people in the house, which was to be expected. After about four minutes, Mason walked back out into the hallway with a little baggie in his hand.

"You'll probably be good doing about a quarter at a time of this stuff. It's been mixed to dilute it a bit because people have been dying from this shit. We like our customers alive," Mason said, smiling that fake smile again. Trouble just looked at him. He'd never had a dealer tell him how much to do before, much less volunteer that his product was cut with something. It struck him as strange. He took the bag from Mason with his left hand.

"Alright. Thanks for the heads-up. You have a number, for when I want more?"

"Sure," Mason said, and told him the number. Trouble pulled out his phone with his left hand and put it in. Then he called the number. Mason's phone started to ring in his pocket.

"There's mine," he said, smiling an equally fake smile back at Mason. Then he walked out the front door and started back toward his bike, his right hand in his jacket pocket, gripping his gun the whole way.

He got to his bike quickly, his gut sounding an alarm that was hard to ignore. He kept thinking he had seen Mason before but couldn't place where. He pulled his gun out of his jacket pocket and shoved it under the inside of his left thigh, against the seat. Something told him to get out of there, and fast, so he did. He sped around corners and risked getting pulled over by the cops. But he never saw a police car, and he slowed down when he felt that there was no one following him. Not for the first time, Trouble was happy to have a fast, maneuverable vehicle.

The feeling had faded from his gut by the time he got home.

# Ten

MURKE ARRIVED IN DENVER approximately twenty-eight hours before Trouble bought the fentanyl. Only arrived wasn't exactly the right word. Came into existence would be a more appropriate phrase. He came to Denver as someone else. Someone whose name he was even now forgetting. He hadn't been that person for long, anyway. Somewhere deep inside of him rested the information that he identified as his real name, birthplace, likes, dislikes, memories, etc. But he never had use for those things in his line of work.

When this job was over, he would take off the facade and go back to wherever it was he came from and do whatever it was that he did when he wasn't working. So he arrived in Denver, shed the identity that he had used for travel, and donned Murke. He didn't really think that he needed a separate identity just for travel, but the powers that be were big on covering their asses, and it's not like it was his money. They always paid for everything because, well, that's the way it was done.

Now, sitting at the little cafe, waiting for his contact to show up, he mentally groaned about how cliché it was to be meeting in a little cafe. He much preferred to meet in offices, which, for much of his early career, he had. Meaning he spent a lot of time in D.C. and New York. Which also meant that he did much more traveling in those days.

One thing remained the same: this part of the job could not be done over the phone. Small mercies, he supposed. In the old days, he would have flown to D.C. for a twenty-minute meeting, and then flown out to wherever the job was—in this case, Denver. He didn't necessarily mind traveling, as it afforded him ample opportunity to read, but meeting in cafes like this to discuss matters of such importance seemed—what was the word? Cheap. He felt like he was always being watched, which he kind of was. That's why it's called public.

He felt that this kind of cloak and dagger shit was overkill. But he would never say that to any of his superiors. It just didn't work that way. So he did what he was told, went where he was needed, and focused on being really fucking good at his job.

He smiled when he saw her come through the door of the tiny cafe. It was a skinny but long coffee shop with a total of twenty chairs, ample sunlight, and great coffee. She was a skinny but tall woman in her late thirties, and Murke had worked with her before. One of the perks of being in the business for as long as he had was that he knew his connections if he was working stateside. There was no silly secret code for anyone to memorize. No doubt about anyone's validity or credentials. It made the meetings much smoother and easier for both parties.

She smiled at him as he stood up and waved at her. They were both dressed like successful thirtysomething Americans, which is exactly what they were. They looked right at home in the coffee shop, and he stood in line with her while she ordered, catching up on small talk. He asked about her kids and she said they were doing great (he was quite sure she didn't have any). She asked about his wife (she must have spotted the wedding ring when she walked in, which was a part of his identity, but he wasn't married). They fell into lying to each other with practiced ease. All for the benefit of anyone else paying attention, although neither of them thought that anyone cared.

The meeting lasted twenty-six minutes. There was no paper exchanged. Only words. And a single key to a storage unit containing supplies for Murke. Supplies that she had gathered from a list that Murke made himself before coming to town. Any evidence of the list had long-since been deleted from secure government servers. She recited the address, the unit number, and the code to get into the storage place. Murke didn't need to write them down.

She had memorized the players in the game and the layout as it stood at that moment in time. Murke, for his turn, memorized everything he was told. She would be around if he needed her for anything. And one other operative whom Murke also knew. He would try to do it alone, as was his preference. But it was always nice to be able to call in backup. That was a luxury that he had quickly grown to appreciate early in his career.

As she told him about the mobile banking operation, he listened intently. This was something new. It was interesting. She described the restaurant it was in, and the house it was being moved to within the next twenty-four hours. She said that they moved the money to a bank in Mexico at irregular intervals. A bank that had no issues depositing and making available drug money.

Once they moved the money, she said, they usually moved locations. They were careful. Half of the dispensaries in the area used the mobile banking operation because they had no other choice. The legit banks in the city couldn't knowingly take money made from selling weed. It was still illegal at the federal level. And banks were insured by the federal government.

It was a colossal clusterfuck in Murke's limited opinion. A failure to see eye to eye in terms of the state and federal governments. But really, it didn't matter. He wasn't about to write his congressman. The dispensaries were doing the only thing they could. Aside from stockpiling their cash and having it guarded all the time.

By the time she finished filling him in, he was actually excited about the job. He started to formulate a plan to achieve his objective. The place seemed like a powder keg waiting to blow. Which was good for him. He figured it wouldn't take him a week to bring the whole thing crashing down.

He felt like a kid left home alone for the weekend. He could get artful with this job. He could think outside the box. He couldn't see any way things could go wrong. He was supremely confident. In all fairness, he had never failed before. Not really. Not in any way that mattered.

When she'd told him all, Murke smiled. The woman smiled back.

# Eleven

TROUBLE COULDN'T MOVE. HE was being choked. He struggled to get his bearings, and things came into focus. He was in a copse of trees, just off a beach, on all fours. There was sand at his hands, knees, and feet.

He knew what happened next. Looking straight ahead, he saw those eyes. Looking at him, pleading with him to do something, anything. Trouble saw the knife at the throat under those eyes. He tried to scream, to move, but it felt like he was underwater, with a forearm around his neck, choking. The man that held the knife smiled and then pulled the blade across the throat. Trouble watched the skin and cartilage separate, watched the artery tear open and the blood spew out, watched as his friend died in front of him. There wasn't a damn thing he could do. Trouble's vision closed in on him as he fought against the immovable weight that held him down.

But no. That's not how it was supposed to happen. Trouble fought. He killed the men who killed his friend, didn't he? His vision expanded out from the pinhole and the scene was the same again. His friend's pleading eyes, the knife, the weight, the panic. No. Not again. How many times would he have to live this, to witness this? A year and thousands of dollars in dope later and he still couldn't escape it. He knew it was all his fault, but it changed nothing. He couldn't go back, as much as he wished he could. So he watched. Again and again. Until finally he gave up and let the darkness take him away.

But oblivion escaped him. His torture wasn't over. This time a different scene materialized before his eyes. An SUV speeding toward him. He had his guns out and was firing at the windshield as time slowed down and the man fell out of the window again. As the wheel rolled over his head, it was as if all other noise ceased and the sound of breaking bone was amplified in Trouble's ears. Another death on his conscience.

No. No, that wasn't right. What would have happened if Trouble hadn't done anything? He would be dead, or they would be waiting for him another day. It was a freak occurrence. He felt for the guy, but ultimately it came down to his ass or Trouble's, and that was a no-brainer.

Then he saw it.

Out of the corner of his eye, he caught a glimpse of the driver as he spun the wheel to get turned around. He had seen him again. It couldn't be a coincidence, could it? Clean cut, Caucasian, nothing really special about him, but he had seen that face again in the dope house. He had sold Trouble the fentanyl. Mason.

Trouble jolted awake on the couch, his heart racing, and proceeded to vomit all over the coffee table. His body was rejecting the drug the only way it knew how. He had done too much. His head was spinning, and he threw up again and again on his way to the bathroom. When he finally got over the toilet, he was throwing up yellow strings of stomach bile.

The fact that he woke up at all meant that he wasn't overdosing, but that he'd come close. He didn't need to call an ambulance, he just needed to stay awake and puke it all out. He forced himself to drink some water from the bathroom faucet, then hovered over the toilet again, waiting. He had done half of what Mason had recommended he do. An eighth of a gram, and even then he didn't shoot it, but snorted it. Had he shot it, he would probably be dead. *No way that's a coincidence*, he thought. *That's the second time the guy has tried to kill me*.

He rarely had dreams when he was high, which was part of the appeal, but he was thankful that his subconscious was working to keep him alive, even as he was slowly circling the drain. He had arrived back at his place excited to get high, but something about the interaction had bothered him, and all the horror stories came back to him about how easy it was to OD on fentanyl. So he started small. Precaution. Survival. Dodging that shit luck of his.

He looked at the bedside clock from his position in the bathroom. It had been just over an hour since he snorted the stuff, meaning he still had a few hours before his last cash run of the day. He tried putting all the pieces together in his head, but was having a hard time staying awake, much less thinking straight. When he thought that he was done vomiting, he stood up to move back to the couch, but that movement made him nauseous again.

Eventually, he crawled back to the couch to lie down. Even though he felt sick to his stomach, he also felt incredibly relaxed. His opioid receptors had soaked up plenty of the drug before his body started rejecting it. It was a hell of a high, and he understood how easy it would be to go just a little bit overboard with the dosage and end up dead, even if you knew what you were doing. He closed his eyes and started thinking.

Sam was the one who had told him where to go. Now, thinking of the phone call, Trouble recalled the two long pauses his dealer had taken. Maybe thinking about what he was doing, maybe weighing his options, maybe getting told what to do from someone there with him. Trouble would have to pay Sam a little visit and ask him.

Best he could think was it had something to do with the guy that got his head run over. If they just wanted the money he was hired to transport, they weren't going to get it with Trouble dead in his apartment. Must be some sort of payback. Maybe they blamed him for the guy dying. Sure, he had caused it in an indirect sort of way, but really the whole thing was the driver's—Mason's—fault.

Mason was the one that slammed on the brakes, and he was the one that backed over the guy's head. Plus, there was the understanding that if you were going to go around robbing people, chances are that one day you'd get maimed or killed. Trouble accepted that and acted accordingly by attempting to be prepared for every eventuality. Obviously, there were some things you couldn't prepare for, like getting your head crushed by your own guy. But that was all part of the game. Although they probably didn't see it like that, seeing as how they'd tried to kill him again. *Oh well. What can you do?* Trouble thought. It seemed like everywhere he went, there was someone trying to kill him. You get used to it after a while.

***

Trouble parked down the road from Sam's house. It was full dark when he got there after finishing the day's second and last cash run from the weed shop. It had turned cool and felt more like spring than summer, which meant that Trouble was comfortable in his leather jacket as he strolled up the block toward Sam's place, on the opposite side of the street.

He hadn't called ahead, of course. But he had remembered what Sam told him the first time they had met. Something about treating him as hostile if he ever showed up there unannounced. That meant that there were surely precautions taken when Sam wasn't expecting anyone. Maybe an elaborate security system, one of those with cameras around the house that you can watch on your phone. Maybe, but Trouble didn't think so. Sam struck him as more of a lock-the-doors-and-windows-and-carry-a-big-fucking-gun type. But you never know.

He walked leisurely past on the opposite sidewalk, looking at the house only through his peripheral vision. He saw that the garage door was closed, and that there wasn't any obvious movement in or around the house. Most of the neighborhood looked the same. Garage doors closed, shades drawn, blue light from televisions or computer screens flickering in some rooms. It was Sunday night. Everyone was getting ready for the start of a new week. Winding down and squeezing the last little bit of their weekend into those final hours before bed.

He walked down to the end of the block and turned left, crossing to the other side of the street, following the sidewalk halfway to the next block. He came to an alley that ran down the length of the block. Sam's house would back up to it. It was just wide enough to get a garbage truck through, which was exactly its purpose. All the yards on both sides of the alley were fenced in, and each one had a gate. Most of the fences were made of cinder blocks, but some were wooden.

Along the right side of the alley sat big black trash bins. Their placement indicated that four households shared one of the bins, since they were placed between every two gates, and only on the right side. They looked like oversized versions of the kind that people in other neighborhoods set out in front of their houses once a week for trash day. He walked down the dirt alley smelling a mixture of old trash, fresh and rotting foliage, damp dirt, faint barbecue remnants, and the rare whiff of chlorine from a backyard pool.

Slowing as he came up behind Sam's house, he made sure to duck a little so his head wouldn't be visible from the backyard. The fence was made of cinder blocks, and the gate was made of a metal skeleton with wood slats fastened securely to the frame. It was locked. Trouble could see bits of broken glass glued or cemented to the top of the fence. Great for keeping birds from shitting on your fence. Also useful for keeping out pissed-off bikers you had conspired to murder earlier in the day. But there were ways around that.

One of the oversized black trash barrels was across the alley and down next to another gate. Trouble went over and lifted the hard plastic lid to look inside. He spotted a few bags, but it wasn't full by any means. He gripped it by the lip with both hands and dragged it across the alley, positioning it against the cinder block fence adorned with broken glass.

He stood up on his toes to look over the fence into the back-yard. It was neatly trimmed and cared for, as he expected. There were some tall bushes against the back fence that he would have to clear, but he didn't see it being much of a problem. He could see into the kitchen through a picture window. Lights were on, and regular kitchen things were set around, but there was no movement. No sign of Sam or his wife.

Trouble wasn't sure if he had any kids, but didn't think so, since he never saw toys in the garage or the yard. Never heard laughter or crying or playful screams that so often accompany the presence of young children. Trouble supposed that there could possibly be a teenager living in the house. Sam was certainly old enough to have sired an almost-grown human, but there was no evidence of this either. Trouble stood on his toes for a few minutes, watching for movement. There was none.

When he was satisfied that there was no one lying in wait for him, Trouble climbed onto the trash bin. The domed lid bowed under his weight and sunk about six inches, but it didn't make much of a difference. Trouble brought one foot off of the lid and, with his boot toe, broke away enough glass so he could put his foot down on the fence. From there, he launched himself over the bushes and came to a roll on the lush Colorado grass in Sam's backyard. He stopped, crouching on the grass, and listened for a minute. Still nothing. No movement, no crunch of a shotgun slide. No hurried footsteps.

He stood up slowly and made his way onto the back patio, careful not to bump any of the outdoor furniture. He peered into the kitchen through the picture window, seeing the same scene he'd viewed from behind the fence, only closer. To his right was a sliding glass door that led into what looked like a den. He started toward it and then stopped. He'd seen something on the ground in the kitchen, just a flash of color. He turned back and looked through the window again, seeing a splash of red on the white tile floor just past the kitchen counter. He stood up on his toes to get a better view of that section of the floor, enabling him to look down at a shallower angle. More red. Blood. A slender hand. A woman's hand, he guessed. The rest of her was blocked from view by the kitchen counter.

He pulled his .45 out of his inside jacket pocket and went to the sliding glass door. It wasn't locked, and it slid back easily on its tracks. He came into the den with his pistol up, safety off.

Straight ahead of him was the guest bathroom that he had used once before. Beyond that, a hallway leading to the garage.

He went through the door on his left, leading him into the kitchen. On the floor next to the kitchen cabinet under the picture window was a woman that Trouble assumed was Sam's wife. He had never seen her before. She had long brown hair and blue eyes that were open in shock and horror. Her throat had been cut, and by the look of the blood, Trouble guessed that it had happened a few hours ago. It was clear that she was dead. She wore black shorts and a muted but colorful tank top. But the shorts were twisted and bunched around her ankles and the tank top had been pulled up, revealing her breasts.

Trouble's still-sensitive stomach roiled at the sight. His recurring nightmare—the memory he had been trying so hard to forget—flashed in his head. He started breathing hard. He didn't want to puke, and he needed to clear the rest of the house.

He turned away from the sight and forced himself to lift his gun and go through the rest of the house. Through the dining room with a small table and four chairs. Through the living room with the flat screen television on the wall and a comfortable-looking couch, small speakers mounted all around the room. Down a hall, past a bedroom-turned-office with two desks, bookshelves, and filing cabinets. One more room at the end of the hall. Master bedroom. The door was closed. Trouble slowly turned the handle with his left hand, entering cautiously, but he already knew what would be waiting there for him. There was no one moving in the house. No one but Trouble.

Sam was lying on the bed, on the side nearest the door Trouble came through. It looked like he was asleep, except for the lack of color in his skin. On the bed near Sam's right hand was a bloody knife. Next to him, on the nightstand, sat all the familiar supplies: bent spoon, lighter, cotton ball, bottle of water, syringe, and a big block of black-tar heroin.

Even at that moment, seeing Sam dead, the addict in Trouble was wide awake. The block of heroin on the table caught his attention and held it for long enough to make Trouble feel ashamed when he snapped out of it. His only thoughts were of how many times he could get high off that much dope. Meanwhile, a man whom Trouble had considered his friend lay there dead from an apparent overdose. *Jesus, I have got to get off this fucking drug,* Trouble thought, fighting an urge to fix right there on the bed next to Sam's corpse, on Sam's stash, while Sam's wife lay dead in the kitchen.

He didn't know what exactly had gone down, but for a second he thought that maybe there had been a fight. Maybe Sam *had* murdered his wife and then, overcome with grief, killed himself with a massive dose of heroin.

It made sense until he remembered the phone call, the strange pauses from Sam, and Mason from the SUV and the drug house. More likely it was Mason and his crew that had made Sam betray Trouble. And then killed them anyway. But why? That didn't make sense to Trouble. Why kill them at all? Surely threatening their lives would have been enough. Why leave bodies behind, even if it was made to look like a murder-suicide?

And how did they know about Sam and Trouble's connection in the first place? There were too many unanswered questions. He thought for a long moment about leaving town. With the dope on the nightstand and the fentanyl back at his motel, he could make it anywhere in the country before he had to face sobriety.

But that was never really an option.

Not for Trouble.

Shooting at him was one thing, but killing Sam and his wife was the crossing of a line. Not just a toe over, either, but a big fucking jump over that line. It had to be answered. Sam had been good to Trouble when he could have easily been just the opposite. He couldn't blame the guy for sending him to the setup at the drug house. If Trouble had been in his shoes, with a wife whose existence was on the line, he probably would have done the same thing. Sam wasn't to blame at all. It was the bastards that did this to him.

Somehow this whole thing tied in with the dispensary, or at least the pop-up bank he was delivering money to. He just didn't know how. Looking around Sam's bedroom, in the roaring silence that sometimes follows death, Trouble decided that he would find out who did this and make them pay for it. Any damn way he could.

It wasn't really a big leap for him. He didn't clench his fist or set his jaw. There was no swelling musical score, no faraway look in his eyes, not even a change in his breathing. It was as simple as thinking about what to eat for dinner. It was like recalling that you have an appointment to keep. Your brain remembers it, shifts some things around, and you keep it there, at the front of your mind, until the task is complete. Only for Trouble, the appointment would involve violence—and lots of it. Simple as that. Once that line was crossed, there was no avoiding it. It was permanently on his to-do list until it was done.

Trouble decided that it was a long shot, but he was going to head back to the drug house to see if there was anyone there who could put his mind at ease. Maybe he could even get a workout in while he was at it. Suddenly, he was itching for a fight. He walked over to the nightstand and picked up the block of heroin, put it in the bag on which it had been lying, put it in his pocket, and went back the way he had come, wiping the bedroom doorknob of his prints.

He went out to the backyard, wiped the sliding door handle, and found that the gate leading to the alley was locked with a simple metal bar that slid into place in the cinder-block wall. He slid it out with his palm, closed the gate behind him, moved the trash bin back into its original place, and walked back to his bike.

# Twelve

For the second time in a day, Trouble found himself riding around the poverty-stricken neighborhood looking for people sitting in cars on the street, cops or otherwise. He had stopped before entering the area to pull out one of his guns. He stuck it under the inside of his left thigh, just as he had when he left the area in the early afternoon. It was dark, and the cars were harder to see into, but he felt confident that there was no one watching him or waiting for him to come back to the house. He didn't really think there was going to be anyone there, but it was the only lead he had.

Once again, he parked his bike down the street and approached the house on foot. This time he kept his .45 out of his pocket, held down by his right leg. The streetlight that would normally illuminate the area around the little house was broken, so Trouble took it slow. He stopped to listen twice as he approached. There was the occasional car that drove by, and one man peddled past on a bike, but otherwise it was a quiet neighborhood.

The lack of blue light coming from windows, the empty driveways, and the general silence told him that many of the houses were probably vacant, or their owners weren't home. Most of the houses certainly looked run-down enough to be unclaimed.

He went up to the porch but didn't step up. He stood on the concrete walkway and listened.

Nothing.

He went around to the left of the house, slowly stepping around the random junk piled haphazardly in the yard, looking for a window that wasn't boarded up. He found one around the side of the house but couldn't see anything. No light, no sound.

He went back to the front of the house and around the right side. He found another board-less window and could see some faint light spilling out. He crept up to it and looked through with the corner of his eye. Through the window was a den of some sort, piled with the kind of trash he had seen in the front rooms. Through the doorway of the den, he could see a small slice of the kitchen area.

A battery-powered lantern sat on the counter. The kind you can get at a big chain store for under five dollars. It was giving off a faint light. Trouble stood there and waited. After a few minutes, he watched a very gaunt and scraggly man walk into view and pick something up from next to the lantern, then step back out of Trouble's field of view. Trouble just had a glimpse of him, and that glimpse screamed "addict." He waited there for another ten minutes, but nothing happened. He was sure the man was alone. So he headed for the front door.

Before he climbed the porch steps, he shut his eyes and counted to sixty. He was pretty sure that his eyes had adjusted as well as could be expected, but wasn't about to take any chances. The front door was unlocked, but not for lack of trying. He noticed that the door frame into which the deadbolt would normally slide was splintered and broken. Like someone had jammed a crowbar in there to break it.

He moved slowly down the same hallway in which he had waited before, checking the rooms as he went. There was no one in them, just the trash and junkie detritus he had seen before. He made his way to the back and peeked around the doorway into the kitchen. The gaunt man was lying there on the kitchen floor, a tattered backpack behind his head, a grimy sleeping bag under him, and a syringe next to him on the floor. He must have been getting ready to fix when Trouble had caught a glimpse of him from outside because he had a smile on his face and looked to be in the land of nod. He hadn't noticed that Trouble was now with him in the kitchen. A look at the homeless man assured Trouble that he wasn't going anywhere.

Checking the remainder of the house didn't take long, and when Trouble arrived back in the kitchen, the addict was still there, still blissfully unaware. Trouble knelt down beside him and nudged him with his left hand. He still had his .45 in his right hand, but as more of a helpful prop to get the guy talking. It didn't seem to Trouble that this guy had anything to do with Mason or the others. It was more likely that he just frequented the house as a place to get high and sleep out of the weather.

Still, he wanted to see if the guy knew anything about them, so he woke him up.

The guy's glazed eyes opened slowly, and he made a sleepy sound, like a grunt, then closed his eyes again. Trouble nudged him, harder this time, and spoke using his outside voice.

"Hey. Wake up, man. This isn't a dream. I want to talk to you."

The old guy started awake and looked around, trying to remember where he was. Then he saw the gun in Trouble's hand. He backed up, now fully awake, into the corner where rotting and doorless kitchen cabinets met. It didn't put him much farther away from Trouble than he had just been, but it was the only place to go. Trouble was kneeling in the middle of the floor, blocking the only way out of the kitchen.

"Whoa, bro. I don't have nothin'. You can see that. I'm just trying to sleep here for the night. I'll move on if you want." He went to stand up, but Trouble stopped him.

"Relax. I am not here to rob you, and I'm not here to kick you out. Just stay where you are. I have a couple of questions for you. No right or wrong answers, just tell me the truth, okay?"

The homeless man looked back at Trouble with shiny, bloodshot eyes and nodded. There was a shame in those eyes that Trouble immediately identified with. He had seen the same look in the mirror many times since he had started using dope regularly.

Having been no stranger to the stuff, Trouble had used it many times in his adolescent and adult life. But he had always understood the power that it held, and so was able to have enough foresight and self-discipline to keep from using too many days in a row, therefore avoiding the physical dependence that was always waiting around the corner. It was only after he started running from something that he let his guard down and didn't stop himself when the usual four-day limit hit.

He wondered if the guy sitting before him had been through something similar. He assumed so. It was like sitting across from a cautionary tale.

"What's your name?" Trouble asked.

"Jameson," the gaunt man said, relaxing a little.

Jameson had on fatigues complete with cargo pockets, holes, and stains both old and new. His sweater was threadbare and had once been a pale gray, but now looked like a grease monkey's hand towel, smeared and stained various shades of nasty.

He had his shoes and socks off, and Trouble could see where the guy had been shooting. The tops of both of his feet were bruised and there was one abscess that looked to be infected. All the visible skin on the guy was yellow and dirty, and his stench was palpable. His clothes were all baggy not because they were too big, but because he was too small. A normal, healthy person would fit into them just fine, but not this emaciated man. He had a reddish-gray beard that looked to be a few months' growth. A dirty black beanie hid the rest of the man's hair. He looked to be about fifty but could well have been forty with a ten-year habit.

A worst-case scenario.

Trouble knew he was one bad day away from living like Jameson. In fact, it was a near certainty if he continued down the road he was on.

Sure, there were plenty of functioning addicts all around. They worked at the coffee shop, the corner store, the office, the local hospital. Many people function just fine for many years, and some even manage to get clean before really digging themselves into a hole, but mostly the drug eats people from the inside out. You can function until you can't anymore. Life changes around you, but your addiction stays there, insistent and impossible to ignore. Number one on your shopping list is always dope because without it, you can't do shit. Not eat, not sleep, not work, not laugh.

"Jameson, I'm Trouble." Jameson groaned at this and tensed again. Trouble smiled.

"No, that's really my name. Not some clever way of telling you I'm about to beat you up or something. Been called Trouble since I was a kid."

Jameson looked at him warily from the side of his eye.

"Were you around here earlier today at all?"

"No. I just found this place like an hour ago, I swear. I didn't see anything. I only just got here. I neve— "

"Jameson, look at me. I promise you I won't hurt you, no matter what. I'm just looking for information. So, were you around here earlier today?"

Jameson shook his head.

Trouble sighed. He could tell that the guy was just telling him what he thought he wanted to hear. Time to change tactics. He stood up, put his gun in his outside pocket, and turned around. He dug out the bag with the big heroin rock in it and broke off a decent-sized chunk. Probably about eighty dollars' worth. He turned back around and knelt beside Jameson again, holding out the dope. Jameson saw it and his eyes came alive with that familiar hope and yearning. He looked from the tar to Trouble, and back again.

"I'm willing to give you this, out of my own personal stash, if you tell me the truth. I'll know if you're not," Trouble said. Jameson was now giving his undivided attention to the words Trouble was saying. He was all ears.

"Now. Were you here earlier today?"

"Yes. But I left for a while to score a couple of hours ago."

"Tell me about before that. Did you see people come into the house?"

"Yes. I still had some dope this morning, so I decided to stay here. I stay here sometimes. When I'm too late to get to the shelter."

Trouble could tell the guy was being sincere with him. The man underneath the grime and addiction was showing through. The promise of free dope was enough for Jameson to let his guard down.

"I don't have a phone and my watch broke a couple of days ago," Jameson continued, "so I don't know what time it was, but I heard some people walking around outside talking. So I went to my secret spot in the attic where I hide sometimes."

"Show me where that is," Trouble said. His search of the house hadn't yielded any obvious attic access, but he hadn't been looking for it, either.

"But... then it won't be my secret," Jameson said, hesitant again.

"Show it to me or you don't get the dope. I'm not going to harass you again. And I won't tell anyone about your secret spot. I promise." Trouble could tell that the guy wasn't quite right, even aside from the obvious issues of extreme poverty and substance abuse. Somehow developmentally disabled, he guessed. It made him feel for the guy even more. Jameson looked at the dope between Trouble's thumb and forefinger, and acquiesced.

"Fine. Come with me," he said as he started the slow process of getting up off the floor. Trouble stood up and waited, then followed the guy out of the kitchen and toward the rest of the house.

They walked to a door off the hallway. Because of its placement between two bedrooms, and the small size of the door, Trouble had skipped over it in his search of the place. It couldn't be anything but a closet. Jameson opened the door to reveal a small square storage space lined with empty shelves on three walls. It was just large enough for a person to fit inside and close the door. If the shelves weren't there, it would probably fit three or four people. Jameson pointed at the ceiling.

"Up there," he said. Trouble leaned into the closet next to Jameson and looked up. There was white painted wood bordering a hole in the ceiling. At some point in the past, there had been an access panel sitting on the wood frames, but that was gone, possibly in the attic. The shelving in the closet was all reinforced and fastened to the walls, making a built-in ladder. Trouble moved Jameson out of the way and told him to stay put. He put the dope back in the bag in his pocket, then climbed up so that his head and shoulders were in the attic.

He used the flashlight on his phone to illuminate the space. It looked like the attic covered the whole house, with enough room to stand up almost straight in the middle of the A-frame roof, and little room on the sides where the roof sloped down to meet the walls of the house. There were loose wide wood planks that made a makeshift floor along the middle of the attic. Trouble could see a wide spot on the planks where the dust had been rubbed away. Jameson's secret spot. He climbed back down and looked at the other man.

"You were up there when the men came into the house?"

Jameson nodded.

"Did you hear anything? Them talking about anything?"

He nodded again.

"Well? What did you hear?"

"It was mostly small talk at first, but then one of them started talking about some job that he did. Something about a kid. Thomas, maybe? Or Thompson? They were laughing about him."

Trouble thought for a second, but the name didn't mean anything to him.

"What else did you hear?"

"They started talking about fentanyl, which is when I really started listening. I even crawled closer to the kitchen. That shit is ten times better than dope. You ever done it?"

Trouble ignored the question. "Did you hear anyone else come in?"

"Yeah, that's what all the fentanyl talk was about. They were waiting to do a drug deal. It sounded like they were going to rip the guy off, but they didn't. They said that the guy was packin', so they didn't want to risk it."

Trouble knew that Jameson was talking about him now.

"Tell me what they said, what you can remember."

"I think they had a guy outside watching, and after the knock on the door the other guy came in the back, I think, and told the others in the kitchen that the one who came to buy the drugs had a gun in his pocket, and his hand was on it. They had some sort of discussion about it. In the end, they just sold him the drugs, and he left. But they sounded pretty pissed that they couldn't rip him off. Especially the one guy who did the deal. It sounded like he wanted to kill the guy. I even thought about coming down and asking them about the fentanyl, but the way they were talking made me think they'd kill me just for being here. Plus, I didn't have any money."

Trouble already assumed that they were trying to kill him, so Jameson wasn't really giving him any new information. He hadn't known about the guy outside watching, which was disconcerting. He also hadn't known how close he'd come to death. His paranoia had served him well yet again. If he hadn't walked into the place with a hand on his gun, he wouldn't be standing here, talking to Jameson. Still, it wasn't exactly what he had been hoping for.

"Did you hear why they wanted to rob the guy? How about names? Did they use any names besides Thomas or Thompson?"

Jameson thought for a second, then paused and smiled wide. "I think some of that dope will help me remember." He thought he was being sly.

"You'll get the dope after you tell me all you know. That was the deal. Or I can walk out now and you get nothing."

"Okay, okay. There was Mason, who I think was the one who did the deal. Colton, who was the guy that came in and told them about the gun in the guy's pocket. There was another guy, but I didn't hear his name. And then they were laughing about Thomas or Thompson, like I already told you. That's all. Honest."

"Thanks, Jameson."

They walked back to the kitchen, and Trouble dug the dope back out of his pocket. Jameson stood in front of him with both his hands cupped together and held out to Trouble. As soon as the dope was in his hand, Jameson turned around and began pulling his supplies together for a shot. He was hunched over and wheezing slightly. It reminded Trouble of Golem from the

Lord of the Rings movies. He wondered if he looked the same way when he was getting ready to fix. The thought gave him chills.

"Be careful, Jameson," he said to the old man's back as he headed toward the front door. Jameson didn't say anything, didn't turn around. He was miles away, lost in dope.

Trouble headed home. His near overdose had sapped his energy, and he wasn't thinking clearly. He had not eaten in several hours and hadn't done any dope since the fentanyl. It was time for a shot, but he knew that even a small one would send him to the land of nod in a matter of minutes.

He craved the bliss and solace that dope sleep would bring him. It was one of the things he liked best about being a junkie: nodding off to sleep while watching something on television. It meant he didn't have to think. About these people trying to kill him. About the mistakes he made in the past. About the fact that he was a junkie. He could escape it all for at least a few hours. Even dope can't totally quell the waking mind. No better drug than black, dreamless sleep.

# Thirteen

W HEN HE GOT HOME, Trouble shot a little bit of dope, still worried about overdose if he did too much. He had no idea how long fentanyl stays in the body. He decided that before he passed out, he would do a little research. He lay back on the couch and pulled out his phone. He found the little white search bar and typed in *Denver thomas news* to see if he could find anything about who Mason's crew was talking about. He scrolled through a couple of pages, but nothing jumped out at him.

He tried *Denver thompson news* and got a hit on the first page. Pressing the little blue text with his thumb led him to a local news website. It was a short article about a guy named Brad Thompson who had been murdered in the middle of the day about two weeks before Trouble arrived in Denver:

**One Dead in Globeville Shooting**

Denver Police Official Denies Possibility of Cartel Involvement

By **Sarah Hiraj** | Posted May 20th, 11:46 a.m.

*The Denver office of the Medical Examiner has identified a 28-year-old male who was shot and killed during an apparent robbery as Bradley Thompson. Thompson was pronounced dead at the scene just after 10 a.m. on May 16th.*

*According to police, the unidentified suspect or suspects accosted the victim when he pulled up to a stop sign at 40th and Fox on Wednesday morning. It is unclear what the suspects took, and whether this was a random or targeted robbery.*

*Police spokesman Roger Ballatte said that it may have been gang-related, although the police have found no evidence of gang ties to the victim. This will be the 30th homicide in the city limits so far this year, putting it on par to make this Denver's most violent year in a decade.*

*When asked about potential drug cartel ties, Ballatte said that the police are looking into all possibilities but have found no evidence that any cartels are operating within Denver. This shooting comes only days after a suspected cartel operator known only as "Mr. G" was captured on camera following a shooting in the Five Points area.*

*The victim, Thompson, was well known locally as the rhythm guitar player for Burned Ego, a Denver band that, according to lead singer Kurt Reynolds, was about to go on tour to promote their new album.*

*Thompson's girlfriend, Katrina Parks, has requested that anyone with any information about Thompson's murder call the police tip line. She will also be organizing a benefit concert for violence prevention this Saturday at the Spotted Owl in downtown*

*Denver. Click Here to visit Burned Ego's website for more information about the benefit.*

*Any tips about this or other crimes are welcome by calling the police tip line at 303-555-1122.*

After finishing the article, he saw another one that caught his eye near the bottom, under a 'Related Articles' heading. He tapped the picture, which featured an armored car, and began to read. Apparently, several months previously, the owner of an armored transport company had been murdered in his home, along with his wife and son. The newspaper was calling it a home invasion, and the police had caught a pair of brothers who had been breaking into homes in adjacent neighborhoods. The brothers insisted that they hadn't killed anyone, pointing to the lack of evidence tying them to the scene. They were currently awaiting trial for the heinous murders.

Trouble didn't think that the brothers were to blame. It was no coincidence that the owner of a top-notch armed courier company had been killed while Trouble was able to find a job as a courier a few months later. But, in his current state, he couldn't think why. If there were cartels in town, he supposed that scaring professional security contractors away from working with certain dispensaries would make them easier to rob. But it was a lot of trouble for only a little money, if what he had been transporting was any indication. Something else was going on.

Pretty soon Trouble was thinking at half speed with half-closed eyes, semi-conscious. A self-imposed delirium had settled upon him, and thinking coherently was becoming increasingly difficult.

Finally, he drifted off into a restless dope sleep.

***

Trouble awoke seven hours later, vaguely uneasy from his fast-fading dreams. The first thing he did was fix. It had become a habit, even on the rare mornings that he woke up without feeling early detox sickness.

He went to the dispensary to pick up the morning's haul, walking through the front doors like he usually did, but instead of heading for the back office he decided to linger a little bit on the sales floor. Bright fluorescents in the ceiling illuminated the glass cabinets in a big square bordering the room. There was enough space behind the glass counters for employees to move comfortably around the square. The walls behind the counters were lined with shelves and boards, packed with baggies of weed. In the glass cabinets sat all kinds of weed-related products.

Trouble strolled casually around the shop, looking at all the different packages of little weed candies and gummies and sodas and suckers. All the different containers of marijuana with funny names like White Widow, Maui Wowie, Starfucker, and Death from Above. There were several customers in the place and three employees. Trouble usually just made a beeline for the back, to get his job done. He'd never really looked around.

He had once been a big fan of weed, but since his heroin addiction had gotten serious, he couldn't find a use for the stuff. Dope was a jealous mistress. He took in the sights, got a feel for the place, and then headed for the back office.

Lori was at her desk, like always. She seemed to be lost in her phone, punching at the screen furiously with her thumbs. She didn't notice him walk in. He looked around the office and saw that nothing much had changed since yesterday. He wondered what she did in here if nothing had been moved. Maybe it was all digital and everything was done on her computer, but then why all the law books and clutter around the office?

He cleared his throat, and she looked up at him from her phone, her face twisting into a rictus of concern. She spun around in her chair and opened up the safe behind her. Trouble caught a glimpse of at least six bank bags identical to the one she pulled out for him. Full bank bags. Lori had never opened the safe in front of him before. She always had the bag ready to go when he walked in.

She handed the bag to him, and the log out book from on top of the safe. He signed out the bag and stepped back into the hallway. Not a word said between them. He glanced back in as the door swung shut. Lori was back on her phone again, typing away, her face unchanged.

In the bright summer sunlight, everything about the dispensary seemed a little off. Trouble scanned his surroundings as he headed for his bike parked on the sidewalk behind the building. He kept one hand on a gun in his pocket and the other on the money bag as he walked. He tried not to lose himself in his thoughts, but it was hard. Something was nagging at him. He dismissed it and reminded himself to talk to Thompson's girl-friend. He had missed the benefit concert, but he was confident that he could find her. It was the only lead he had gotten from Jameson the night before.

Riding back to the house that doubled for a bank, he had the feeling that he was being followed. That feeling seated itself in his stomach, insistent and somewhat comforting, but he didn't see a tail. If someone was following him, they were doing a good job of it; using at least two cars. Mason and his crew didn't have that in them, he thought. So, after doing a couple of large and small circles in some random neighborhood, he headed for the house.

Arriving there, the place looked the same. It was an older, middle-class house. Two stories, two-car garage, basketball hoop out front, beige paint with brown trim. It sat on a non-descript street that ended in a cul-de-sac some hundred yards further on. Looking at it, there was no way to tell that it was being used to hold money. How much money, Trouble wasn't sure, but probably not an insignificant amount.

He parked on the street and walked up to the porch. As he came to the door, it opened and the same big, tough-looking guy stepped out with a clipboard and a bored look on his face. Trouble handed him the bag and took the clipboard to fill out the deposit information.

"How long before you guys change locations again?" Trouble asked without looking up. The guy said nothing.

"Something happen to the last place? Or is it regular to move once in a while?"

Still the guy said nothing. It was clear he wasn't going to tell Trouble anything or, for that matter, even change his expression. This came as no surprise. Everything about this crew and this setup told him that these were professionals. There was no way for him to tell for sure, but Trouble was confident that there were at least two guns pointed at him as he stood on the porch. Probably high-powered automatic rifles. Surely with extended magazines and in perfect working order. Big Tough Guy took the clipboard back from him, did some signing and tearing, and handed over the receipt. Trouble folded it up and put it in his pocket, and then headed back to his bike.

Trouble started his bike and rode up to make a U-turn in the cul-de-sac. He looked over the house as he passed slowly by. He still didn't see anything out of the ordinary. No gun barrels sticking out of windows, no barbed wire, no mounted cameras, no guys in sunglasses sitting on the roof, not even a 'beware of dog' sign. These guys were good. If, in fact, there were guys.

It wasn't all that important, anyway. Trouble didn't think that these guys had anything to do with those who had tried to kill him a couple of times now. If they were in cahoots, he would surely be dead already. Plus, why would they try to steal money that was going to be handed to them anyway? It didn't make any sense. But Trouble was curious by nature, insofar as being curious had helped him avoid getting killed many, many times in his life. But by the same token, it had gotten him into a lot of shit, too. There was some sort of cost-benefit analysis in there somewhere, but Trouble had never tried to run the numbers. He was confident that his curiosity had saved him more times than it had put him in harm's way, and that was enough for him.

He brought the receipt back to Lori, who was still looking miserable, but this time she was just staring at her desk, lost in thought. She took the paper from him and put it in a drawer without looking at it. Trouble just stood there in front of her, waiting. She looked up after he cleared his throat.

"Oh, right. You need to get paid," she said with a dismissive wave of her hand. Swiveling in her chair, she opened the unlocked safe about six inches, then stopped herself. She looked over her shoulder at Trouble and smiled an apologetic smile, indicating that he should leave the room like he had done every other time she had to open the safe. Trouble stepped out, shut the door behind him, and started puzzling over what he had seen. She had opened it just enough to give him a glimpse into it for the second time today.

All of the stuffed bank bags he had seen just over an hour earlier were gone.

# Fourteen

K ATRINA PARKS WAS DAYDREAMING about Brad again. She sat at her desk in her small office, staring at her computer, seeing nothing. It had been like this every day since he died. No, not died—that wasn't the right word. Since he had been *murdered*. It still struck her as strange. She had never known anyone who had died before, much less anyone who had been murdered. To be fair, she had lost her grandmother when she was little, but that was barely a memory. She hadn't really known her grandmother. Not the way she had known Bradley Ian Thompson.

She had been waking up every morning resigned to the fact that the day ahead would bring a roller coaster of emotions. One minute, she would remember something funny he had done, and she would smile or laugh quietly to herself. Then she would think about something sweet he had done, or a fight they had, and she would start bawling her eyes out. Right there in the middle of work. She wasn't an overly emotional girl, despite the fact that she still thought of herself as a girl and not a woman.

She didn't want to forget about Brad, and knew she never would, but she wanted this part to be over. She felt like a slave to her memories and the emotions they triggered. But everything she read said that there was still a long way to go in the grief stages before she would be done with it.

At the moment, she was remembering a time when they had been dating for about six months. He had come over to her horrible little apartment in Central West Denver and they fell right into the routine of dinner, movie, sex, sleep. But halfway through the movie, she'd decided that she didn't want to do the same old thing that night. She liked their routine, but doing the same thing every night got boring, so she suggested they go for a ride. It was a warm summer night, and she wasn't about to let it go to waste.

They got into her car and she started driving while Brad asked with amusement where they were going. She wanted it to be a surprise. Thirty minutes later, they were sneaking into Cherry Creek State Park on foot. Ten minutes after that, they had their clothes off and were swimming in the reservoir. It was a warm night, but the water was still cold enough that they didn't stay in for long and instead opted for laying their clothes out on the sandy beach like a blanket and making love on top of them. No one was around and they had the beach and the water and the moon all to themselves.

That was a great night. They stayed out too late and laughed a lot. When they got back to her place, they decided to shower to get the sand off of them, and made love again in the shower.

This was a good memory. A great one. But as soon as Trina snapped back into reality and realized that Brad was gone forever, the happiness she was feeling came crashing down and before she knew it, she was choking back sobs. Then her desk phone rang. She composed herself and picked it up on the fourth ring. It was Bethany from reception telling her that there was a man to see her. A Mr. Rubble. Bethany said it with a question in her voice, like she didn't really believe that it was his real name. Trina checked her calendar program on her computer, but she didn't have any appointments set for right now.

"Did he say he had an appointment with me?" Trina asked.

"Yes. He said your full name and everything. Should I send him up? Or call security? He doesn't look like the type that wants insurance." Bethany spoke in a whisper because the reception area was small, and the man was no doubt sitting within earshot of her.

To Trina, Bethany was one of those people that you had a relationship with only because you had to. She was always talking gossip and making these broad judgments about people based on the way they looked. It drove Trina crazy, so she didn't lend much credence to this last statement. Holding back a sigh, she told Bethany to send the man up. She checked her makeup and composed herself further while getting her mind back into business mode, assuming she'd simply forgotten to log the appointment.

Her office was on the other side of a large room from the reception area. The room was filled with cubicles and junior agents taking or making phone calls. It was where Trina had sat for the first four years of her career at the company, through two promotions, and then finally escaping the rat race with her latest promotion about a year previously. She was young to have her own office, but she had proved herself and it was a point of pride.

Her door was made of clear glass and it sat at the end of the main hallway through the grid of cubicles, so she had a long time to look at the man as he strolled down the hallway toward her office.

Bethany was right. He didn't look like he wanted insurance. He was tall and sturdy looking. The words *self-assured* came to mind for some reason. Maybe the way he walked. He looked left and right and glanced down into cubicles with open curiosity, his dark green eyes constantly moving as he walked. He wore a light leather jacket like the kind Trina had seen on biker shows on television. Under the jacket, he wore a black rock-band t-shirt with red and white lettering. His pants were dirty and worn blue jeans, and he had on sturdy boots that looked years old. He looked like he hadn't shaved for a few days, his stubble a brown so dark it looked black. His dark, thick hair wasn't long or short or styled.

Trina took in the sight of him like a person at the zoo. Like someone who knows lions exist, and they've seen them on TV several times, but it was rare to see them in person. *This is a biker*, she thought, making her own broad judgment about the way he looked. But it made sense. Perfect sense, in this case.

*** 

Trouble caught a glimpse of Katrina when he was about halfway down the long walkway in the center of the wide room. She looked like her many pictures on the internet. Selfies, they called them. Most of Trina's seemed to have been taken in a car, presumably hers. He wasn't in the habit of taking pictures of himself—or posting things on the internet—so he wasn't the savviest person. But he had called in a favor from a good friend back in California. The same friend, in fact, who had hooked him up with Sam.

Trouble had decided not to tell his friend, Dylan, about what happened to Sam. First off, he didn't want to involve any more people in this mess than need be, and second, it seemed to him that Dylan was always saving his ass in some way or another. Better to just handle this one himself. But he had asked him to find out about Katrina and send him the information. It took Dylan all of an hour. Child's play for him.

As Trouble took his time walking between the cubicles, hearing little tidbits of conversation, he was still deciding how he wanted to play this. He wasn't sure if honesty was the best policy. *Hi, I'm Trouble, I think the people that killed your boyfriend are trying to kill me and anything you can tell me about what he was doing before he died would be super helpful. Why? Oh, because I'm going to find these people and kill every single one of them. Okay? Thanks.*

Most people—normal people—prefer to hand these types of situations over to local or federal police forces. That was the last thing Trouble wanted. In his experience, police were slow, ineffective, stubborn, sloppy, prejudiced, and occasionally corrupt.

As he stepped up to her glass door and pulled it open, the only decision he had made was to wing it. She stood up to greet him, but didn't move from behind her desk.

"Nice to meet you, Mr. Rubble. Please, have a seat and tell me how I can help you." She gestured at the two chairs that Trouble stood between. They looked new and comfortable, but by no means luxurious. As he sat down, Trouble thought that she looked better in person.

She wore a gray skirt, made from some sort of thick but stretchy fabric, that ended just above her knees and clung tightly to her legs. Her spaghetti-strap blouse was black and tight and made of some sort of high-end material that gave off a shine. The matching gray top of her ensemble was hanging on the back of her chair.

He remembered someone saying that pictures on the internet were never indicative of how someone looked in real life, because of the filters and editing and general ego-energy that goes into the picture or the post before it's published. It made sense to Trouble, given the state of American culture and the age of the instant celebrity. *She must be the exception to the rule,* he thought.

It kind of surprised him to be instantly attracted to someone such as he was now. His libido had been nonexistent since he'd started doing dope. He couldn't remember the last time he had thought about sex. It was kind of a relief, honestly. A respite from a part of his biology that was constantly on, and working overtime, ever since he'd been about thirteen years old. But now, sitting across from Katrina, he was right back to being a teenager, having trouble collecting his thoughts and formulating sentences.

"So listen," Trouble said after a long moment. "This is going to sound strange, but I don't need insurance. I came here to talk to you about Brad." He let that hang in the air to see what her reaction would be. It wasn't much, at least not outwardly, but he had a sense that she was on the verge of breaking down. He immediately regretted not thinking of some small talk before delving right in.

He had never been the best at talking to people about nothing, and when faced with a particularly attractive member of the opposite sex, his linguistic skills evaporated away in an instant.

He saw a small blue square stack of paper on her desk. The kind that you can peel off and stick to smooth surfaces. He pulled a plastic pen with the name and number of the insurance company stenciled on it out of a pen holder on her desk and grabbed the small square of paper. He started to write *Trouble* on the paper, but stopped himself and wrote *Terrence* instead. Under that, he wrote his cell phone number. When he looked back up at Katrina, she was sobbing into her hands and trying to say something at the same time.

"Ssss... huuhhh... ssssoorry," she gasped between sobs. Then she got it a little under control and grabbed a handful of tissues off of her desk.

"I'm so sorry, Mr. Rubble. This is so embarrassing. If this is about Br-Br-Brad, then you know wh-what happened. It has been a rough month for me."

Trouble nodded in silent consternation. Then he stood up and peeled the top blue paper off the stack and presented it to her.

"How about later today? It's urgent, so the sooner the better, but I understand that now is not a good time. Here's my cell number. Just call me when you're ready to talk." He turned to walk out of the room as soon as she took the paper. She held it up in front of her with one hand and held the wad of tissues up to her nose with the other.

Trouble was about halfway down the cubicle corridor when he heard her shout for him to wait. He stopped and looked back over his shoulder to see her hurrying to catch up with him, swinging on her jacket as she came.

"How about a beer?" she asked him when she had caught up. She looked much more composed now, mere seconds after the initial outburst. Trouble was puzzled, but nodded his head and then let her lead the way out of the building.

***

Trina didn't know why she had decided to go out for a drink with this strange, rough-looking man in the middle of the day. Part of her was sick of sitting in her office thinking about Brad all day. Part of her was sick of crying over him. Another part of her was sick of herself for thinking that way. She was also curious. Something she admitted to herself as she drove the mile and a half down the road to a little Tex-Mex restaurant that she frequented for lunch, glancing into her rear-view mirror at the man who was following her on his loud black-and-chrome motorcycle.

She had offered to drive them both in her car without thinking. She'd immediately regretted making the offer, thinking of all the bad things that could happen, and was relieved when he'd refused—insisting that he follow her on his motorcycle. She got the feeling that he didn't like to go anywhere without it.

She parked and then got out and walked with him to the door of the restaurant. He had parked next to her, backing his bike into the spot. She had seen other motorcycles parked like that, but had no idea why people did it.

She paused a moment and looked at the biker as he held the door open for her. It seemed to her that he was impatient about something and wanted to get this conversation over with so he could take care of some sort of pressing business. Or maybe he was just afraid that she would start crying again in the middle of this eatery. Maybe that's why he parked his bike facing outward, so he could make a fast getaway if she started bawling again. The thought made her chuckle to herself as the hostess led them to a table. Trina thought it strange that the young hostess kept staring at Mr. Rubble, but she shrugged it off as she sat down.

A waitress appeared promptly, and they each ordered a drink. Trina felt a sense of comfort as she got situated. The restaurant was familiar territory, and that's what she needed. Since Brad's unexpected and horrible murder, all Trina wanted was a normal routine with no surprises. She wanted comfort and warmth and familiarity.

Most of all, she wanted someone to talk to. Even if she wasn't conscious of it, that was the reason she had decided to skip out on work with this complete stranger. She told herself that he was probably a friend of Brad's, come to give his condolences. Or he was a fan of the band and just had to talk to her about it. Something like that.

The truth was that she had become somewhat of a pariah. People avoided her if they could, and when they couldn't, they tried to limit their time around her as much as possible. She was a walking reminder of the cruel indifference of the universe. She didn't have too many close friends around. Over the three years of her relationship with Brad, there had been a kind of gradual phasing out of any serious friendships that may have developed. She had spent most of her time with Brad, after all. That was how it was supposed to be, wasn't it? You find your best friend, soul mate, and lover all wrapped up in one person. Then you eventually get married and have kids and that's your family. You have friends that you get together with once a month, but your real friends are your husband and kids. Only that path had been violently interrupted.

The few friends she did have had been supportive for the first couple of weeks—as supportive as they could have been, she supposed—and then they stopped returning texts as quickly, stopped calling her to see how she was doing every day. She knew it wasn't on purpose. They all had their own lives to live, their own boyfriends or husbands and kids.

It had occurred to her that she was being a little selfish and high maintenance, but she also felt that she deserved a little selfishness. She knew she was a drag to be around. She would break down crying at random moments, and all she wanted to talk about was Brad.

She knew that there was really nothing anyone else could do to help her move on. That was something she had to do herself, but dammit, she wanted to talk to someone. With the loss of Brad came the loss of her sounding board, her confidence-builder, her "sound sponge" as she sometimes called him because he was so good at just listening to her talk and talk without feeling like he had to get a word in edge-wise. He knew that sometimes people just needed to talk, and he had been happy to listen.

Maybe she sensed that in Terrence, or maybe she just wished she did. Either way, she found herself across from him in a booth at eleven in the morning, hearing herself order a strawberry margarita from the waitress.

***

Trouble released a small sigh of relief when it was clear that they wouldn't be seated in earshot of other lunch-goers. He had no idea how this conversation would go down, but judging from her reaction in the insurance office, he wasn't hopeful. If she broke down crying again, it would be just his shit luck to have some machismo wannabe cop sitting in the place who would undoubtedly walk up and try to start some shit with him. He glanced around the place, half looking for anyone who fit the bill, and half out of habit.

It would be another hour before the lunch rush really got into full swing, which was why they had been seated so quickly. Their booth was against a wall of windows, and there were people sitting at booths and tables around the restaurant, but none directly behind or ahead of them.

Ever since he could remember, Trouble had possessed what they call situational awareness. It was one of his few God-given talents. He was always acutely aware of his surroundings, even if he was drunk or doped to the gills. Although being inebriated dulled that awareness somewhat, it was always there in the background, working away. Having terrible luck had simply helped him cultivate and hone that skill over the years. This awareness alerted him to the hostess, who'd been staring at him. He looked over at her and whispered to himself, "What the?"

"What is it?" Katrina said, turning to see what Trouble was looking at.

"Nothing," he said, but kept his eyes on the hostess. She had her phone in one hand, and she smiled at Trouble like she was embarrassed and then turned around. He watched her head back to her station near the doors. It wasn't an uncommon occurrence for him, considering how he dressed and his demeanor, to receive stares in "polite company." He shrugged it off and turned back to Katrina Parks.

"What were you looking at?" Katrina asked in an amused voice.

"Oh, uh, nothing. Just looking around. Looks like a fun place," he said, not hiding his sarcasm. Trouble hated kitschy restaurants with all sorts of weird stuff on the walls. This was his idea of dining in hell.

The waitress came back carrying Katrina's strawberry margarita and the beer that Trouble had ordered. They both declined to order any food but told her to check back. Trouble was hoping to be out as soon as he finished his beer, preferably with details that would help him find out who exactly was trying to kill him.

The attraction he had felt upon their first meeting had dulled significantly under the need to gather information and complete his task of ending the lives of those who would end his. It was the sort of task that, at least to Trouble, needed to be dealt with as soon as possible, and really shouldn't wait for anything as trivial as getting laid.

Not that he thought he had a chance of that with the beautiful stranger sitting across from him. Aside from the very obvious fact that she was still mourning the loss of her boyfriend, there was also the fact that they seemed to be worlds apart on that invisible and intangible spectrum of sexual attraction. People on her side of the spectrum simply weren't attracted to people on Trouble's side. Obviously, nothing was impossible, and there were examples of stranger things happening, but those examples were the exception, not the rule.

But biology is a funny thing, and Trouble's libido, despite having been forced into hibernation by heroin for the past year, was trying its best to crawl into the sunlight. Nothing like the attention of a beautiful woman to wake a sleeping giant. Okay, maybe not a giant... but the sleeping part was accurate.

He was of two minds about how to start this conversation, and he decided to split the difference and try for a few minutes of small talk. It would give him a little more time with Katrina, and it may even prove useful in extracting information.

Had he taken a slightly larger dose of dope that morning, he would have been able to easily sweep these instinctual thoughts and feelings aside and get on with his mission before things went to shit, but he hadn't, and he couldn't.

And things went to shit very, very quickly.

# Fifteen

**M**URKE WATCHED AS RUBBLE and the girl walked into the Mexican restaurant. He had been following Trouble via the GPS locator he had placed on his bike at the motel the day before. Following the biker back from the bank house had been more difficult than he'd anticipated—clearly this career criminal was paranoid—but Murke had managed it. When he'd first laid eyes on Trouble, his instincts told him that this was the guy he'd use. A little bit of research on him simply solidified that notion. A loner with no family and few friends who'd been in and out of jail his whole life. He couldn't have hoped for a better subject.

Murke sat in his van, doing research and determining how best to go about his job. He re-read for the fourth time all the information he had on Terrence Rubble, aka Trouble. He'd figured that the guy's heroin addiction would make manipulating him that much easier.

He was making notes on his laptop when a Jeep pulled up into the restaurant's parking lot. The three men that got out looked like they were in a hurry. One of them headed to the back of the restaurant. *Oh shit*, Murke thought, while pulling out his burner cell phone.

***

Trouble kept hoping to steer the conversation delicately to the subject of Brad, but it was clear that Trina wanted to get to know about Trouble before spilling anything about Brad. Finally, after letting the frustration build, he asked her directly. "So, what was Brad doing for work?"

The question hung there between them. Up until that point, fifteen minutes into their conversation, Katrina had been asking Trouble questions about himself. Trouble had been lying half the time.

She took a breath and said, "How do you know Brad?"

"I used to play in a band here, and we had a couple of shows together a while back. I was just so shocked to hear about his death. The article I read about it said it might have been gang related? But that doesn't sound right to me." The lie about playing in a band was easy enough, and the article he'd read had mentioned something about the shooting being gang related. He thought it was believable enough.

Katrina stopped making eye contact and was staring at the table as she answered. "No, it doesn't sound right to me, either. I don't really even know what he was doing for work. He said that his boss asked him to keep it a secret. We had a big fight about it. I didn't like him keeping secrets from me, but he was bringing in good money. He finally told me that he was working for a dispensary. He just couldn't tell me what he was doing or which one he worked at."

*Bingo.* Trouble's hunch was right. He figured the crew that killed Brad was probably the same one that came after him. His mind reeled as he sat back to think about this.

"Are you okay?" Katrina asked, looking at him again. He was about to answer when his phone made a little sound that signified a new text message. It was a sound he knew, but not well, and he was immediately curious. He could count on one hand the number of people that had his number, and one of them had been killed recently. On top of the fact that he preferred talking on the phone, it was a rare occurrence that someone would text him unbidden. Trouble had never been what you would call an outgoing person. Much less so since he had been doing heroin daily, which was by no means a social drug.

He pulled out the phone and looked at the message. It was from a local number—303 area code. He started looking wildly around the restaurant. He shoved his phone away and reached into his inside jacket pocket for his gun.

\*\*\*

Ray walked around to the back of the restaurant, taking care to not walk too fast. Joseph and Tim would wait two minutes for him to get into position before making their move.

There was a young man at the back of the building dressed in black slacks, a black t-shirt, and a black, food-stained apron. He had the rear door of the restaurant propped open with an almost overflowing rectangular trash can as he stared at his phone in one hand and puffed on a cigarette with the other. He looked up as Ray opened the door all the way and walked past him.

"Hey!" the guy said.

Ray stopped, turned, and stared at the young man.

"Whatever. I'm on break," the employee grumbled before returning his attention to his phone.

Ray found his way through the large and somewhat busy kitchen to stop short of a set of closed swinging doors that led to the seating area of the restaurant. The workers glanced at him briefly, then returned to their work. Ray had learned a long time ago that acting like you belong in a place is all you need to convince people you did belong there.

He couldn't see everything from his vantage point, as there was another identical set of doors on the other side of the kitchen. From where he was, he only had a view of about half the restaurant.

He was about to move through the kitchen to the other doors when his eyes landed on the back of a guy's head that matched the photo they'd been sent. He was sitting across from a rather attractive young woman.

Ray could see the top of the guy's shoulders over the back of the booth. He was wearing a leather jacket. Ray pulled out his phone and checked the picture that the hostess had taken.

It looked right, so he texted Joseph, "Right side booth against window." He looked at the picture again and put his phone away. This was the guy that the Jiménez Cartel wanted, and word was they wanted him bad. He didn't know why, but his orders were clear. Ray pulled his gun out of the waistband of his pants and checked the chamber. He was ready to go.

They were under orders to get the guy alive, but the last thing they wanted was the guy making a scene in the restaurant. So, they had discussed it and decided that the guns and the element of surprise would do nicely to convince the guy to leave quietly. The girl sitting there was an added benefit. If they threatened her, the biker would surely come along. Unless he was a total monster.

Ray looked around the restaurant, noting the other people enjoying an early lunch. Luckily, there were precious few people in there. He counted ten total before he eased open one of the flimsy kitchen doors and took a step out into the seating area. Joseph and Tim walked into the restaurant and into his line of sight on the other side of the building. They were about twenty yards away from him, near the front doors at the end of the corridor between the booths on his left and tables on his right. He saw Joe and Tim recognize the guy from the picture, pull out their guns, and start toward the seated couple.

The first thing to register with Ray was someone yelling "Oh, shit!" behind him, followed by the sound of ceramic plates breaking and silverware ringing off the tile floor. Ray turned around to see a waiter running away from him, his dropped tray of food on the floor.

The girl sitting with the biker screamed.

Ray turned back in time to see that the guy's head was no longer there in the booth.

Gunfire tore his attention away from the screaming girl. Joe's left knee exploded in a blast of blood and bone, then his right shin a second later. Two shots, but where had they come from? Joe screamed as Tim, who had been a step behind him, dove into an empty booth for cover.

Some people were running out of the restaurant while others were hiding under tables, calling 911. A head poked out from floor level at the booth the biker had been sitting at, only it wasn't the back of his head this time. Eyes locked onto Ray's and then two shots rang out and Ray dove back into the kitchen. Both shots missed him, but barely.

Ray heard two more shots and then glass breaking, then four more shots. Two from the biker, two from Tim, Ray thought. He chanced a glance back at the booth and didn't see anyone there anymore. The window had been shattered, and he guessed that they had jumped out.

It was deathly silent in the place as Tim poked his head out of the booth he'd hidden in. Ray had never seen him look so angry. Joe was unconscious in the middle of the floor, bleeding out.

\*\*\*

Katrina didn't have time to register what was happening. She was sitting there at her favorite restaurant having a normal conversation when this perfect stranger sitting across from her (who said his name was Terrence but who really knew, now?) got a text that said god-knows-what and then started looking around the restaurant like a crazy person.

She had been puzzled at that point, but not worried. Then the next thing she knew, Terrence was pulling a gun out of his jacket and sliding under the booth like his bones had just turned to liquid. Seeing him slide under the table like that, like a snake holding a gun, made all manner of heinous and horrible possibilities accost her mind. She thought that maybe he was going under there to do something to *her*. To her legs or her feet or her *other* parts, with that gun of his.

She had been terrified and had screamed and gone to slide out of the booth. But before she could move to the edge of the seat, there came a gunshot from under the table, followed quickly by another one. She screamed louder and froze in place, waiting for the pain to come, for the blood to spill out of her legs or her feet or wherever the crazy man had shot her. Then her scream was joined by another.

It shocked her enough to make her stop screaming for long enough to twist around in her seat and look at the man lying on the floor behind her, bleeding onto the fading orange and purple carpet. Looking at the holes that the bullets had made in the man's legs, her first feeling was that of relief. She was happy it had not, in fact, been her that Terrence had shot. A second later she felt shame for feeling that way. A second after that, she heard two more shots from under the table and she twisted back around to see Terrence pulling himself out to stand up on his seat across from her.

He pointed his gun at the window and shot twice more, and then reached out and yanked her up with his left hand and kicked at the two bullet holes in the large window. The glass tumbled down onto the table and out into the dirt in the small swath of landscaped earth that bordered the restaurant. He pushed her toward the window and turned back around to shoot twice more at someone behind her. She jumped out the window and rolled off the manicured earth and onto the hard concrete of the parking lot.

Terrence landed next to her on the concrete as two shots rang out from inside the restaurant. She didn't know when, exactly, but the guy inside had stopped screaming. Instinctively, she knew it was because he was dead or unconscious. She scrambled away from Terrence and got up to run. She was no longer hysterical, but fight or flight had kicked in and she wasn't going to stick around to see how the fight turned out.

She got to her car and realized that she had left her purse sitting on the table at the booth. Her keys were in her purse. She hit the pavement and slid her body under her car and listened. There were no footsteps. No gunshots.

She waited.

***

Trouble only had one bullet in his pistol. One left. He rolled up off the concrete, vaguely aware that Katrina was running in the opposite direction. *Good.* He ran to the back of the restaurant and found the back door propped open by an overflowing trash can. He saw no one else around as he eased the door open and moved swiftly inside.

He thought of the spare clips and his other gun that were sitting in his saddlebags on his bike in a parking spot at the front of the restaurant. So close yet so far. He didn't know where all the cooks and servers and managers were, but he was thankful that they weren't there. Most people, smart people, run far and fast when they hear gunshots.

Trouble cleared the kitchen and came to the flimsy hard-plastic doors that led to the seating area—front of house. He remembered the term from his short stint as a food service worker. He was in the same spot where one of the gunmen had been hiding before. Trouble had taken two shots at the guy and was fairly sure he'd missed. The fact that there was no sign of him now gave credence to that theory.

He had no idea how much time had passed since the shooting started, but his best guess was coming up on three minutes. Maybe four. He would hear sirens soon, and he didn't want to be around when those sirens grew loud enough to make him wince. He crouched down behind one of the doors and got as low to the ground as he could. Then he pushed it open. The lead guy—the one that Trouble had shot in each leg—was still on the ground, not moving. Trouble scanned around as he stood up slowly, gun tracking around the restaurant with his eyes, the thought of one round left in the gun a nagging worry that he could do nothing about.

Well, that wasn't exactly true. He could leave. But that wasn't really a serious option in his mind. Not when he still had one bullet left. It was a bit of a paradox. But then again, that was par for the course in his life so far. He saw movement to his right and swiveled his gun that way, only to see a gray-haired woman poking her head out from under a table and just as quickly ducking back for cover when she saw Trouble.

Suddenly, he heard movement behind him. He spun around to see the guy he had missed earlier with his two shots. He was opening the back door of the restaurant from the outside. Trouble cursed himself for not moving the trash can when he came in. He fired his last shot at the guy. As soon as he pulled the trigger, he knew he missed, so he started running as the guy fired back.

*** 

Ray opened the back door slowly, but it still made a low sweeping sound from the plastic liner on the bottom. He peered around the door, leading with his gun, when he saw the biker take a shot at him. Ray took three shots as he ducked behind the door, shooting and swinging the metal door in front of him simultaneously. He knew that all three shots went wide, but they were cover shots to give him some time.

He was breathing hard as he put his back to the door to think of his next move. It was a heavy-duty door, and he knew that handgun bullets wouldn't get through it. He looked down at the trash can that was still propping the door open when he heard fast footsteps coming from inside. His eyes went wide.

***

Trouble hit the door with his right shoulder, putting all his weight into it. He had gotten up to full speed before launching himself against it. He wasn't a gifted athlete by any means, and fast for him was about average, if not a little below, but that didn't change the fact that he weighed just over two hundred pounds. And two hundred pounds slamming against an unlatched door—even a heavy-duty metal door—will create a violent reaction.

He would have preferred that the door opened onto a wall ninety degrees through its arc. That would have meant that the guy hiding behind it would be slammed into the wall and incapacitated. But as it was, he knew that the door had to swing through one hundred and eighty degrees before contacting the wall. Plus, he guessed that there was some sort of mechanism or doorstop to prevent that from happening.

Still, in the moment, Trouble was pleased with the result as the door flung the man away at a bit of an angle. Since he'd had his back to the door, the gunman was able to keep his feet for a few steps before the top of his body was too far forward for him to stay balanced. He fell onto his hands and knees on the concrete slab between the back of the restaurant and the squat, fenced-in dumpsters that stank of old food and rotting vegetables. He still had his gun in his right hand, having used the ball of his palm to break the fall with that hand. Trouble's momentum carried him almost directly toward the man.

A split second after Ray landed on the ground, Trouble smashed into him and they wound up in a tangle of limbs. Trouble had been hanging onto his empty pistol, but he dropped it and used both hands to grab Ray's right wrist and hand, trying to wrench the pistol away from him.

They struggled on the ground for a few long seconds before Ray got off a shot right next to Trouble's head. His left ear exploded in pain from the sound of the shot, but he didn't loosen his grip on the gun. They rolled around again, and Trouble got on top of Ray and held him there. He was larger and stronger than Ray was, but he still couldn't get the gun from him. He felt his arms tiring, and panic crept into his mind. He couldn't keep this up much longer. His stamina was not what it used to be.

Then he had an idea.

They were struggling with the gun between them, each of them trying to point it at the other. Trouble twisted the gun around to where it was still pointing away from both men, but the slide was pointing at Ray. Trouble pulled the trigger by forcing Ray's finger down, and the gun fired. The bullet left the chamber and traveled through the wood fence and into the dumpster behind, creating a hole in the fence and a shallow dent in the dumpster.

The shell casing, however, ejected from the slide and into Ray's left eye. His eyelid closed on reflex, but not quick enough. He made a small sound and flinched in reaction. Trouble almost missed his opportunity for the wonder that it had actually worked, but was quick enough to take advantage of that flinch and the momentary slackness of muscle that it caused. He yanked the gun away from Ray by twisting and pulling it as hard as he could. He heard something crack in the guy's hand and Ray made another sound, this one louder and full of pain.

Trouble got the gun in both hands, stood up, and pointed it down at Ray, who was holding his right wrist in his left hand, eyes shut, body writhing. There came the screeching of tires on asphalt and Trouble looked behind him at the sound. A jeep was rocking on its struts as it came to an abrupt stop. Trouble recognized the guy in the driver's seat from inside the restaurant. He'd wondered where he had gotten off to. His driver's side window was closed, but it didn't stop him from raising his pistol and taking a shot at Trouble. Trouble shot back and moved toward the dumpsters at the same time. The jeep was about twenty feet from him, and he hit the back passenger window just after the front window shattered from the driver's shot. Then he was tripped.

He twisted in mid-air to land on his right shoulder, his back toward the jeep. He looked down at his feet and saw the half-blind culprit there, left hand on Trouble's foot. A shot rang out from the jeep and Trouble felt a spray of broken asphalt hit his back. Since he landed on his shoulder with the pistol still in his hand, he only had to pick it up off the ground a couple of inches to shoot the guy hanging onto his foot. Which he did.

The guy's forehead caved in and the back of his head exploded outward. Trouble rolled away from him and heard another ricochet off the asphalt where he had just been a second before. He rolled to face the jeep and pulled the trigger, hitting the driver's side door right under where the driver's head and shoulders were framed in the broken window. The guy flinched in pain and looked down. Trouble fired again, but the jeep was already moving. He fired again, but this time the gun was empty.

He got up, gasping at the pain in his upper back and the ringing in one ear, and listened as the jeep's engine noise died away. Trouble hoped to hear a crash, but it never came. He knew he had hit the guy through the door, but it may have been only enough to bruise at that point. He had no way of knowing.

Trouble put the pistol in his outside jacket pocket and reached over his left shoulder to feel the wounds on his back. He brought his hand back and inspected his fingertips briefly. They were bloody, and he felt like he had maybe a dozen little holes in his back from the asphalt and possibly little bullet shards. He had an idea that none of the wounds went too deep, and there was nothing he could do about it right now, anyway.

He collected his pistol from the ground further toward the restaurant and intentionally avoided looking back at the man he had just killed, although he thought about getting the guy's wallet. It wouldn't do him much good. It wasn't like he had access to police files, and most criminals didn't advertise their criminality online. Plus, most professionals that he knew didn't bring any identifying information if they knew they were going on a job.

He jogged back into the restaurant to the table they had been sitting at, and his heart sank when he saw that Katrina's purse was gone. He ran outside, hoping that she had come back to get it, but when he saw her car sitting right where she had parked it, he knew that wasn't the case. His motorcycle was parked in the spot next to hers, and he grabbed his other pistol out of his saddlebag, along with a full clip, which he swapped out for the empty one in his other .45.

He glanced into her car and tried to open two doors, but they were locked. He stepped to the trunk and tried to open it when he heard what sounded like a sigh or a small moan from under the car. He got down on his knees and looked into the terrified eyes of the poor woman he had gotten into this mess.

"We should probably go now," he said.

# Sixteen

I T TOOK TIM ALL he had not to speed once he was on the road. He passed two police cruisers hauling ass the other way, lights flashing and sirens screaming. He watched them fade away in his side mirror. Feeling at the spot on the left side of his chest where the bullet had hit him, he counted himself lucky. It would be a hell of a bruise, but not much more. Maybe a cracked rib.

Joe was probably dead from his leg wounds, and Ray was dead. It was a clusterfuck like he'd never seen. How had the guy known they were coming? *No one is that fast.* He kept replaying it in his head as he drove. Sure, he and Joe had pulled their guns out when they walked into the place, but the guy was reacting even before they raised them. He had to have known they were coming. But how?

It took Tim twenty minutes to get to the house. Twenty minutes of replaying the whole thing over and over. Seeing Joe get shot and then Ray, over and over. He grew more and more angry as the minutes ticked by, and the only thing that made him feel better was the thought of finding the biker and his girlfriend and making him watch as he took his time with the girl. Then he would take care of the biker with a bullet in each leg and one in the head.

As he pulled into the driveway, he glanced over at the passenger seat and smiled. The girl's purse sat there. It was all he needed to find them.

He grabbed the purse and jumped out of the car, running up to bang on the mansion's door.

"Who the fuck is that guy?" Tim yelled at his boss, who opened the door with a smile on his face. A smile that faltered immediately.

"Calm down, Tim. Come inside and we'll talk about it."

Boss wasn't the best word for what Diego was to Tim. More like a commander or a shot caller. But Tim just thought of him as Diego. They had come up together, Diego, Tim, and Joe. The three musketeers of petty crime in Denver. But things had changed, and quickly, when Diego spearheaded a kind of cartel franchise opportunity here in Denver.

Tim walked into the mansion and straight to the kitchen. He dropped Katrina's purse on the counter, grabbed a can of beer out of the fridge, popped it open, then leaned back on the counter by the oversize fridge and took a deep breath before going to work on the beer.

"What happened?" Diego asked. "Where's Ray and Joe?"

"Ray's fucking dead. Probably Joe, too. The guy knew we were coming. No one's that quick. No one."

"What?" Diego looked crestfallen. Joe had been his friend since high school, and Ray he had known for several years.

"Who the fuck is this guy? Why do they want him so bad?"

Diego had a faraway look in his eyes as he came to terms with what he'd just been told. "Word is he killed one of Jiménez's head honchos. Mr. G," Diego said finally, his voice tightening with resolve.

"No shit? Damn." Tim's anger was flagging for the moment. "No wonder they want him. But why do we want him? Shouldn't we be patting him on the back?"

"He's a bargaining chip. With him, we can get a meet with Mr. Z, who's apparently still in town. Emotion will run it, and they won't be thinking straight. We will never get a better opportunity to make a move for the whole city. I was thinking we could rig the biker with explosives or some shit. Take out half of their leadership in one go..." His voice trailed off as his eyes unfocused again. "Goddamn. He killed them both? Who the hell is this guy?"

"Does anyone know who he is?" Tim asked.

"I guess it doesn't matter. He has to die now. If we can get him alive, great. If not, we kill him."

# Seventeen

*K*IDNAPPING. THAT'S A NEW *one for me. Maybe I should've just left her there.* Trouble was having a hard time figuring out what to do with Katrina. He was currently headed back to his place because he couldn't think of anything better to do. She had her arms wrapped around him to keep from falling off the motorcycle. But turns out it's impossible to hold a gun on someone who is sitting behind you on a motorcycle and drive it at the same time.

She hadn't jumped off at a stoplight yet, which would be easy for her to do. He was kind of happy about that, but part of him also hoped that she would jump off. Then she would no longer be his problem. He didn't feel like he was in any sort of shape to be taking care of anyone but himself, and he wasn't doing such a great job of that lately. But if she did run, she would probably end up going back to her place and getting killed by whoever the hell had tried to kill him at the restaurant. The guy who got away had her purse. The bad guys knew where she lived, so she had to stay with him until he figured this whole thing out. That she hadn't jumped off the bike said something. Maybe she was coming around to his way of seeing things.

She had refused to come out from under her car when Trouble had asked her nicely. He could hear sirens by then and was in no mood to chat with police, so he'd pulled out a pistol and threatened her with it while she cried under the car. It didn't take long for her to squirm out and join him on the bike. By then, there were people staring at them from all around. They all kept their distance, but he was sure that the police would have a relatively accurate description by now. He needed to lie low for a while.

Another nagging question on his mind was about the heads-up he got at the restaurant as a text that read "3 men with guns coming for you. Get out NOW." What the hell was that about? *Just what I need*, he thought, *some shadowy figure trying to do god-knows-what, and somehow I'm involved. This shit is lame.*

It never occurred to him that there may actually be someone out there rooting for him, hoping he would find the people that had killed Sam and his wife and tried to kill *him* twice. It just wasn't plausible. He had decided a long time ago that *he* was the only person who would ever be rooting for him to win, and even then it really came down to what mood he was in. Thinking that there was some person—or force—out there pulling strings in his favor was as smart as walking onto a crowded freeway with a blindfold on. It just wasn't a good idea, and it made staying alive difficult.

Trouble had never feared death, but did his absolute best to avoid it—although lately something told him that he was losing that fearlessness. He did, however, think that other people deserved to live long and happy lives—unless they were murdering assholes. He had never really been a big fan of people in general, but the few encounters he'd had with those rare saintly few who grace the world with their presence gave him a glimpse of how wonderful people could be—if they wished.

So, here he found himself with another person to protect, although this time he felt that Katrina's involvement in this situation was more his fault than anything else. It appeared that her boyfriend had gotten himself into something that led directly to his death, but Trouble would have to find out more before he was sure. For the time being, he decided as they pulled into the rear parking lot of his motel, he would enjoy the company of this beautiful woman while he could and keep her alive while he was at it.

She got off the motorcycle first and looked at the squalid motel like it was covered with cockroaches. Her eyes were rimmed with tears, her makeup smeared and running. Trouble thought she still looked as wonderful as when he'd first seen her through the glass door at the insurance office.

He led the way to his room on the second floor without a word. She followed along in stunned silence. Trouble was glad that he didn't have to use his gun to get her into the room.

"It's not much, but it's a good place for you to lie low for a while," he said while he took his two .45s and the spoil-of-war

9mm Beretta out of his jacket and placed them on the coffee table.

"Why won't you let me go home?" she said. The force in her voice startled Trouble, and he suddenly realized that he had been in such a hurry to get out of that parking lot that he didn't tell her about her purse.

"Listen. Sit down, will you?" he said, gesturing at one end of the couch. She hesitated for a second, standing on the other side of the coffee table, hugging herself protectively. Right when Trouble thought she was going to make a run for it, she stepped over and sat on the couch, as far from Trouble as she could get.

"I went back into the place after all the shooting stopped," he began when he saw she was as settled as she was going to get. "I was looking for your purse, but it was gone. The one guy that got away must've taken it. So he knows where you live now." He could tell she didn't believe him as she looked at him from the corner of her eyes, skeptical and on edge. He couldn't blame her.

"Did you see me carrying a purse? Do you want to check my bike? I don't like this any more than you do, but I can't in good conscience let you go off and get killed. I'll end this whole thing soon, and then you can go home. Okay?"

"Why don't you let me go to the police?" she whispered, pleading.

"Well, in general, the police are pretty good at killing people, but not so good at protecting them. They can't seem to make the two work together. More to the point, if you go to the police, you'll have to tell them about me, which I can't have you doing. They would just gum up the works. Plus, there's something funny going on here, and I can't be sure that the police aren't involved."

"Involved? Like dirty cops? There's no way." Her tone was sure, like that of a law-abiding taxpayer who had grown up trusting the police.

"Well, I don't have any proof of that, but I find it's best to assume that there are a handful of dirty cops in every city. It has served me well so far," he said. She didn't look convinced.

"Okay, look. I think that whoever killed your boyfriend tried to kill me and killed a friend of mine. That's the whole reason I came to see you. I need more information about what Brad was doing. I never met him before. I don't play in a band. I'm not even from here. So please, think of this as a vacation. A shitty one, but still a vacation. Can you call off work for a couple of days? I promise you I'll have this all sorted out by then."

He was surprised to see a little glint in her eyes, like maybe she wanted revenge for Brad and was hoping Trouble could do it. Or maybe that was wishful thinking on his part. She looked him full in the face for the better part of a minute, apparently judging whether she could believe him. He stared back. Finally, her face softened, and she spoke. "Do you have anything to eat here? I'm very hungry."

Trouble smiled.

\*\*\*

He had nothing to eat, but he fixed that with a call to a pizza place. He let her pick the toppings and go wild with sides and desserts. It was his treat and a sad excuse for an apology.

By the time he hung up with the pizza place he could hardly turn his thoughts away from dope. He was overdue for a shot, and he was starting to feel it. Or at least he thought he was starting to feel it.

All his dope paraphernalia was around, but not visible. His spoon, cotton ball, and most of his dope were on top of the coffee table, sandwiched in a hand towel. His syringes were in a paper bag underneath the table. His water bottle was on the floor next to the bag. He had the rest of his epic supply of dope and the fentanyl in a hidden pocket in the lining of his jacket. He had been using it for his "in case of emergency" stash. He felt better having it on him, even though it was a risk.

The pocket was just a hole cut into the lining of his jacket in a strategic place where whatever was put inside wouldn't find its way further in. Said hole was sealed with stick-on Velcro to keep it closed. A diligent searcher could find it, but for any sort of regular cop pat-down, it would be essentially invisible.

He turned on the TV after ordering the pizza and offered Katrina the remote. She shook her head. He put on some nature documentary just to have some noise in the room. Trouble was thinking of a way to take all his supplies into the bathroom to get well without her noticing. The thought of her running off while he was in the bathroom getting high occurred to him, but it was a secondary concern. Number one priority was to get high. After he did that, he could think just fine.

"Can I take a shower?" she asked, shifting her blank gaze from the television over to Trouble. "I think it will help me feel better." Trouble noticed that she was scuffed and dirty from crawling underneath her car.

"Sure," he replied, trying to conceal his excitement. He would be able to get high while she was showering. *Perfect*. She stood up and paused, looking around.

"Oh, right. Bathroom is over there." He pointed to the only door it could be, given the layout of the place. "There are clean towels in there," he said as she walked away.

As soon as the bathroom door shut, Trouble sprang into action, excitedly sliding down off the couch to sit on his legs in front of the coffee table. He pulled all his equipment together and was ready to find a vein in about three minutes. It took him another five to find a usable spot in his left leg. He remembered to pull up his pants and put away his equipment before slouching deep into the couch and letting the warmth overtake him.

Trina was still in the shower when the pizza guy knocked on the door. Trouble was nodding off when the knock came and he jumped up and opened the door cautiously with a pistol hidden in his right hand, forgetting that he had ordered a pizza. He tucked the pistol in the back of his pants and paid the man after he realized there was no threat, aside from possible heart disease some time in the distant future.

He was enjoying his high, and he knew that if he ate right now, his high would go away that much quicker, so he set the pizza down on the coffee table and went back to the land of nod on the couch.

# Eighteen

Detective Gibney surveyed the scene outside the restaurant. The initial shock he always felt when seeing a dead body was dulled now. He had started inside the building, seeing the large pool of blood from a man who had been shot in each leg and had died in the back of an ambulance.

Now, looking at the second victim, Gibney felt like he was quickly losing an already unwinnable battle. The dead man lay between the back door of the restaurant and the wooden structure that held several dumpsters. The back of his head and all that it had previously held in were scattered and smeared on the asphalt. The corpse's pockets had held a wad of cash, but no wallet or ID. He figured the man in the ambulance wouldn't have ID, either. They were professionals. He silently expressed gratitude that there were no dead civilians in the immediate vicinity.

His phone chirped from the clip on his belt. It was Wane, texting him from inside the restaurant. He clipped his phone back onto his belt, took one last look at the scene outside, and headed inside to watch the security footage Wane had texted him about. He walked through the kitchen and stopped briefly to watch a young crime scene tech work methodically to pull a bullet out of a tile-coated wall.

It was clear what had happened. The uniforms had gotten plenty of statements from several witnesses who had been enjoying an early lunch when the shooting started. Both detectives remembered the description of a biker from daily briefings. He was a person of interest in another case and was quickly becoming the prime suspect in this one.

Gibney found Wane standing next to the restaurant manager in the main office.

"So, this guy—if it's the same guy—is involved or implicated in three out of five homicides in the last month, and now he's kidnapping women," Wane said, shaking her head. They were looking at the security footage. There was a frozen shot of the biker on the screen, holding a gun and looking under the camera.

"It's the same guy. I can feel it," Gibney replied, staring at the wall of the office just above the computer. "Now we know what he looks like."

Wane snorted and then laughed, breaking Gibney out of his reverie.

"You can 'feel it'? Ha! Please tell me you're joking. You sound like a damn TV cop or something," she said, chuckling. "Is it in your bones or your gut? I'm sure the judge will love to hear your testimony." With that, the restaurant manager—a large man in his early forties—couldn't hold it in any longer. He snorted laughter out of his nose and turned from his seat next to Wane to glance back at Gibney. The look he found there made him stop laughing.

"I'd concentrate less on me and more on how the dead bodies are going to affect your business, *sir,*" Gibney said. The manager slumped in his chair and turned back to the computer screen.

There was an awkward silence until Wane spoke up a few seconds later. "Well, let's get his face out there and see if anyone recognizes it." Her tone was more businesslike now.

"Let's go," Gibney said to her, paying no mind to the dejected restaurant manager.

# Nineteen

THE CALL CAME THROUGH on a cell phone. A man in cowboy boots, a plaid shirt, and a wide-brim cowboy hat answered it. "Sí," he said, then listened. He had to listen hard because his English wasn't so good, but he could pick out some of the rushed and excited words. His eyes traveled over the unfamiliar surroundings of the kitchen in which he was standing. He had been looking for something to eat, but now he thought he better bring the phone to his boss on the other side of the house. He told the man on the phone to wait and then held the phone down by his side.

Stepping past an overturned chair in the small and tidy kitchen, the man made his way toward sounds of pleading and crying. He passed through the entryway, squinting his eyes at the bright bar of sunlight coming through the open doorway. Even if he wanted to close it, he couldn't. The door itself was lying on the floor in the hallway with faint boot prints on its white face, splintered wood all around. He paused briefly to shift his weapon's strap further up onto his shoulder. Continuing down a narrow hallway decorated with pictures of a very large and happy family, he could hear the pleading rising in volume and intensity. Not just because he grew closer, but also because the cries grew more frantic and desperate.

He kept his face impassive. He had never been a big fan of this part of the business, but he would never let his brothers-in-arms know it. Not by words or deeds or a furrow in his brow. It was sad but true that these kinds of things grew easier for him the more he did them. But still, if he didn't have to be the one doing them, he would just as soon wander around looking for something to eat. He knew that some of the other men had grown to enjoy this type of thing, but he didn't understand that. Not at all. He, Eduardo Ruiz, thought himself a good man, if not for his line of work.

He came into a small bedroom at the end of the narrow hallway to see four men. There was a woman on the floor, but she was dead. Two of the men held another on a bed by the arms and legs. The fourth man, Ruiz's boss, Hector, leaned over the captive's head and whispered something inaudible to the crying man. Ruiz was about to get his boss's attention when he looked up and out of the room's only window. His eyes went wide. He stuffed the phone in his pocket and slung his AK-47 off his shoulder while shouting "Mira, mira, mira!"

Two trucks had just stopped on the street in front of the small house. There were three men jumping out of each truck and milling around looking at one of the drivers, who appeared to be the leader. Two of them were armed with pistols, the other four with rifles. They were about fifty feet away from the house. It was clear that they couldn't see into the room. The bright sun shone through a cloudless sky to reflect off the window glass. The men fanned out toward the house. There was still confusion in the room. The two men holding down their captive didn't want to let him go, and Hector had set his gun down earlier.

Ruiz took two steps closer to the window, raised his weapon to his shoulder, and fired through the glass. Two of the men outside went down as glass shattered and Ruiz swept his AK from left to right, trying to get as many of them as he could. The gunshots in the enclosed space slammed painfully against their ears, and right away the men in the room lost hearing as a reliable sense. Ruiz stopped firing and fell onto his knees and then his elbows. A single shot cracked to his right, and he looked up to see that Hector, el jefe, had grabbed his pistol and shot the man on the bed. With that obstacle taken care of, the other two men, Rico and Tomas, went for their guns and hit the floor as the men outside started firing into the room.

This was not a new situation for any of them. They crawled out into the hallway and Ruiz told them how many, what kind of weapons, and likely positions. Hector nodded and spoke briefly. The three of them listened intently, eyes hard, no fear visible. Rico took his pump-action shotgun and crawled into another bedroom in the back of the house and opened the window, checking for shooters in the backyard.

Ruiz stayed where he was and fired a few shots blindly around the doorway and out toward the sound of gunfire. He didn't think he would hit anyone. Tomas ran the short distance down the hallway to the entryway with his AK and peeked his head around. This caused more gunshots from one of the rifles, peppering the front of the house and walkway. Whoever was firing the gun couldn't aim well at all. Tomas smiled and ran back up the hallway and ducked into the room Rico had gone into.

Hector and Ruiz were sitting in the hallway with their backs to the wall. Gunshots died down outside, so Ruiz fired blindly around the door and then went down the hall to do the same at the entryway. They didn't fall for it this time. They were conserving their ammo, probably waiting for backup. One of the men Ruiz had shot was moaning and crying. Ruiz sat back down next to Hector. They looked at each other and couldn't help but smile. It wouldn't be long now. After another minute, Ruiz crawled back into the bedroom facing the street and set up next to the window, out of sight.

It was the simplest of plans. If the men outside had been anything more than farmers and shopkeepers and salesmen, they would have been able to defend against it, or at least leave before they all got killed. They were just citizens who were tired of doing nothing, tired of letting the drug cartels destroy their neighborhoods and cities. They had no formal training, and their weapons were no match for the ones the cartel members had. They were dead the moment they had decided to stand up for themselves. This Ruiz knew all too well.

***

Tomas went one way around the back of the house, and Rico the other. They each went two houses over, crossed through the yards, came to the street—the one that the soon-to-be-dead men were on—and crossed it. They each went behind the houses on the other side of the street and made their way back toward their targets. They met behind the house directly across from their targets and talked briefly and excitedly. A woman in the house opened the back door, looked at the two men as they slowly raised their weapons toward her, and then shut the door and locked it. They split up again, with each man going through the side yard on either side of the house. They found as much cover as they could and picked a target.

Tomas shot first and hit his man several times in the back. Before they knew what was happening, Rico fired at his target and the man's head was gone in a red mist. Tomas hit another one in the legs, but the last one made it around to the other side of the trucks. He quickly realized his mistake and scrambled to jump into one of the trucks, but Ruiz popped up at the window and shot him four times. By now, everyone was dead but the one that Tomas hit in the legs and that was soon fixed with a shot to the head.

The four men met on the sidewalk and strolled to their car up the street as people peered through drawn shades at them. At these treacherous, evil men that made their living through murder and mayhem. As they arrived at the car, Ruiz remembered the phone call and told Hector about it. Hector returned the call right away.

***

Tim watched as Diego set his phone down and breathed out a heavy, ragged sigh before raising his eyes to meet Tim's. From the one side of the conversation that Tim heard, it didn't sound promising, but he looked a question at Diego anyway. Part of the agreement from the beginning was that the Colorado crew would handle its own problems, and Tim knew this. He had pressed a reluctant Diego to make the call, which he had, eventually.

Diego had called his other lieutenants together and the five of them had spent the last twenty-four hours together trying to figure out what to do. They were all in Diego's mansion, having agreed that it was the most easily guarded place. After talking late into the night, they had all decided to look at the situation with fresh eyes in the morning. When they all approached the issue again, three hours ago now, the numbers were still the same. All four of Diego's lieutenants were in favor of calling in the big guns. Diego hated the idea. It felt like he was giving up. Like he couldn't handle a little bloodshed.

He would never admit it, but he was shaken. Joe and Ray had been two of his best. They knew their shit, no doubt about it. And now they were dead. But what bothered him most was how the biker had known they were coming. Tim seemed to think the guy had been surprised when they walked in, but then he started firing before they had even shown their guns. None of it made any sense. So, in the end, he made the call. Hector had listened silently and then agreed to send two men. Men who specialized in this sort of problem solving.

Tim breathed his own sigh of relief when Diego told him. He would have preferred more than two, but at least they would be seasoned. Tim wasn't really a superstitious man, and he didn't have much of a problem killing people who were in the game—they knew what they signed up for—but ever since they'd killed that woman, he hadn't *felt* right. It wasn't even his shot that killed her, but he felt responsible somehow.

Then, seeing two of his coworkers—his friends—die was almost too much. He was close to walking away. He probably would as soon as he took care of that fucking biker. It was the only reason he was sticking around. No better motive than revenge.

He stood up to go tell the news to the other three, who were playing video games in one of the mansion's several living rooms.

***

Diego leaned back into his plush white couch and put a hand over his eyes as Tim walked away. He still didn't feel right about calling in help. Even after the surprisingly painless phone call. This was the problem with dealing with these ruthless cartel types. Although Diego was in business with them, he preferred to stay far away from them whenever possible. Calling them in willingly made his skin crawl.

He slouched deeper into the couch and remembered what seemed like a lifetime ago, which was only two years ago, how scared he was, but how fucking excited he was, too.

He had flown to El Paso, Texas. He'd barely had enough money for the trip, but he had family in Juarez, right across the border. He visited with his aunt and uncle, claiming that he missed them, that it had been too long. But he, and his older cousin Guillermo, knew better. It was Guillermo who had the connection. Who had finally agreed to hear Diego out after several weeks of daily calls.

Once Diego had explained it to Guillermo, it was just a matter of time. It wasn't a bad idea. In fact, it was a good idea, by all accounts, but it was so simple that Diego half expected to be laughed at when he brought it up. But when the phone line went silent for a beat after he finished his explanation, he knew that he'd made his cousin think hard about it.

He had been growing marijuana illegally for years in Denver. It was one thing that he was exceptionally good at, but he had never been much of a networker or marketer. He grew enough weed to keep his head above water, but that was it. His operation never took off like he hoped it would. No matter how much he worked to increase demand, he always found himself back in the same spot, selling to the same people. When medical marijuana became legal in Colorado, he saw his chance, but there were too many regulations and laws governing the industry. He tried half-heartedly to find investors, but once again, his lack of networking and marketing savvy kept him locked into the status quo.

Two years before the state legalized recreational weed, Diego's house had been raided by law enforcement, and they found his grow operation. They also found a gram of cocaine in his bedroom. He spent just under a year in prison and was released on probation with a felony on his record.

When recreational use was legalized, Diego allowed himself to get excited at the prospect of going legit. It didn't take long to find out that the state made it almost impossible for anyone with a felony conviction to break into the legal marijuana business. He was stuck. Then the state announced that they would allow private citizens to grow marijuana in their homes. Up to twelve plants for personal use. He also learned that the state also levied all sorts of taxes on recreational marijuana. Dispensaries were selling a gram for $60 while Diego was selling that same gram—and the same quality—for $30. So the idea came to him.

A couple of months after the idea came, Diego flew out to El Paso and Guillermo drove him to a little beat-up house in Juarez. There, they met two men with guns. These armed men transferred Guillermo and Diego to another car and blindfolded them. In the front seat, the two men with guns joked and talked in Spanish as the two blindfolded men sat and listened. Diego didn't speak much Spanish, and what he did was mostly slang. Guillermo was fluent, which was why he came along instead of just vouching for Diego.

It was a twenty-minute drive during which both Diego and his cousin went through the same thought process in their own private darkness. They both had the idea that they were in over their heads, that everything would be fine, that they were going to die, that they were going to be rich. Really, when dealing with the Marquez Cartel, it could have gone any which way.

They were kept blindfolded until they were inside the entryway of a massive stone house. As the armed men removed their blindfolds, two curved staircases leading up to a shared landing filled their vision. Ahead of them and between the two stairways was a marble fountain with water softly bubbling out of the top of three tiers and flowing down into the base. The floors were white, the walls and ceiling a red velvet. It looked, to Diego, like a stereotypical drug dealer mansion, but it was also the nicest and, without a doubt, the most expensive house he had ever been in. Dollar signs filled his eyes as his fear bubbled away like the water at the top of the fountain.

They were led to Hector on the back porch, which overlooked a series of stepped pools surrounded by perfectly manicured landscaping. The white walls surrounding the estate were high, and all around the inside were platforms, allowing men to patrol the wall without being on top of it.

Guillermo spoke first in Spanish to Hector, who sat at a table with Ruiz, both men sporting sunglasses and looking stoic. Hector nodded his head once at the gratitude Guillermo expressed, then they got down to business. It turned out Hector spoke English, and he listened intently as Diego hurried through his plan, his voice tight with excitement.

"So, you think we can get away with growing all of our ganja in Colorado?" Hector asked when Diego had finished. He sounded genuinely interested, if a little disbelieving.

"I think," Diego began carefully, "that we can start small and see how it goes. But growing it there will make it easier to transport around the country. You won't have the border to contend with."

Hector and Ruiz looked at each other. "Getting across the border isn't too hard, though. We expect losses," Ruiz said, sounding skeptical. He began to say something else, but Hector stopped him with a hand as he leaned forward. "I've heard that the banks won't do business with the marijuana stores," Hector said. "Is this true?"

Diego nodded.

"So that means it's a cash business, yes?" Hector asked, a smile showing on his face. Diego and Guillermo nodded in unison this time, both leaning forward.

"What do they do with all of their money, then?" Hector said this through a grin. Ruiz was smiling now, too. As were Diego and Guillermo, although they didn't know exactly what at.

The four men had talked for several more hours before coming to an agreement that suited them all.

# Twenty

G IBNEY AND WANE ARRIVED around the corner from the motel a few minutes behind the SWAT team and the hostage negotiator. Wane, unusually silent during the ride over, was quick to exit the car before Gibney even got it in park. It was the first time he'd seen her move so quickly and was surprised that she could. In his experience tall, muscular people like Wane were slower than those with slight builds like himself and the other compact individuals that made great Rangers and Navy SEALs. To be fair, though, it was the first time he had ever been close to a live-fire situation such as this with her, given his short tenure as her partner.

The tip had come within two hours of them getting the biker's picture on the news and all over the internet. A motel manager claimed to have rented the guy a room. Said his name was Terrence Rubble. Second floor room. Had seen him only a few days previous.

Wane talked to an officer in uniform for a minute and then came back over to Gibney, who stood watching the SWAT team check each other's gear and visibly struggle to keep their fingers off of their triggers. It was like watching a junkie wait for a fix, and Gibney was starting to feel the same way. The tension in the air was palpable, and he suddenly wanted to be first through the door, despite it being a flagrant violation of proper breaching procedure.

"The clerk said he doesn't know if the guy's here now or not," Wane said, looking visibly disappointed. "No motorcycle around. He also said he's never seen the girl before."

"Well, is the room occupied?" Gibney said, trying to stay patient. Wane nodded. "Says it's under the last name Rubble. But that sounds fake to me."

Gibney was quiet for a moment, wondering if they had really gotten so lucky. Then he started wondering if maybe this was the wrong guy. Or maybe he was just really dumb. Any halfway smart criminal would know that the police had his face. Only a real idiot would head back to the place under his own name. Either way, they had to check it out.

"I don't know. Maybe he's just an idiot. Let's get into position and then we'll go through possible hostage protocol."

***

Trouble woke with a start for the second time in half an hour. This time it wasn't from the front door, but the bathroom door. Trina had slammed it. Trouble figured she had done it to wake him up. When the hazy cloud surrounding Trouble's thinking processes lifted as much as they would, he was greeted with a scene that struck him as the best thing to ever happen to that particular motel room.

Calling the towels available in the bathroom large was being generous, to say the least. They were somewhere in size between a hand towel and a regular towel, but leaning toward the former. Trina had one wrapped around her midsection, barely reaching below her lap and above her nipples. It took a moment for Trouble to realize that she was asking him a question, and that she looked like she would rather be anywhere else in the world than standing in front of him like she was in that moment.

"Do you have any clean clothes I can wear? Or do I need to get back into my dirty ones?" She asked for the third time, clearly agitated. Trouble felt the hot flush of guilt as he looked away and snapped his jaw shut in a gesture that would have been comical under different circumstances.

He hurried to the bedroom and pulled out a backpack that he had stuffed between the wall and the side of the bed. He rooted around for a moment and selected a pair of boxer shorts and a *Dead Kennedys* t-shirt that smelled and looked somewhat clean. He handed them to her while looking purposely at the floor. She snatched them from his hand and padded back into the bathroom, slamming the door shut once again. Just then, a red light on the phone on the small nightstand in the bedroom began blinking. Trouble didn't notice it. He had turned the ringer off after the night clerk had mistakenly called the room his second night here, interrupting a particularly peaceful heroin nap.

***

Gibney held a pair of headphones to his ear and listened to the ringing. A hostage negotiator held the phone a few feet away from him. All told, there were five people listening to the persistent ring, one through the telephone and four with headphones hooked up to a machine designed for such a purpose. It kept ringing. They let it go on for a full two minutes before deciding to breach and hope that they didn't find the worst-case scenario: a dead woman and no sign of the biker.

From their position around the corner from the motel, it took the breach team under thirty seconds to get to the door of the hotel room. The lead SWAT officer tried the doorknob, found it locked. He then signaled to the officer carrying the battering ram. The man stepped in front of the door and swung the heavy object back to gain some momentum and then forward into the wood just above the knob, splintering the cheap door.

***

The door swung open as Trina stepped out of the bathroom, dressed in the boxer shorts and t-shirt Trouble had given her, both of which were several sizes too big. She noticed the red light blinking on the phone. "Your phone's ringing."

Trouble looked at her, perplexed, as he pulled his cell phone out of his pocket.

"No. That phone," she said, gesturing toward the bedroom.

"Oh. Probably a wrong number," he said as he started to put his phone back in his pocket. But before he could, it chimed with the text notification sound. *Answer your phone*, the message said. Just above that message was the one he had received earlier in the day. At the Mexican restaurant. The one that had probably saved his life. He got up from the couch and walked past Trina into the bedroom to pick up the motel phone.

"Look out your window," a man's voice said as soon as Trouble put the handset to his ear.

"Who the fuck is this?"

"My name is Murke. Now, look out your window," the voice repeated, the tone not changing at all. "I'll wait."

Trouble set the handset down on the nightstand and walked past Trina again.

"What's happening?" she said. He ignored her. He cracked the curtains on the large front window. Sunlight streamed in and he blinked a few times before looking at the motel across the street, which was now crawling with police. They were clustered around the room that Trouble had held previously. He had purposely paid for another week's rent—to see if this exact thing would happen.

The police across the street didn't really worry him. His bike was parked around the back and he had managed to get his current room without putting his name down, a convenience that had cost him a hefty, non-refundable deposit. What worried him was this voice on the phone. The mystery text messages. How the hell did this guy know where he was all the time? Who was he? Trouble walked back into the bedroom as Trina took his spot at the window.

"Yeah, and?" Trouble said when he picked the motel phone up again. There was a pause before the guy chuckled.

"And it will take one phone call to put you in jail for a long, long time," the guy said, a smile in his voice. Trouble rolled his eyes and groaned about as loud as the guy had laughed.

"Listen Murke—which is a terrible fake name, by the way—whatever game you're playing, just get on with it. I've got someplace to be soon."

"Ahh, yes. The little cash run for the dispensary. Without the money from that, you won't be able to keep up your little habit, will you?"

*Jesus Christ*, Trouble thought, *this guy must be some sort of professional. No one else could have tailed me like that without me knowing.* He was starting to get a little worried, but mostly it just pissed him off. At times, heroin gave him a shorter fuse than normal, which meant a damn short fuse. "What the fuck do you want, man?" he nearly screamed into the phone.

"I want you to open a door for me. A door at the bank. Day after tomorrow," the voice on the phone replied sweetly.

"What fucking bank? What are you talking about?"

"The house on Pleasant View Road that you'll be dropping money off to later today. That bank."

"You want me to, what? Kill the guy at the door and then wait for you to come? Meanwhile, the rest of the guys in that house will be serving me lunch and definitely not shooting at me."

"Look in the nightstand drawer," Murke said.

A chill ran up Trouble's spine as he opened the drawer. Inside was a Gideon's bible and a red bank bag Trouble had never seen before.

"You can open it if you want, but I wouldn't. The less you tamper with explosives, the better. All you have to do is give the man at the door the bag and walk away. Quickly," Murke said. "If you do that, you'll get away in time and the door will be open for me and my friends."

Trouble stood up, suddenly feeling all the frustration of the day coming down on him. "Call the cops, I don't care," he said. "Or, better yet, do your own fucking robbery," Trouble yelled and then slammed the phone down into its cradle. Fuming, he turned around to walk back into the front room when he saw Trina standing by the bedroom door, next to the bathroom. She looked more curious than frightened. He opened his mouth to say something as he approached her, but the sound of shattering glass in the bathroom stopped him.

It took him a second to realize what was happening, because he couldn't hear the shots. Plaster dust spewed out from the walls as bullets passed through the drywall above his head. He lunged at Trina and brought her down to the floor with him as more bullets passed through the bathroom window, the walls, and lodged somewhere in the ceiling. Since he couldn't hear the shots, the shooter was probably using some sort of high-powered rifle with a fancy silencer on it. Special Ops shit. Probably over ten thousand dollars' worth of rifle and accessories.

A couple of seconds after the shooting stopped, Trouble's phone chimed again with a text notification. He pulled it out, knowing who it would be from. *Don't fuck around with me. Do what I ask or I'll kill her before I kill you. Morning run. 10am Wednesday. -Love, Murke.*

Trouble read the text and then looked at Trina, who was now more frightened than curious, lying next to him in the small doorway between the bedroom and the main room, the two of them coated with white plaster dust. She had landed on his left hand, and he could feel her warm, soft skin through the t-shirt. His t-shirt. He looked into her eyes, a sudden urge to kiss her almost uncontrollable. She looked back at him for a moment. He thought he saw something there. *Is this really about to happen?* Trouble thought, his libido getting ready to redline.

"What the fuck!?" Trina yelled suddenly. Trouble snapped out of it. They'd just been shot at, and he was expecting a make-out session. *I watch too much fucking TV*, he thought, pulling his hand from under her.

Trouble remembered the gaggle of cops across the street. He scrambled over to the front window on his hands and knees. Apparently, they hadn't heard the shots because none of them were paying any attention to the motel from which Trouble gazed at them. It made sense. The bathroom window faced the opposite direction, and there was a residential street behind Trouble's motel on which a truck or van could be parked easily. Open a window and fire a few shots from a fancy rifle, no problem. Plus, it was still early afternoon, with normal city sounds to drown out silenced gunshots.

He let the curtain fall back into place and then made his way over to the couch. Sitting with a sigh, he looked at the dozen or so holes in the walls and ceiling. "Definitely not getting that deposit back, now."

"What the fuck!?" Trina said again from the floor.

*** 

Murke took one last look at his tablet, which showed three wide-angle views of Trouble's motel room. Trina was getting up off the floor and Trouble was still slumped on the couch. He powered it down and then pressed the button to close the wide window on the side of the van, through which he could see the back of the motel. Then he placed his rifle on the back seat, climbed into the driver's seat, and pulled his phone out of a jacket pocket. He typed in a number from memory and put the phone to his ear.

"Hey! How are you?" he said, sounding like a PTA dad calling his son's teacher. The person on the phone responded. Murke listened for a few seconds and then continued, "Great, great. I just wanted to let you know that I'm enjoying Denver. Do you think you and your husband will be able to make it out here tomorrow?" He waited for the response, and when it came, it made him smile. "Excellent. I'll see you soon."

\*\*\*

Trouble made his evening run, leaving Trina in his crummy motel room to either stay or go, once again ambivalent about which he would prefer. He'd brought the bank bag with the explosives in it, deciding that it was better with him than it was with her. She might go snooping around and open it and blow up. And, if he was being honest, he didn't want that on his conscience.

He thought about Murke's threats on her life as he rode through the slowly dying daylight, wondering if he should have told her. Wondering if there wasn't another way out of it. Wondering if Murke had been serious...

Of course he wouldn't let any harm come to her. He would figure something out. But telling her that her life had been threatened once again wasn't something he was ready to do. In truth, he didn't think she would go anywhere. If she did, it would be to the police, and hopefully they could protect her. Not likely, but still...

He had left the motel a little early simply to escape the flurry of questions Trina had directed his way. It seemed as though her initial fright had given way to anger. He couldn't blame her. When you weren't used to getting shot at, twice in a day was a lot to handle.

Only after he had left did he curse himself for not grabbing some fixin' materials. He had meant to, but Trina's insistent questions made him forget. He had his massive dope stash in his secret jacket pocket. He had put it in there after getting high while Trina was in the shower. He didn't want it left out where she could find it. Who knows what she would do with it. Probably throw it away.

He could have stopped at a dingy gas station bathroom and fixed himself a good one, if he'd remembered. But, as it was, he would have to wait until he got back. Of course, if he really wanted to, he could dilute some dope in water and snort it up his nose, but the high wasn't nearly as good. Once you got used to the feeling of shooting dope directly into the bloodstream, there simply was no substitution.

He decided to use the cash run to case the bank house more closely, trying to think about how he would rob the place if he was going to force someone to blow up the front door and the guard tasked with protecting it. As he rode up, the place still seemed like a fortress, and the setting sun wasn't helping. The minivan was still out on the street, surely occupied by a highly trained killing machine with a rifle and a radio.

After dropping off the cash, an act which comprised Trouble talking nonsense while the stone-faced security guy said nothing and finally gave him his receipt, Trouble decided to see about a back way.

The neighborhood wasn't your normal grid-type. The houses were in lots of various sizes, most of them large, and set among hills with winding roads. The nearest house behind the target house was on the other side of a large swath of land through which ran power lines. It was like a big alley between backyards, with only a small dirt service road for city employees. Approaching from behind wasn't possible. If they had one halfway decent spotter covering the back, any approach from there would be seen a good quarter mile off. There were pine trees dotting the approach, but no bushes or other real cover. Darting from tree to tree only worked in the movies.

The houses on either side of the target had high wood fences, so getting in from a neighbor's house would prove difficult. There was really only one tenable option: the front door. Which is why the black-ops douche picked Trouble, no doubt. He had an excuse to be there.

The problem was that once the door was opened, there was a three-hundred-pound gorilla blocking entrance. But the explosives would take care of that, no doubt. Trouble didn't particularly like the big bank guard—he didn't want to grab beers with him—but he also didn't want him blown up during a madman's robbery attempt.

*And what about me?* Trouble thought. *First, I have to get away from the explosion. Then I have to hope that whatever other hidden guards there are just happen to miss when they shoot at me.* He figured they would have at least four guys there, all armed to the teeth.

He tried to see the logic in Murke's plan. So what if the front door was blown off its hinges, and the guard reduced to little bits of himself? They would still have to be close enough to get through the door quickly. Where would they hide? There was no place in the front yard. Maybe they would come around the corner in a vehicle. That might work. But still, Trouble had a sneaking suspicion that there was someone in the van at the end of the driveway. Or maybe that was his paranoia...

He shrugged and told himself there was a way out of this. He just had to find it. But soon enough, his thoughts drifted away from the task at hand and toward dope. It hadn't been that long since his last shot, back when Trina was showering, but it felt like an eternity. He needed to get back and get well again. Then he could think straight.

Trouble rode back to the dispensary, the last of the sunset fading out behind the mountains, his mind a flurry of anxiety about the black ops guy on the phone, about Sam's death, and about Mason's crew trying to kill him. It had to have been those guys at the Mexican restaurant. No one else was after him. At least, not that he knew of.

He parked his bike and walked in the front door of the dispensary distracted, hoping to give Lori the receipt and get paid as quickly as possible. He made a beeline for the back and noticed that the place was emptier than usual. In fact, he only saw a few customers, their backs to him.

He didn't see any employees.

Even stranger, the customers seemed to be moving toward him.

By the time he realized what was happening, there wasn't much he could do to stop it. He broke one guy's nose with an elbow, and some toes with a stomp of his boot-clad foot, before someone hit him in the head, hard. After he hit the ground and before he lost consciousness, he recognized one face looking down at him below bright fluorescent lights: Mason.

# Twenty-One

TRINA MANAGED TO RESIST the urge to rummage through Trouble's stuff for about an hour. She was impressed with herself for holding out that long. He had told her nothing about anything before leaving. He'd muttered something about a job he had to do, and that was it. She had known men with some heavy defenses before, but this guy was something else. He gave new meaning to the term "stone-walling." He was distracted, depressed, relaxed, and guarded all at the same time.

The effects of Trina's adrenaline rush had taken a long time to die down after the shooting had ended. She felt incredibly tired for a good long time. But then her appetite had come back, and she had eaten two small slices of the lukewarm pizza that Trouble had ordered. She felt much better after that.

Now, as her search moved from the bedroom to the living room, she was convincing herself to go to the police with every dirty piece of clothing, every fast-food wrapper, every half-smoked cigarette butt. How would this slob of a human protect her? She had never been in a situation like this before but felt more confident in her own abilities to protect herself than those of this—she hated to think it—this loser.

Sure, he seemed to know a little bit about what really happened to Brad, but what good was that if he wasn't willing to tell her anything? She was leaning heavily toward picking up the phone and calling the police when she opened a brown paper bag and saw a dozen dirty syringes. She unfolded a hand towel that had been stuffed under the couch and found a bent spoon and a torn cotton ball. She flinched away from the drug paraphernalia like it was contagious. Like she'd become addicted by just touching the spoon.

He was a *junkie*. She had never known a *junkie*, but her head had been filled with images of them from popular movies, news stories, and urban legends. She ran to the phone in the bedroom and dialed 911. After all, it was an emergency of sorts. The *junkie* could come back at any moment. And there was no telling what he would do.

She remembered what Trouble had said earlier. About assuming that there were dirty cops in any city. She remembered the name of the detective who had spoken to her about Brad's murder. She refused to talk to anyone else.

Finally, after several minutes of standing firm with the operator, she had the detective on the line.

"This is Sharon Bailey," she heard through the phone. The voice sounded right.

"This is Katrina Parks. I think you're looking for me."

***

Katrina was waiting in the small, dingy lobby of the motel when Bailey pulled up. She saw her through the dirty glass of the front door. A young Indian man sat behind a bulletproof partition across from her, glancing up from his laptop occasionally, as if to see if she was still there. He hadn't asked her anything when she came in and sat down on one of the two metal folding chairs against the wall, next to a mostly empty brochure rack.

She felt uncomfortable in the large t-shirt and boxer shorts, regretting her decision not to change back into her own dirty clothes, which sat in a grocery bag by her feet. When she saw Bailey get out of a silver and black jeep, Trina wondered briefly why the detective was driving her personal vehicle for police business. She shrugged the thought off, stood up, and walked out to meet her.

Trina started to tell Sharon Bailey about her day, starting with Trouble showing up at her office, but the detective told her to wait before walking a short distance away and making a phone call. She was back in less than a minute. Trina didn't hear what the phone call was about, but she figured she was calling a unit to come sit on the motel until the biker came back, at which point he would be arrested. With some soothing words, Bailey ushered Trina into the front seat of the jeep. They pulled out of the parking lot, and Trina told her the story.

***

Murke watched all of this from inside his minivan parked in a fast-food restaurant's parking lot up the street. He ran over the moving parts in his mind. Really, he could do without the biker. It just wouldn't be as fun or profitable. His objective was clear: chaos. But, with his teammates coming in tomorrow, he could easily create chaos without the biker. The whole plan with the biker was just a way to keep from getting bored, really. Murke had been getting too good for his own good, and he was purposely putting obstacles in his way. Plus, it was an experiment of sorts. Was he really that good at profiling people? Would the players act as Murke thought they would? He figured they would. They had so far, for the most part.

He opened an app on his phone and located the GPS device he'd placed on Trouble's bike after he'd seen him that first time at the bank house. Murke had tailed the biker home and stuck the device on the bike when he'd disappeared into the crappy motel. Too easy. The challenge would be Wednesday morning. Either way, he didn't think the biker would make it out alive. Guys like that died young, in Murke's considerable experience.

In the end, he decided to let the girl go. It wasn't worth killing a cop over it. Besides, it might still work. He started his van and pulled out into traffic, heading to where the app said Trouble's bike was located.

# Twenty-Two

WITH A DULL THROBBING came the slowly dawning realization that he was sick. It took a few moments for consciousness to fall enough into place for Trouble to have such a coherent thought. Shortly following the initial thought of sickness came the further realizations of what had happened to him at the dispensary, and the trouble Trouble now found himself in.

He groaned as he willed himself back into the blissful blackness of unconsciousness, but to no avail. He kept his eyes closed while trying to move his right hand to his secret jacket pocket. His eyes shot open, revealing only darkness. He couldn't move. His arms were tied out to his sides, fastened to whatever it was he was lying on. And someone had taken his jacket. Panic set in.

It wasn't so much the fact that the guys who had tried to kill him a couple of times had caught up with him. It wasn't so much the fact that he was helpless, tied to what looked to be a couple of wooden pallets in the middle of what looked to be a windowless, dingy warehouse. It wasn't so much the fact that he was surely facing an unpleasant and drawn-out death. He had been in similar situations before and had made his way out.

No, he wasn't worried about those objectively scary cards stacked against him. It was, in that moment, the fact that he was beginning to feel the sickness of heroin detox. The fact that he no longer had his lucky jacket was a two-fold gut-punch. It meant he was no longer protected from those malicious forces that had been hounding him since the day he was born. It also meant that the only thing that could keep detox at bay was out of his reach.

His thoughts quickly focused in on heroin, to the exclusion of all else, as if he could will it into his veins. He lay uncomfortably, thinking that he could die happy if he could die high. He could handle anything that was thrown at him, if only he was high. Detox made everyday life almost unbearable, so Trouble could only imagine what kind of effect it would have on a torture session.

He let his eyes adjust and turned his head to see that his arms were tied to a wooden pallet. His legs were similarly bound to another pallet, which he could lift a few inches off the ground, but the effort it took was draining. He could see some dark shapes on either side of him. Not people, but those items you usually find in deserted warehouses the world over, he supposed. He wasn't in the habit of exploring deserted warehouses but, for some reason, shady characters seemed to gravitate toward them like raccoons to a dumpster. Since he made his living from shady characters, he had become familiar with warehouses of all different kinds. And he had never been in one that didn't have some shit stacked in one corner or another.

He gazed around in the dark, figuring he was alone, when he heard a small moan coming from the spot on the floor directly above his head. It had to be coming from there, because that was the only place he hadn't been able to look. He craned his neck back, the crown of his head pushing into the slats of the wooden pallet. If he had been standing up, he would have been looking directly at the sky, but since he was lying down, he was just looking along the floor.

It was too dark to see details, but there was definitely a person on another two pallets only ten yards away. A woman, by the sounds that he heard. Trouble called out a greeting, hoping that she wasn't tied down. But even as he thought it, he knew it wasn't true. She only answered with pain-filled groans and didn't speak a coherent word. His first thought was that it was Trina, and he really, really hoped it wasn't. Whoever it was, they were as dead as Trouble.

A door opened from the direction of Trouble's feet and rows of fluorescent lights, suddenly flooded with electricity, shone their sickly buzzing illumination down on him and on all the previously dark corners of the dusty warehouse. He craned his head down and looked between his splayed legs to see four men walking toward him. One of them had his jacket on. *You're fucking dead,* Trouble thought, his temper flaring and his pulse quickening. He was fighting to rid himself of the dread he felt creeping up his spine. Of the knowledge that he, within an hour or two, would essentially be completely useless under the oppressive weight of detox. Never mind whatever these guys had in store for him.

As the men got closer, he recognized one of them from outside of Sam's house the last time he'd scored. The last time he'd seen Sam alive. They'd passed each other; Trouble on his motorcycle, the guy in a white SUV. He'd figured Mason and his crew had killed Sam and his wife, but didn't know exactly why. He hoped to find out. Not that it would help his position any, but it was a nagging question. If he could somehow get out of this, he'd know who to kill.

Trouble heard a small sound, remembered that there was someone else next to him. He looked back up to see who the woman was and immediately recognized her. They were positioned head-to-head, and when Trouble looked up, she was doing the same. Their eyes met. It was Lori—his boss from the dispensary. She was gagged and couldn't speak, but the look in her eyes spelled terror. Trouble didn't know what was going on, but he knew it wasn't good. He knew why they wanted him, but Lori was a different story. What had she done to piss them off? He knew he was probably going to find out, and it wouldn't be pretty.

He yelled and bucked up and down, lifting the wooden pallets a couple of inches off the ground at most. He heard wood cracking, but felt no difference in the strength of his bonds. The men laughed at him. The one he knew as Mason was carrying a small red duffel bag, which he put on the ground. He pulled out an extension cord, a rectangular box with a power cord, and a small mechanism that Trouble immediately recognized as a tattoo machine. The guy in Trouble's jacket took the male end of the extension cord and plugged it into the wall. Mason was making little adjustments on the machine, while the other man looked down at Trouble with something like hate in his eyes.

Trouble could see that the tattoo machine had been modified. But to what purpose, he couldn't glean from simply looking at it. The box was the power supply. It had two input jacks: one for the machine itself and one for the foot pedal that activated the needles when pressed. There was a large rubber grip around the metal of the machine, big enough to be gripped in one hand comfortably. It took a few minutes for Mason to set the whole thing up. Trouble watched, saying nothing, his mind reeling, his panic building. He noticed, as Mason knelt beside him, that the wires coming from the power supply to the handheld machine looked different.

He had spent a fair amount of time under various tattoo machines throughout his life, and had been curious about how they worked, in a detached sort of way. It had given him something to think about to take his mind off the annoying and persistent pain necessary to put ink in skin. Now, as Mason placed his right knee on the pedal and the familiar buzz of the machine filled the air, Trouble knew that this pain was going to be far worse than any tattoo he had ever received.

*\*\**

Trina thought it strange that Detective Bailey said they were headed straight for a safe house. Although she'd never experienced anything close to this, Trina had assumed that they would go to the station first, surely. She thought that safe houses were only used by spies and CIA agents and people like that. But Sharon—that's what she insisted Trina call her—was comforting and confident. Trina got no bad vibes until they reached the house, and even then, she wasn't too alarmed. She was with a cop. She'd been taught to trust the police.

She looked at the street sign as they made a left into a nice neighborhood. *Pleasant View Road*, it read. They pulled into the second driveway on the right. The road ended in a cul-de-sac. There was a van parked next to the driveway of the safe house. It all looked normal to Trina. She supposed that was exactly the point. A big man dressed in a dark suit came out of the front door, looking around as he did so.

"Stay put for a second, please, Trina," Sharon said as she got out of the jeep and walked to meet the man on the wooden porch. The two looked like they were arguing about something. After a few minutes, the man threw up his hands in exasperation and Sharon came back and got into the jeep. A few seconds later and the garage door opened. There was a sleek black passenger van inside, but the other spot was empty. Sharon pulled in and the garage door closed behind them.

***

The tattoo machine had been modified to pass electricity. Mason, as the wielder of the apparatus, was protected from the electrical current by a large rubber grip. Some electricity was routed to power the vibration of the needles while the rest flowed into Trouble's body. The funny thing was—and Trouble had experienced this phenomenon before—that when the current was flowing through his body, he had a kind of irreverent inner dialogue going. It was only when Mason stopped touching the needle to skin, allowing Trouble's body to register the whole of what was happening, that his mind reeled incomprehensibly. He cried out for mercy or death.

So, as to be expected, Trouble began to yearn for the touch of the electrified tattoo needles. He was able to think clearly then, in his strange way, under and around the pain. Being no stranger to the occasional electric shock, he had learned the basics of electricity at a fairly young age. He knew, as the needles touched his skin, that it wasn't the voltage that could kill him—it was the amps. He knew that one or two milliamperes were enough to cause a tingling sensation, while fifteen milliamperes could cause muscle paralysis and the pain he was now feeling. Anywhere between twenty and one hundred milliamperes could cause lung and heart failure, among other unpleasant happenings.

It seemed to him that they had rigged the power supply to increase and decrease amperage, because when Mason had begun—what seemed like hours ago but was really no more than ten minutes—Trouble hadn't experienced paralysis or even much pain. It was clear to him that they wanted this to last. They wanted him to pay for what he did to "Mr. G," as Mason called him when he occasionally broke his smile to speak to Trouble.

Mr. G: the man who had, in fact, been killed by Mason when he backed over the guy's head.

Sure, Trouble had been firing on them in defense of his life, but he hadn't killed the guy. Mason had done that all by himself. Mr. G wasn't without blame, either. After all, he was the one who could not keep himself from falling out of the car when Mason slammed on the brakes. But people like Mason couldn't be expected to take the fall. That's not how these things worked. Trouble knew the type. He was probably trying to cover his own ass by having a fall-guy.

After a half-hour of persistent shocks and breaks and the guys taking turns, they finally caught on to the fact that letting Trouble sit, untouched, seemed to have the most torturous effect. While at first they were shocking him longer and letting him sit less, they began to shock him for shorter periods, letting him sit for longer and longer. His detox was coming on hard, his body was pouring sweat and clearing out any remnants of dope in his system. Time warped in his mind, and he no longer knew the difference between ten seconds and ten minutes.

He began to yearn for the touch of the electric needle as thoughts of dope stretched the seconds into what seemed like hours. After a while, his torturers left, talking about what food they wanted to eat, arguing about the place to go. After all that,

Trouble felt the worst for lying there alone, tied to wooden pallets, sweating and shivering, every inch of his body excruciatingly uncomfortable, his dope-sick brain losing itself in the true torture that every junkie knows all too well.

The only good thing was that, in putting their attention on Trouble, they hadn't even glanced at Lori. For all the noise she made, Trouble assumed she was asleep or dead. When they had started in on him, he forgot that she was there, and only remembered that he wasn't alone in the situation when his mind managed a respite from the pain they were inflicting on him.

"Lori? You there?" Trouble asked soon after the men left for their lunch break.

No answer.

"Lori? Can you move? Can you get loose at all?"

Nothing.

"Lori, wake up!"

Muffled moans came from above him, and Trouble craned his neck to look at her. She was doing the same, but her mouth was stuffed with a gag and she looked out of it. She had a bruise forming on the side of her head.

Trouble's energy was nearly gone, and the sickness was coming on strong. He couldn't hold the position long, so he relaxed his neck and let his head down. No escape.

The room grew dark as Trouble's eyes slipped closed, whisking him into a restless and uncomfortable sleep, the only sounds those whimpering whines made by Lori. Even those faded away as his exhausted and traumatized body tried to shut down. He lost consciousness.

When he woke again, he had no idea how much time had passed. But the men were back and Lori was screaming as they tortured her. They had turned Trouble around, apparently, so he could watch what they did to Lori, but he was still bound securely to the two pallets.

He raised his head and looked down between his feet to see Colton and Mason standing over Lori. The other two men that had been here earlier were nowhere to be seen. The soles of Lori's feet were facing Trouble's, so he had a clear view of the bloody and disturbing show. Her screams seemed to bounce around the warehouse and vibrate Trouble's body in a thrum of empathy, anger, and desperation.

The wet *thunk* of knife striking flesh issued again and again as Colton and Mason took turns dropping knives into Lori's legs. They had pulled the trousers of her pantsuit down around her ankles, revealing white cotton underwear and smooth, trim legs—which were bleeding in a half-dozen places. Lori's gag was around her neck, but only screams of pain came from her mouth, as if coherent thought had left her.

Trouble flexed his muscles, fighting the sweeping sickness that threatened to make him vomit. Colton pretended to drop his knife into her leg. When she flinched and whimpered, both men laughed. Mason did the same thing. Then Colton dropped his knife. Trouble watched it as it fell, willing it to miss. But it didn't. It struck her kneecap with the tip, then tumbled down onto the wooden pallet, leaving a gash in her skin. Lori cried, biting her lip. Mason dropped his knife. It thumped solidly into the meat of her upper thigh, wavering as she screamed and writhed and shook uncontrollably.

"Fuck you," Trouble yelled when it was clear he couldn't break his binds and rain holy hell on the two men.

Colton ignored this outburst, but Mason turned to Trouble, a surprised smile on his face. "Oh, you won't be saying shit in a minute," he said. "Not once you learn what this bitch was willing to do to you."

Mason turned back to Lori and yanked his knife from her leg. "All right, bitch," he said. "We know what you did, but we want to hear you tell it. We want your friend here to hear what it was." Mason gestured at Trouble when he said this. "So take us through it. If you tell it all, I'll let you go. Promise." Trouble knew they would never let her leave. Just like he knew he would die here, in this dingy warehouse, at the hands of a couple of genuine psychopaths.

"We understand each other?" Mason asked.

Lori nodded, her face a mask of dismay and pain. Mason smiled at her and then slowly turned that smile to Trouble. It was clear that he liked this even more than he had liked electrocuting Trouble.

"I'm sorry, Terrence," Lori said. "I'm so sorry. I was glad when you came back. I was glad." She sobbed through her words. Trouble had no idea what she was talking about.

"Start from the beginning," Mason said brusquely.

It took her a moment to gain her composure. The holes in her legs leaked blood continuously as the two men twirled their respective knives over her. "They gave me no choice," she began. "They came in right after I'd opened and said I had to pay them every week. For protection, they said. I—"

"Who, bitch? Who came in? 'Cause it sure as fuck wasn't me." Mason yelled down at her, gripping his knife in a white fist.

"I—I don't know. I don't know who they were. All they said was Marquez. The guy said his name was Tim, but I don't know if that was his real name. I ignored them the first week, and they came in and trashed my store. Three of them. They took all the money in the register. One of them ripped my clothes off and put one of my employees in the hospital. I had to close for four days. I talked to the police, but they did nothing. They watched the place for a few days, but as soon as they were gone, the men came back. When I went to the police again, they told me to hire security. But all the companies in town refused me. They said that I was too much trouble. They knew, somehow, that the cartel had taken over. They wouldn't work with me. So I started paying."

"Those fuckers in the Marquez are brutal," Mason said, with a hint of humor in his voice. "Just smash and grab. No finesse. They don't know how to talk to people. They don't understand the finer points of a protection racket."

Mason looked expectantly at Lori, who continued after a moment.

"So... I found a way to contact these guys here. I had read all the news reports about the possibility that cartels were operating in the state. I... I just wanted to get them off my back. To make them go away. I was losing my life savings to the Marquez cartel. So I found their rivals." She gestured at Mason, who seemed to stand a little straighter when she did. "I found a low-level dealer and paid him to pass word up about the courier," she continued. "Paid him to keep me out of it. To say it was his idea." Lori stopped, gathering a sobbing breath. "I just wanted them to take the money. I didn't know they would kill him. I just wanted to be able to say to the Marquez cartel that someone was stealing from my couriers. I didn't think they would hurt him."

"Hurt who? Who was it? Brad Thompson?" Trouble asked, starting to get the picture.

Lori nodded. She was barely holding it together.

"You were trying to start a war," Trouble whispered, more to himself than anyone else. Mason heard him.

"That's right. The bitch was trying to get us to go at each other in the streets. The police here only put up with so much, no matter how much you pay them. The only problem was that they—those Marquez pussies—went after one of ours. From one of our dispensaries. They killed him and an innocent civilian. A woman. That got the pigs pissed. So that's where you came in. We couldn't start an all-out war in the streets. So we went after another courier—you. She knew it, too. And she didn't say shit to you, did she?"

"That's why you were willing to pay so much?" Trouble asked Lori, who had her eyes screwed shut, tears spilling down her cheeks.

"I couldn't just ask them to call it off," she whined. "I wanted to take it back, but I couldn't. I couldn't."

"You doubled down, didn't you?" Trouble asked, anger in his voice. "Hoping something would happen to get the police involved. Or hoping that I would kill one of them?"

Trouble was shivering and sweating, and his body felt like it was crawling with bugs. He wanted so badly to stretch out his limbs, but he couldn't. Even if he could, they wouldn't feel any better. It felt like his bones were itchy, and he wanted to pop them out of his skin, if only to stop them from feeling this way.

All this, added to the story about why he was in this situation in the first place, made him feel a welling hatred for not only the two warring cartels, but also for Lori for not warning him about what she'd set in motion. She had let one innocent guy get killed, and was perfectly willing to let another one die, too. It explained the look on her face when he'd come back and told her about the incident in which Mr. G had died. He'd lied to her about it, saying they just shot at each other. She had seemed disappointed. Maybe if he'd told her the truth, her face would have lit up.

"I didn't see any other way out," she said to Trouble. "I'm sorry."

"But she didn't even tell you the best part," Mason interjected. "She was barely sending any money with you guys. She started stashing the rest of her profits somewhere else. Isn't that right? She knew that her couriers would be hit—hell, she's the one that set it up. So, instead of sending the money to the bank house, she sent it somewhere else. She told the guys from the Marquez cartel that we were stealing all her money, so she couldn't pay them. Meanwhile, she was stashing it somewhere." Mason had been talking to Trouble, but he turned to Lori. "That means you've got a fat pile of cash somewhere. Which is the only reason you're still alive. So you need to tell us where it is. Story time's over. Now I want a location."

Lori said nothing. Her eyes were closed again. Trouble remembered the day that he'd seen inside the safe. She'd been distracted and had left it open when he walked in the room, and he'd seen a good half-dozen red bank bags, all of which looked swollen with money. When he'd come back later, they were gone.

Colton, still wearing Trouble's jacket, dropped a knife into Lori's upper thigh. She screamed. The guy hadn't said a word since he'd been there. But the look in his eyes as he tortured Lori told Trouble all he needed to know. Trouble decided that if he somehow lived through this, it would be a pleasure to remove the fucker from the earth.

"Where is it, Lori?" Mason asked. Colton removed his knife from her leg, leaving another wound that immediately started dumping blood.

Lori looked pale. Deathly.

"Where's the fucking money?" Mason yelled, dropping his knife into her shin. It struck and bounced off. Trouble swore he heard the sound of the bone chipping. He couldn't watch any longer. He shut his eyes and laid his head on the wood. He wished for sleep, but he knew it wouldn't come.

He lay there, his eyes closed, and listened to Lori's screams and Mason's yelling. Time morphed and stretched and folded as Trouble thought about how nice it would be to shoot some dope. He tried to block everything else out and imagine the feeling of the drug spreading through his body, taking everything and everyone away. Faintly, in the back of his mind, he willed Lori to hold out. They were going to kill her anyway, so why give them the money?

*You're stronger than I am,* he thought. *Don't give it to them.* Maybe she had a wife or girlfriend or husband or boyfriend that would take off with the money. He hoped so.

He dozed into a nightmare realm where his discomfort grew and time turned incomprehensible. He wasn't asleep, and he wasn't really awake. But it wasn't comfortable. There was no oblivion, just delirium and fever nightmares. It was the opposite of restful. He came back to reality with Mason yelling at Colton.

"Goddammit Colton. I knew these fucking crates were a bad idea. We couldn't see how much she was bleeding. Fuck!"

Trouble raised his head and looked at the two men.

Colton simply looked from Mason to Lori and back again before reaching down and grabbing the bottom pallet she was on. He slid the two pallets backward, Lori's still-bound body holding them together, to reveal a large smear of blood that had seeped down in between the wooden planks and pooled on the concrete floor. Trouble wasn't surprised that she was dead, seeing how much blood was there. Evidently, she hadn't given them any information.

"Fuck!" Mason yelled, stomping his right foot like a petulant child. He had his knife in his fist, gripping it so hard his whole hand was mottled white and pink.

Slowly, Mason turned toward Trouble. He stepped close, a vein on his forehead pulsing and his face flushed pink. "Your turn," he said.

# Twenty-Three

"G Give me a shot and I'll tell you about the bank." Trouble's voice didn't seem like his own. The pleading quality permeating every word shamed him to his core, but he was unable to stop it. The need to get rid of the pain and sickness had become his only priority. And he was playing the only card he had: the bank-house.

In the hours since Lori had died, Colton and Mason had taken turns going in on him with the tattoo machine. His detox had only gotten worse, and ending it was his main concern now. The electricity going through his body was now amplifying his need for dope. He no longer had the ability to use the pain as an escape from the detox. It was all blending into crushing anguish and anxiety.

If he had been asked to describe the mental state he was in, he would have been at a loss for words. In fact, words had all but left him. He had begun to think about the world only in shades of pain. The warehouse was a light pain, as its drafty interior served to settle on his sticky, sweaty skin like a thin blanket made of steel wool. Even when the torturers took a short break, he found no respite in the surrounding air. In those moments, he simply wanted to tear off his skin.

His clothes felt like they were made of sandpaper, scratching his skin with every breath and slight movement. The bindings around his wrists and ankles were zip ties, but they felt like razors digging into his skin. Whether his eyes were open or closed, they felt like they were bulging and popping out of his skull, too wet and too dry at the same time. The electricity pulsing through his body constantly made him feel like vomiting, which he did twice. Both times he got a kick in the ribs. The fact that he probably had a couple of cracked ribs was low on his list of ailments.

All of this came together to lay a black cloud on him. He'd never been tortured like this before, per se, but he'd been in similar situations—hopeless ones. Each time he'd been able to keep a level head, to piss off his captors by being bright and cheery. But he'd never been detoxing before.

As he lay on the pallets now, shivering and sweating and waiting for Mason to respond to his words, he saw no joy in the world. Where once was seated an unshakable confidence in himself, there was now a dark void. Where once he could have looked up and smiled at the pain inflicted upon him, he could now not even meet Mason's eyes. He was like a beaten dog, groveling to his master. He had no past, no future. There was only now. And now was completely unbearable.

He needed dope.

It would fix everything.

So he decided, in his weakened state, to offer them a way into the bank. He didn't really think they would take him up on it, but he wasn't thinking that far ahead. He only wanted some dope. He figured they would kill him soon, even if it was an accident—like Lori. He could die happy with some dope in his system. For the first time in his life, he really feared death. He didn't want to die dope sick. It was no way to live and an even worse way to die.

"Give me a shot and I'll tell you about the bank," he repeated in that same whiny voice.

Mason smiled at Trouble. The kind of smile a knowing adult gives a pitied child. "We already know about the bank. You think we're morons? The place is untouchable. Just because you've been to the door doesn't mean you know anything we don't."

"But I *do* know something you don't." That whining voice again—like nails on a chalkboard to the remaining vestiges of Trouble's true self, the part of him untouched by addiction. Never in his life had he been so disgusted by the sound of his own voice. "So give me a shot and I'll tell you. What have you got to lose? You'll still have me. It's not like I'm asking you to let me go. Just get me well and I'll tell you, Mason."

At this, Mason looked up at Colton from his position kneeling next to Trouble. There was some sort of communication there, and the two of them walked out of earshot and stood in a huddle, discussing the proposition. Trouble closed his eyes and listened to the dull murmur of their voices, searching their tones for any positive signs to support what he wanted so badly. He told himself to resist as long as he could if they refused his offer, but he knew deep down that his will was gone.

Finally, after what seemed a long time, Mason came back to Trouble as Colton walked into the small office at the opposite end of the warehouse. Trouble sneezed suddenly and unexpectedly, spraying snot and mucus down over his chest, chills wracking his entire body. He knew all about the no-warning sneezes and what came next in the sickness's progression. While regular sneezes felt good, like relief, dope sneezes made him feel worse and were impossible to suppress because they came without warning. Pretty soon, he would be vomiting regularly and probably shitting himself. Unless he got some dope in his system.

Mason looked down at him in disgust. "I'll give you your shot," he said. "You'll tell me what you know. But if I'm right and it's nothing worth hearing, we're just going to kill you. So enjoy your high while it lasts, you disgusting fucking junkie."

The relief Trouble felt was immediate. It was almost as if he didn't hear the part about being killed. All his focus was on getting well again. There was no future but the rush and relief of opioids in the bloodstream. He felt better knowing that he would be well soon, but he was sick enough that it did little to stop his physical discomfort.

Colton walked out of the small office carrying a bottle of water and what looked like a shoebox. He set the bottle next to Mason's feet and handed the box to him. Mason knelt and opened the box. He took out all the little things he needed to fix an injection.

Trouble watched in anticipation, wishing that Mason would hurry. He sneezed again, the violent motion jerking his head down and sending a sharp pain along the left side of his rib cage. As he sneezed, the pallet his upper body was fastened to lifted and clattered back to the concrete floor with a loud slap. The men ignored this. They had clearly dealt with sick junkies before. Trouble thought that was half the reason for fixing him the shot. They didn't want to deal with vomit and diarrhea if they could help it. Or maybe this had been the plan all along. It would explain the kit they just happened to have in the back office.

Mason took a dark brown clump of heroin from the box and cut off a little piece with a pocketknife. "More," Trouble said, whining. "Please."

Mason cut off another piece almost equal in size and put them both in the spoon, then continued to fix the shot. It took them a couple of minutes before they found a usable vein in Trouble's left foot. He worried briefly about the cleanliness of the needle, but it wasn't important enough for him to say anything to stop the progress. With his neck craned to watch the brown liquid disappear into his body, Trouble breathed a sigh of relief as Mason pulled the needle out. Trouble laid his head back onto the pallet, closed his eyes, and waited for sweet relief. He waited for the blossoming of warmth to permeate his body. For his chills to stop. For the no-warning sneezes to stop. For the reeling of his mind to slow to a dull crawl.

But they never came. Not really.

He felt marginally better, but something was wrong. There was a nagging voice gaining traction in his exasperated mind. A voice vastly different from the one that had been crying for heroin just minutes earlier. There was relief in that he felt the chills receding and his mind slowing. But with that slowing came a certain clarity that he couldn't avoid. Worse than being angry, the voice—a facet of his own—was disappointed. The self-imposed weakness that had been plaguing him for the last year had slowly given rise to that voice, and his pleading was the last straw.

Here he was. He'd gotten just what he wanted: a big shot of dope. But it hadn't really changed anything. It had solved none of his problems. It was a band-aid, and one that did little to stop the bleeding. Instead of thinking about a way out, Trouble had allowed himself to think about only one thing: heroin. To what end? There was nothing on the horizon for him but death. Best-case scenario was one more shot of dope before he died.

The voice told him he'd been fundamentally changed. That quitting heroin was as simple as refraining from its use. *But it's not that simple,* he argued. *I can't function without it. I need to get out of this first. I need to...* To what? Death is staring you in the face and all you can do is worry about your next shot, the voice said. This is not you. This is not us. We're stronger than this shitty fucking life-sucking drug.

Trouble realized that the voice had been there all along, telling him to resist, clear as ever. But he'd been ignoring it. Even when he was being tortured, it was there. It was him, that was for sure. It was stubborn and brusque. *Maybe it's right. Maybe...*

Trouble had all but forgotten about the two men standing over him until Mason kicked him in the ribs and told him to spill it. Trouble opened his eyes, his inner dialogue interrupted. Not caring whether he lived or died at the moment, he decided to press his luck.

"Just tell me one thing. Why did you kill Sam and his wife?"

At first, Mason wasn't sure what he was talking about. He looked at Colton, who said, "Over by Sloan's Lake. The small-time dealer."

"Oh, right. His name was Sam? Didn't strike me as a Sam. Hmm." Mason seemed to contemplate holding back the information, but something made him speak, his voice matter-of-fact. "You showed up at Sam's house not long after you killed Mr. G. But by then, we already had the word out to look for you. One of our guys said he saw a biker riding up to the house. Funnily enough, that guy, Sam, gets his dope from us. Or *used to* get his dope from us. Small world, huh? Anyway, when I finally heard about it and got to the guy's house, you were already gone. So we wanted to wait. But that neighborhood was crawling with witnesses, so I decided to enlist the help of your friend Sam." Mason stopped abruptly, looking up as if remembering.

"You know, the more I think about this, the more I realize you're a fucking pain in the ass," he said, kicking Trouble in the ribs again. "I thought your name was stupid when Sam first told me, but now I realize that it's pretty fucking apt. Anyway, the guy didn't really want to give you up, but we put a little pressure on him. Then Colton here got a little carried away with the wife, and Sam got mad and wouldn't calm down when he saw her dead in the kitchen like that. So we didn't really have much of a choice. It did take five of us to hold him down, though. He went out fighting. And high as fuck, too. Not a bad way to go, really. Much better than getting raped and murdered by Colton here," Mason said this last laughing, and Colton laughed too.

Trouble felt sick. He regretted asking the question.

"You know the rest," Mason continued. "We would have taken you at the trap house, but you're a paranoid bastard. Had a finger on the trigger the whole time you were in there, didn't you? In that stupid fucking jacket of yours."

"Hey, I like this jacket," Colton said.

"Then you somehow avoided overdosing on the fentanyl I sold you. Granted, that was a long shot. I was just thinking on the fly. Let me ask you, did you do the dose I suggested?"

"No. I'm not a fucking idiot," Trouble said.

"Sure. You know, I kept waiting for you to recognize me from when you killed Mr. G, but you never did, did you? You do that much dope? Is your mind that fucked up? Don't answer that." Mason sighed before continuing. "We tried to follow you home, but turns out following a guy on a motorcycle is damn near impossible unless you have your own motorcycle. Anyway, we knew where you worked. And it didn't take too long to figure out that this bitch was hiding her money away. So I decided to take you both at the same time. Here we are. One down, and one to go. Now, tell me what you promised so I can kill you already."

Trouble knew that his only hope of getting out alive was to tell them about the Murke guy and his plan to raid the bank-house. So he did. He told them about the guy on the phone, the shots fired through the motel wall, his appointment to get inside the fortified house, and the little explosive device in the bank bag he was told to deliver.

"You can wait for him to come out with the money and then take it," Trouble said in a sleepy voice. "But if I'm not there and the explosives don't go off, he'll know something's up. I have the explosives in one of my saddlebags."

While Trouble talked in a low, sleepy voice, suggesting anything he could think of to keep them from killing him, the two men exchanged looks. Their wheels were turning. They saw an opportunity.

What Trouble left out was Katrina's involvement in all of it. During the little torture session, it had become apparent to Trouble that Mason's crew was entirely different from the one that had come to the Mexican restaurant. There was only anger over Mr. G. No mention of two other dead comrades. Plus, there was a difference in style between the two groups. Nothing concrete that he could point to with certainty, but a feeling that they came from different places, had different training and modes of operation. Then, when he'd heard Lori's story, he figured the guys at the restaurant worked for the Marquez cartel.

So he left Trina out of his explanation. Why involve her any more than he already had? It was easy enough to say that the threat was to his life instead of hers. That the Murke guy would find him and kill him if he didn't show up on time at the bank-house on Wednesday morning.

The two men standing over Trouble asked him question after question, trying to find any holes in his story. He used the high to his advantage, occasionally closing his eyes like he was nodding off to go over his answers in his mind before he said a word. It wasn't difficult to keep it all straight because he was telling most of the truth, but he knew that one wrong answer would probably get him killed.

Finally, when they didn't have any more questions, they left him alone with Lori's corpse in the warehouse. It didn't take him long to nod off again.

# Twenty-Four

TROUBLE HAD NO IDEA what time it was when he woke up again. He'd been captured Monday night. He assumed this was Tuesday night, or even Wednesday morning. He couldn't see any daylight in the windowless warehouse, and so had no idea whether the sun was even up.

When two men Trouble had never seen before came in to dispose of Lori's body, he asked them what day it was. Neither man answered. He'd managed a peak behind them when they entered, but there was some sort of anteroom they came through first. If it had been a door directly to the outside, he would've at least known whether it was day or night.

The two men took Lori's body through a door at the other end of the warehouse and Trouble heard the whirring of electric saws and other sounds that made it clear they were working hard. At one point, one of the men came to Trouble and pulled off his boots without a word. Trouble simply watched, knowing that anything he said would do no good. He watched the guy walk off with them, wondering vaguely why the man had stolen his pair of ratty old boots.

For the first hour or so after he woke, Trouble felt good, considering. The conversation he'd had with himself about dope was in the forefront of his mind. But as the hours passed and detox settled on him, that conversation left his mind, replaced by thoughts of dope and the miracles it would surely bestow upon him.

The depression that settled on Trouble was absolute and crushing. The need for dope grew even more powerful the longer he lay there, sweating and shaking, his muscles on fire. He knew that if he could just get high, the seemingly insurmountable obstacles that stood before him would seem less so, if only because he would be numb to any potential consequences.

Slowly, his sickness ramped up again. He thought he slept very little, but it was hard to tell. He lost consciousness and regained it several times as the minutes passed. He gave barely a thought to Trina or Lori or anyone else during his moments of clarity. All he could think about was ending the feeling that gripped his body and mind.

He woke to panic and feverish delirium when seven men walked into the warehouse some time later. Mason and Colton, and five more. They all wore bulky jackets to cover body armor and were clearly a little jumpy and tense. *Wednesday morning*, Trouble thought.

The look on Mason's face gave Trouble no hope whatsoever. He began, in his whiny junkie voice, to plead his case to Mason. It was almost an automatic action. He felt as if he had no choice but to plead with the murdering psychopath for dope. With dope, all would be well. He hated himself for it, but did it anyway. He hadn't gotten three words out before Mason kicked him hard in the ribs and told him to shut up.

"You're going to listen, and that's all. I'm not giving you any dope. Not until this thing is over with, so don't even fucking ask. It'll be your reward if you survive this. Now, here's what we're going to do."

Mason explained the GPS device and small remote controlled explosive device that they had placed on his motorcycle. He explained the second tracking device they had placed in one of his boots. He explained the route Trouble would take, and that any deviation from that route would result in the explosives being detonated.

Mason told him how they would track him in two cars at a safe distance, and that if they saw anything they didn't like, they would simply kill him. It came down to a sure death being torn apart by explosives, or a chance at making it out alive at the bank-house.

"You're going to take the same bag," Mason said. "The one that the guy on the phone gave you. Hand it over and then walk away. We'll do the rest."

"What's your plan?" Trouble asked. "Take him when he comes out with the money?"

Mason smiled at Trouble but said no more. For a few seconds, his sickness briefly abated, and Trouble almost laughed at the silliness of it all. He felt like he was in a low-budget spy film, where Mason and his minions were the bad guys, and Trouble himself was the hero. Then, thinking of himself as a hero got him going even more, and he bit back a smile. But before he knew it, his sickness was back in full swing and the dark cloud had once again settled over his mind.

They let him up from the pallets and gave him a minute to stretch out and get feeling back in his arms and legs. One of the guys threw Trouble's boots at his feet. He put them on, his reeling mind thinking about a dozen different outcomes to the coming events. All of them were bad. Part of him kept thinking about ways to give everyone the slip and go find some dope.

Brainpower that he should have focused on evading his almost certain death was instead devoted to thinking about heroin and how everything would be okay if he only had some. It was incessant. Every step he took toward the door of the warehouse was a reminder of how shitty he felt. He wanted to curl up into a ball on the ground and go to sleep, but he knew sleep wasn't possible. Not in his state. *Maybe it's a good thing I'm going to die. Put me out of my misery,* he thought as he walked into the clear, bright Colorado morning.

Someone had driven his motorcycle to the warehouse. Presumably when he was unconscious and being kidnapped two nights before. The keys were in the ignition. There was some foreign object attached to his right front fork with zip ties. It was right in line with the gas tank. That was intentional, he guessed. Trouble knelt to inspect the object that might explode and kill him on his way to get killed at the bank-house. It would be a shame, he supposed.

The only bombs Trouble had ever seen were in movies, and this would have been right at home in a Bond or Bourne movie. It was maybe six inches long by four inches wide and deep. It looked like a cheap phone attached to a plastic box with some wires. Thus far, he was able to inspect the object with a certain detachment that was natural to his character. But, in not more than a second, his mind turned on him and a wave of nausea, swiftly followed by panic, swept over him. He sat on the ground and put his head in his hands. *I can't do this. I can't fucking do this. God, I feel like shit.*

Privacy fencing surrounded the front of the warehouse. The gate was closed. Passersby could not see into the space. Parked near Trouble's motorcycle were two vehicles: a four-door American truck, and an expensive, late model SUV. Both had been stolen that morning. All seven men had been checking their various automatic weapons and sidearms at the vehicles, talking excitedly and crackling with nervous energy. As Trouble moved from kneeling to sitting on the ground, his muscles aching from the early stages of withdrawal and his time tied to the pallets, they all stopped to look at him. Trouble kept his eyes down but knew that their faces held nothing but open disgust. He knew how they felt.

Mason walked over, the look in his eyes one of amused disdain, and knelt in front of Trouble, who kept his eyes to the ground, head in his hands. "This is why I never touch the stuff. Dope. It turns you into a little bitch when you don't have it." Mason spoke slowly, quietly, as if to a dear friend. "I saw the way you handled yourself the other day. That was some quick thinking. The thing with the dumpster. But you had dope in your system, didn't you? Now look at you. Crying like a bitch. A little. Fucking. Bitch. I could never do anything that made me lose my shit like that." Mason paused, looking around briefly before continuing. "I know you could have killed me that day. I'll never understand why you didn't."

Trouble forced himself to meet the other man's gaze. They were close enough that Trouble could smell Mason's breath, a mixture of coffee and toothpaste.

"I bet you regret it now, huh?" Mason continued. "You wouldn't be in this situation if you hadn't wasted your shots. But that tells me something about you. It tells me that you are a weak piece of shit, even at your best. Even when you're doped up and in the zone. That's what makes you a loser. A fucking loser on a motorcycle. So the least you can do is die like a man today. Make your final act one of redemption for what I'm sure has been a shitty, weak, useless life."

The wave of nausea ebbed as Mason finished up his obligatory villain monologue, bringing Trouble's mind back from focusing on the acute discomfort he was feeling and to the problems that lay ahead.

Mostly, at the moment, the problem of the soon-to-be dead man kneeling beside him. His first instinct was to strike out with his right leg, sending his boot heel into Mason's crotch. Then he would stand up and stomp his head until it turned into sludge. But he knew he wouldn't get that far. Sure, he could accomplish the first part, but before he got to the second, he would take a beating and he would still have to ride his motorcycle to the bank-house. Or they would just kill him and take their chances without him. No, better to deal with this later, when the odds weren't stacked so heavily against him.

Trouble stood up, straddled his bike, started the engine, and waited for one of the seven men to open the gate. He knew he only had a few minutes before another wave of sickness swept over him and he turned into a simpering, useless weakling once again. He needed that time to figure something out. Something that could keep him alive through the coming ordeal.

The SUV, with four men in it, including Mason and Colton (who was still wearing Trouble's jacket), followed Trouble. The truck took another route, presumably getting somewhere ahead of Trouble just in case he tried something.

It was a perfectly brilliant summer morning. The sky was bright blue and empty of clouds. Birds chirped and squirrels hopped about on front lawns. There was an easy breeze, the temperature right around sixty-five degrees. Trouble saw all of this, but through a haze of anxiety and unease.

A shiver wracked his body, followed by a violent sneeze without preamble. It surprised him so much that he swerved on his bike, almost spilling onto the pavement at forty miles an hour. Without his jacket and only a t-shirt to protect him, he would have shredded his skin had he gone down. He got the bike back under control and glanced down toward the improvised explosive device that sat about a foot in front of his right knee.

He took a breath and tried to collect himself. His anxiety was building, and all he could do was think about getting some dope into his system, stopping the terrible feeling that was only getting worse.

Getting close now. Every block seemed somehow long and short at the same time. The way days are long and years short. His thoughts oscillated between heroin and the fact that he was probably going to die. The fact that he didn't have his jacket made him feel sure that his last shred of protection was gone. The universe was about to right the wrong of Terrence Rubble's birth some thirty-two years before. Not even a blink in the eyes of the cosmos, this life that seemed so hard to live and even harder to give up.

And again, if only he could face this thing with a fresh high, it would be okay. He would die happy, he told himself. Heroin had become a crutch, a catch-all, the solution to all of his problems. Even death.

He made a turn off the main road and into the subdivision in which the house was located. He pulled over to the side of the street a good half mile from Pleasant View Road, as he had been told, to wait for the truck and SUV to get into their predetermined positions.

The SUV pulled up, and Mason handed over a red bank bag. Trouble looked at it, wondering if there was actually a bomb in it or if Mason just wanted him to think there was. As if reading his mind, Mason told him in no uncertain terms not to open the bag. They sat there for several minutes, waiting on the truck to show. There was some kind of holdup, but Mason didn't seem to mind. Finally, Trouble got the go-ahead and reluctantly began the last half mile to the bank-house.

The cul-de-sac looked much the same as it had every other time he'd been there. A quiet, suburban neighborhood. Houses constructed in a time before the norm became alternating cookie-cutter designs that stamped out any uniqueness or personality. While these houses were identifiable as such, they were patently different. Probably as different as their various occupants. There were nine different domiciles surrounding the teardrop-shaped street. The bank house was second on the right. Three houses facing three others across Pleasant View Road, with three more around the semicircle that dead-ended the road.

The first house on the right looked to be two stories, but chances are it had a basement, as most houses in this part of the country do. It was white with dark blue trim and wide, staring windows for eyes. Trouble saw no movement there. The houses sat on a slight hill—fifteen degrees or so—with the ground leveling out at the top of the cul-de-sac and at the bottom of the road where the cross street ran. Trouble parked his bike at a right angle to the curb to keep it from rolling away, next to the driveway of the bank-house. Not that he felt certain he would be alive to retrieve it—he didn't. But it was a habit. He left his keys in the ignition.

There was no movement visible anywhere. All was quiet, bright, and warm. Trouble stared at the blue minivan parked on the other side of the driveway, its dark-tinted rear window not twenty feet away from him, his reflection the only thing visible as he peered ahead. He felt certain that there was someone in there, pointing a rifle at him, finger resting on the trigger guard, breathing slow and easy, conscience clear for miles ahead. Trouble sniffled and shivered and felt ill. He grabbed the bank bag, turned to his right, and started up the driveway.

\*\*\*

Across the street, approximately seventy yards away, one of Mason's men, a guy named Kade, unslung his Stag Arms M7 Hunter rifle. Behind him, his good friend and literal partner in crime, Julian, covered the rear with his H&K UMP submachine gun. They were in someone's backyard. The house looked empty, but you never knew in situations like these. It hadn't taken them long to find the right yard when they had jumped out of the truck on the street parallel. They'd looked at Google Earth beforehand in preparation.

Kade found that the wooden fence was just a little too high, but he was in luck: there was a wheelbarrow not far behind him. Julian brought it over and Kade stepped into it tentatively to make sure it wouldn't tip. It felt solid.

He set his rifle barrel in between the top of two fence slats, seating it perfectly. He put the butt into the dip between his shoulder and his pectoral muscle and looked through the short-range scope fixed to the top. The biker came into focus, walking away from Kade and up the driveway of the target house, carrying a bank bag.

Kade got ready.

Orders were to kill the biker and whoever opened the door. He wondered if he could do it in one shot. Possibly. If they didn't line up, he could do it in two, for sure. It wasn't far. Eighty yards and change was nothing. A slight breeze had kicked up, but it wouldn't matter. Not this close. Not for a pro like Kade.

*\*\**

The two-story house loomed ahead, bulky and flat-topped, filling Trouble's vision. It looked like a miniature wooden castle with dark red paint and brown trim. The garage was ahead. Next to that, the porch. Four steps up on stained wood. Each step felt harder than the last. Trouble sniffled, his eyes burning and his stomach in knots. The heavy-looking wooden door sat in a recess ahead next to shuttered windows, dark and constant.

Trouble heard no movement in the house. Sensed no movement. He thought for a second that maybe they had left. Changed locations. They'd gotten wind of the plan against them. Or maybe it was just time to move again. They'd done it before. But his hope dissipated when the door opened and the blank, rough-faced man that was so familiar to Trouble stepped out from the shadows, dressed in his dark suit, as always. Trouble suppressed a shiver as he stepped toward the guy. His senses were fucked. No way he was getting out of this alive.

He stepped toward the man slowly, expecting the bag in his hand to explode at any moment. The guy looked at him a little funny, and Trouble tried a small smile as he handed the bag over to the guy. Then he stepped back once. The guy looked up. Trouble's eyes were fixed on the bank bag. He stepped back again.

Before he could turn to run, something hit him.

# Twenty-Five

I T WAS A SNEEZE. It racked his upper body forward in a startled spasm. He thought he heard a loud bang over the sound of mucus and snot leaving his nose and mouth. Still bent over, he felt drops of wet on the back of his neck. He opened his eyes and lifted his head slightly to see the guard topple backwards into the doorway, a gaping hole in his head.

Senses fucked or not, Trouble knew enough to not stand up straight again. He didn't know whether the porch railing was blocking the shooter's view, but he wasn't about to leave it to chance. He jumped forward like a swimmer off the starting block, grabbing the bank bag from next to the dead guard. He was about to toss it when he had a better idea. He yanked the dead guard's body up and shoved the bank bag under his back.

He scrambled over the dead guard and into the entryway. He could hear the *thunk thunk thunk* sound of bullets hitting the house from outside. From inside, he could hear the raised voices of several men and footsteps coming his way.

The bag exploded underneath the dead guard, sending pieces of bone and meat and wood splinters flying in all directions.

Trouble was facing away when it happened, still on his knees, and he felt the stinging impact of a dozen small objects hitting his back.

He turned back around to see that the guard had been blown in half near the waist. His torso and arms had flipped around with the explosion, and the man's guts were spilling toward Trouble like a nest of giant worms. The guy's legs were out on the porch, canted against the wooden railing.

More gunshots sounded from outside. Men were yelling. And they were close.

Panicking, Trouble tried to shut the front door. It wouldn't close—there was half of a dead security guard in the way. He jammed his hands under the guard's jacket and found a gun in a shoulder holster. The footsteps behind him in the house were drawing near. The sound of gunshots and shattering glass issued from nearby—the next room over, Trouble thought.

He was yanking on the gun with his sweat-slick hands, but it wouldn't come out. Everything was happening too fast. His heart was about to burst. But his mind could think of only one thing. He was about to die, and still, he could only think about getting some dope. With a little heroin in his system, he felt he could deal with this situation properly. Or at least less like a little bitch.

There was more gunfire now, from both inside and outside. Impossible to tell how many shooters. It sounded like a war zone. Trouble looked at the dead guy whose gun he was failing to steal. He looked at the hole that had obliterated the bridge of the guy's nose and his left eyeball. Then he looked at the place where the man's legs used to be. Inside he saw nothing coherent. No answers to questions. No explanation for why the guy had done what he'd done. Why he'd been here to get killed today. What he had been thinking before Trouble came up the steps. Nothing. Just red and pink sludge, guts, and bone particles.

Then Trouble realized that he had the gun in his hands—a Heckler and Koch 9mm—and that his heart had slowed. He looked at the unbuttoned shoulder holster, not remembering that he unfastened it, wondering why he hadn't been able to do it before. *Never mind*, he thought. *Get out of your fucking head*.

And he did.

It was a good thing, too, because otherwise he might not have registered the heavy metallic sound that came from the porch. *THUNK thunk thunk.* But it wasn't gunshots again. This was something different. Something heavy and metal, bouncing and rolling... *Oh fuck.* Trouble jumped away from the doorway and into the house, coming to rest face down on the hardwood floor just before the grenade exploded.

The front of the house seemed to turn into something other-worldly as it rushed past Trouble in a flurry of speeding shrapnel. At least it felt that way to him. When it was over, he took his hands from around his head (one of them still holding the pistol) and tried to move, but something was on his legs. He twisted around to see that the legless and scorched torso of the security guard had landed on the backs of his thighs. He wiggled out from under him and got to his feet when a guy came walking out of the adjacent room.

Trouble raised the pistol but didn't fire. The guy was walking, but he was already dead. He had been too close to the explosion, and the front of his body was a mess of blood, glass, and wood. There was what looked to be a piece of window frame sticking out of his neck. Trouble was staring, distracted by the stumbling man, when he heard footsteps coming up the front porch, which was now half destroyed.

Someone out there laughed loud and crazily and said, "Holy shit." Trouble stepped backward a few paces and into a little room leading to the garage. A mudroom, he'd heard them called before. He peered with one eye toward the porch and the near-destroyed front door.

One of the guys he'd seen getting ready at the warehouse walked in first, assault weapon up and ready, sweeping as he went. Behind him came Trouble's leather jacket—and the asshole wearing it: Colton. Where Trouble had gone left, the first guy went right, toward the central staircase. Trouble had instinctively gone away from that staircase. It went up to the second floor and down to the basement, doubling back on itself each way. Hard to cover both up and down at the same time. Unless you had good communication and teamwork. Apparently, Mason's guys didn't. At least not these two.

The guy Trouble saw with the shrapnel wounds was somehow still standing, leaning against a support beam next to the stairs, bleeding to death. The first guy in, Fuckface, Trouble decided to call him, shot the guy two quick ones and then, fatally, put all his attention on the stairs to the second floor. There were a couple of guys shooting at the street from windows up there. Trouble could hear them. If Colton had been on his game, he could have saved his friend. But he was taking his sweet time getting to the staircase.

The gunshots came from the dark basement stairwell. Whoever was down there was shooting almost straight up through the thin gap between the railings. Fuckface gave out a scream as his skin, bones, and organs were ripped to shreds by the spray of bullets. Colton ran over and fired down into the dark stairwell, his back facing the mudroom. It sounded to Trouble like he got the guy, but not in time to save his buddy. Too bad, so sad.

Trouble, not wanting to damage his jacket, walked swiftly over to Colton and put his gun to the back of the man's neck. At the same time, he gripped his jacket's collar with the other hand. "I told you I'd kill you," he whispered just before pulling the trigger. The bullet severed Colton's spine. His hands went limp, his gun clattered to the floor. Then he went to his knees. Trouble, hand still gripping the collar, let him. Trouble set the pistol on the floor and used both hands to yank the jacket off from behind. Colton's body fell forward and slid down the first flight of basement stairs. For a moment Trouble felt regret. But then he pictured Sam and his dead wife. He remembered Lori's scream every time Colton dropped a knife into her. And he didn't feel bad anymore.

Trouble got his jacket on quickly. There was still a firefight going on, though not as intense as it had been before. He felt better with his jacket and took a second to feel for the secret pocket. His heart raced and his throat was suddenly dry. His fingers found a lump the size of a small rock through the leather. Dope.

Trouble picked up the H&K and went deeper into the house, looking for a back door.

***

"Fuck. I missed the biker," Kade said, awe in his voice.

Julian looked back over his shoulder at his partner. "You missed him? How's that?"

"I don't know. He just... ducked—contact left!" Kade picked his rifle up from the fence and pointed it at a figure moving through trees up and across the street, but he no longer saw anyone there. Julian had turned toward Kade, expecting gunfire. Someone started firing from the bank house then. One of their crew fired back. Then more gunfire erupted. Some coming from the house and some from their crew spread out around the neighborhood.

"Let's move," Kade said. He turned around to step off the wheelbarrow when his head flew apart and rained down all over the fence, most of it ending up on the other side.

"Fuck!" Julian said, spinning around toward the sound of the gunshot. Julian got around in time to see a man standing not five feet behind him, a pistol leveled at his face. He didn't know it, but that man's current name was Murke. And when Murke pulled the trigger, the stuff that Julian *did* know disappeared in an instant.

***

Sharon Bailey had made a tough decision before everything went to shit. She'd wanted to talk to her father, to get advice, but that wasn't possible. So she ended up acting on instinct. Which was why she'd brought the Parks girl to the bank-house in the first place. Instinct. Plus, she didn't have anywhere else to bring her. The ex-cops at the house—some of whom she knew—weren't really happy about it, but they knew she could blow the lid off their little operation if she really wanted to.

Finally, when it became apparent that the biker wasn't going to come back to his shitty hotel room, she had a decision to make. She had no idea that the biker—Terrence, the Parks girl said his name was—was a courier who had been visiting the bank-house every day twice a day for more than two weeks. Which was why Bailey had a sudden jolt of hope when she heard the motorcycle outside and looked out the window to see him walking up the driveway. She thought her gambit had worked. That the threatening note she'd left in his motel room had led him here. After all, she couldn't sit on his place day and night. She'd tried that for twenty-four hours. Not physically or mentally possible. Maybe if she had a partner. But no, she was in this alone.

She had pulled her Jeep into the bank house's garage not five minutes before Trouble rolled up. Not five minutes before everything went to hell in a bank bag. Her thinking was this: if the biker wasn't going to show (he'd been MIA for nearly two days at this point) then Katrina Parks served no purpose. Letting her go was out of the question. Bailey had gambled and lost, now she had to pay the price. Which meant taking Katrina Parks someplace quiet and putting a bullet in her brainpan. No way around it. At least, that's what she'd thought before Trouble showed up.

Bailey had just reached the top of the stairs when she heard the motorcycle. She ducked into one of the second-floor bedrooms and looked out the window. There he was. She'd seen the security footage from the Mexican restaurant. Every cop in Denver had. It was him.

Elation struck Bailey then. Of course, she'd still have to kill the girl, but it would be worth it now. Maybe she could get out of this hellhole after delivering the biker. Bailey laughed a bit as she headed back downstairs. Then she heard the first gunshot. She went back to the window and someone shot at her, shattering the window and striking the house with dull, insistent thumps. She hit the floor, listening as a firefight erupted. Someone was actually trying to rob the bank house. She wondered who would be stupid enough—

A small explosion shook the house slightly, sounding and feeling like it came from the front door. A few moments later, a second, larger explosion seemed to move the floor underneath her. Everything got real for her. She had to get out of here. But first she had to cover her ass. The Parks girl could die here and now. She'd be considered a casualty of this robbery. Wrong place, wrong time. If anyone else survived, they'd keep their mouths shut. Ex-cops were good at that. She'd keep hers shut, and they'd do the same. She crawled out of the room and down the hall toward the locked bedroom where Katrina Parks was now screaming.

***

First the Mexican restaurant, then the junkie biker's hotel room, and now this. Trina was surprised to find herself getting used to being shot at. Not that she was necessarily getting shot at now. She heard bullets hitting the house, but they didn't sound too close to her room. They had boarded up her window so she couldn't see out. The attached bathroom had no window. Whatever was happening out there wasn't good. But had she heard a motorcycle before it all started? Could Terrence be shooting up the place for her? To rescue her? That would be the ultimate flattery. *No, no, no, silly girl. You're hysterical.* She didn't even really like the guy. But who doesn't want to be rescued in a hail of gunfire? *Normal people*, she thought. *That's who.*

An explosion shook the house, and Trina cursed. Another, louder explosion sounded, and Trina cursed louder in response. Then she had a thought. The men in the house had gone out of their way to check on her, bring her food, ask if she was okay, make clear that they had nothing to do with this. Guys like that couldn't resist a screaming girl. So she screamed. And before long, she noticed someone working the handle on the other side of the bedroom door. She smiled.

Her bed was a mattress on the floor with a pillow and a blanket. The toilet tank's lid had been removed. She had a plastic cup for drinking water and a paperback book she'd begged off of one of the men holding her captive. There was nothing else in the room. They always took away her plastic plates and utensils when she was done eating. They had even taken her shoes. Not much for weapons. Clearly, these people had done this before.

She kept screaming, staying as far away from the door as she could.

Trina decided just to plead with whatever man opened the door. It was her only chance, really. They were all too big for her to do any damage with her bare hands. She didn't expect to see the Bailey bitch come in. She hadn't seen her since the day she arrived in this hell. But, as someone worked the doorknob from the other side, she heard a woman's voice come through the door. Sharon Bailey's voice. Telling Trina sweetly that they were going to leave together.

Trina made a snap decision.

Bailey opened the door with a gun in her hand, but Trina timed it perfectly. The gunfire outside blocked the sound of her running feet as she charged the door, not running straight at it, but from the side.

Bailey stepped into the room.

Trina, with all her momentum, planted both her hands on the side of Bailey's head—one palm on either side of her right ear—and shoved with all her might.

The door opened onto a wall, so Bailey's shoulder and then the side of her head crashed into the door with the force of one-hundred-twenty pounds of pissed off Trina. The door, which wasn't quite open all the way at that point, gave two inches and then stopped against the wall. Bailey's shoulder folded out of the way and her head took the brunt of the door-wall impact. Her other shoulder knocked Trina's breath out as the younger woman bounced against her before stumbling back.

Bailey was dazed. Trina was hurt, but not badly enough to stop. She ran at Bailey again. This time she swooped an elbow up and into the bridge of the woman's nose. Bailey went down, her eyes swimming and blood pouring out of her busted nose and into her mouth. Trina yanked the gun out of Bailey's hand by the barrel. It came easily. She didn't mean to do it, but in her fury, she brought the butt of the gun down on the center of Bailey's forehead. As soon as she did it, she sucked in a regretful and shocked breath, unable to believe for a moment that she had actually done it.

She ran out of the room and toward the stairs, still gripping the gun by its barrel.

***

Trouble found a sliding glass door on one side of a massive rectangular living room. The gunfire was sporadic now. One side was losing, and it sounded, unfortunately, like the bank-house's protectors were the unlucky ones. He opened the door and stepped out onto a large porch, but scrambled back inside when he heard someone stomping through the bushes toward the porch steps. One of Mason's guys, surely.

Trouble crossed the living room at a run, heading for the other side of the house. He looked back over his shoulder at the large windows facing the backyard, unsure whether to risk breaking one. The house shook with another explosion—this one coming from the basement—and Trouble tripped, not remembering that there was a step up out of the sunken living room. His pistol fell out of his sweaty hand as he tried to keep from smashing his face on the hardwood floor.

He scrambled toward his gun and stopped when he saw bare shins and sock-feet between him and his weapon. He looked up from the floor and met eyes with Trina Parks.

"What the fuck?" they both said at the same time.

"What're you doing—" Trouble asked as Trina spoke over him.

"You came for me?"

"What? I didn't even know you were here. I figured you would have gone to the police," Trouble said, standing up and grabbing his gun. He heard shouting from the front of the house. He grabbed Trina by the wrist, noticing for the first time that she was carrying a pistol by its barrel, and yanked her toward the mudroom.

The garage was right there, which wasn't really a great option because he'd have to raise the door. Hard for anyone outside to not notice that. But he hadn't considered that there might be a regular door in the side or back of the garage that would lead outside. It was worth a check.

More shouting—now from the basement—and more gunfire. He let go of Trina and used his free hand to open the door to the garage. A light came on automatically when he stepped in, and there it was: a side door in the garage, leading to the side yard.

"Let's go," he said.

Trina didn't hesitate.

Trouble poked his head around the side of the house and saw that his motorcycle was still where he'd left it. He could hear sirens in the distance. The neighborhood was silent, aside from a few barking dogs. All the commotion was now in the house. Trouble saw no one. They were all in the basement, he thought. "Run," he said.

They did.

They made it near the motorcycle without incident before Trouble remembered the bomb that Mason had strapped to it.

His heart sank. There would be no getting away from the police on anything but his motorcycle. He supposed they could just sit and wait for the cops to show up or try to get away on foot. If the police swooped him up, he knew he wouldn't get out of this clean. He'd be looking at ten to fifteen, easy. But all these concerns faded when he rounded the motorcycle and saw that the bomb was gone.

"What the hell?" he said, looking on both sides of the bike to make sure.

"What?" Trina asked, dancing around like she had to pee, the gun barrel still gripped in her hand. Trouble noticed that she was still wearing the t-shirt and boxers he had given her two days ago. Poor woman.

"Nothing. Let's go," he said, swinging his leg over the bike. "I can drop you off away from this mess so the cops will see you, if you want. You don't have to come with me."

"Nope. No more cops for me. Not now, anyway. Let's just go."

Trouble wasn't about to argue. He fired the bike up and tore off down the street. He had to swerve out of the way to miss an SUV racing onto the street. It was one of Mason's crew, driving up to the house. The guy didn't even look at Trouble. *They found the money*, he thought. *Good. Maybe they'll leave me the fuck alone.* But he still owed Mason. He wasn't about to forget that. But it could wait. Right now, he had something he really had to do. And he knew just the place to do it. It wasn't far.

Trouble turned away from the sirens and gunned it. He swerved through the neighborhood and came out onto a major street, not exactly sure where they were, but his main concern was putting some distance between them and the bank-house. He sensed the mountains, which helped him get his bearings, but he didn't change direction yet. He just kept going, the ground passing beneath him providing some level of comfort.

***

Mason threw the last large bag into the back of the SUV and jumped into the front passenger seat. It was too bad about Colton and Mack. The biker had kept his promise to Colton, as evidenced by the lack of the stupid jacket on his corpse. That meant that the biker had gotten away. His motorcycle was gone, after all. Mason thought briefly about calling the cell phone and setting off the bomb, but figured the biker had probably cut it off before he'd left. Instead, Mason thought about the piles of money in the back. And he found they did much to lift his heavy heart.

He wondered about Kade and Julian, but feared the worst. No time to go looking for them now, anyway. If they were still alive, they were on their own. Felix jumped in the driver's seat and Louis in the back. There was no one left alive inside the house. At least not in the basement, where they'd found the money. Mason wondered about the Murke guy Trouble had told him about. Maybe that's who got Kade and Julian. But it didn't matter much now. *He* had the money.

The sirens were getting much too close, and Mason was anxious to leave. Instead of going back the way they'd come, they headed up into the cul-de-sac, making it to the top just as the first police cars sped onto Pleasant View Road behind them. Mason spun around in his seat, eyes wide. "Shit," he said. "Get ready. They're gonna be on us quick."

But they weren't.

The nose of the first car bumped slightly up over something and then scraped the ground as the tires shredded on tire spikes spread across the road. Same with the next two cars, effectively making a roadblock at the mouth of the street.

As the SUV turned and bumped over the sidewalk and into a vehicle-sized gap between houses, Mason laughed out loud. So did the other men as they drove down this no-man's-land between houses. Power lines arced down above them as they drove next to support poles on the right and tree branches on the left, which scraped the SUV as it passed.

"Damn! I didn't even see that you guys had that stuff in here this morning!" Mason made a whooping sound and pounded the roof of the vehicle with his fist. He didn't notice the puzzled look on the other men's faces.

"Where did you even get fucking grenades and road spikes?" he said, still jubilant.

"We... We didn't," Felix said. "That stuff was in the truck, wasn't it, Louis? We thought you guys did that."

"No," Louis said from the back. "I thought that was you guys."

Mason's cheery expression dropped. "What? No. We didn't have any of that."

Silence from the men as the SUV bumped down into an adjacent cul-de-sac.

"So who the fu—" the driver's side wheel well exploded, the sound of rending metal and breaking glass huge in the small space.

The SUV came to rest near the middle of the teardrop street, tilting madly where the tire had once been. Everyone was okay, but dazed. It hadn't been a huge explosion.

Before they knew what was happening, two men in tactical gear and ski masks were at the SUV, one on either side.

"Put your hands up, gentlemen. Or you die," the one on the passenger's side said, sounding too cheery for Mason's liking. He raised his hands anyway. Felix hesitated, his hand reaching uncertainly toward a gun in the center console. The guy in tactical gear on the driver's side shot him through the window. One shot, straight to the head. Blood splattered Mason.

"What the fuck? He was just—"

"Shut up, Mason. Or you can die, too," the guy said.

Three minutes later, the living men in the SUV were hand-cuffed to various parts of the vehicle. All but one small bag of money was gone. That bag of money would tie them to the crime. That and all the guns in the SUV.

The black-ops guys walked away, laughing.

Not long after they left, several police officers were loading Mason and what was left of his crew up into squad cars.

They were laughing, too.

# Twenty-Six

TROUBLE FELT LIKE ABSOLUTE shit again. Now that he had a second to think about it, he realized that he was shaking and sweating. He felt bad for Trina, her arms wrapped around his waist. He was sure he smelled like an outhouse with a corpse in it. Not only because he'd been tortured and locked up for almost two days, but because detoxing made him stink something awful. He was grateful for the wind in their faces.

*Fuck*, he thought. *I've got to*—the shrill notes of an unfamiliar ringtone cut through the engine noise. *Oh god. Oh no. The bomb.* Trouble pulled into the bike lane, a car behind him laying on the horn as he came to a stop, almost spilling himself and Trina to the blacktop in the process.

"Get off!" He yanked Trina off and they stumbled between cars in a shopping center parking lot. They crouched behind the cars and Trouble stared at the bike, waiting for it to explode.

"What is it?" Trina yelled. "You've got to stop yanking my damn arm!"

The ringing continued. Trouble looked at her, his mouth open and eyes wide. Finally, he stepped tentatively toward the bike. If it was going to explode, it would have done so by now, he figured. The ringing was coming from a saddlebag. He looked inside and found that the phone and the bomb had been disassembled and placed in the bag. The phone was just a phone again. Trouble answered it.

"Hello?"

"Glad to see you made it out alive," the caller said in a deadpan tone. "It was touch and go, but I knew you could do it. And you got the girl. Great job."

Trouble recognized the voice. It was the black-ops shithead. Murke. He could think of nothing to say. He just stared at the passing traffic, dumbfounded.

"I thought this conversation would go better," Murke said in mock frustration.

"How..." Trouble trailed off.

"Listen, it's been fun. I left something for you with the clerk of a motel just up the road from yours. It's the Blue Room Inn. You earned it. There's instructions for contacting me there, too. You get off the dope, let me know. Couldn't have done this one without you, man." Murke laughed then, the sound grating on Trouble's brain.

"You fucking asshole. You sicked those guys on me? What? How?" He was going over it all in his mind, confused and mad and... confused.

"Listen. Mason's going to be in jail soon. Just thought you should know. Figure you guys have some unfinished business. Anyway, that's it. Get clean, will you? You on dope is a waste.

You did good work back in California. You remind me of—well not me, really—but someone else kind of like me. Just dumber." Murke laughed again, then the line went dead in Trouble's ear.

Trouble stared at the phone, trying to figure out what he meant. *Couldn't have done this one without you,* he thought. *What the hell does that mean?* He turned back to a puzzled Trina.

"What was that about?" she asked.

"I'll tell you later," Trouble said, shaking his head. "I've gotta do something now. I need to get my head right."

The look Trina gave him was unlike anything he'd ever experienced before. He read pity, disgust, and disappointment in it. There was something else, too, but he couldn't make sense of it. He opened his mouth to say something, then thought better of it. He got on the motorcycle, and after a moment's hesitation, so did Trina.

Fifteen minutes later, they pulled up outside a house in a seedy neighborhood. Trouble told Trina to stay put, that it wouldn't take long. He walked into the house, digging the dope out of his secret pocket. He walked to the kitchen and cursed under his breath when he found it empty.

"Jameson? You here, man?"

No response. Silence. Trouble started shaking in earnest from lack of food, withdrawal, and adrenaline fading from his bloodstream. He walked to the little closet, opened the door, and climbed up into the attic. Empty. Trouble looked at the dope in his hand for a long minute, then set it in the middle of the attic floor. He climbed back down, determination now a factor in his shaking, willing himself not to turn back for it.

Trina seemed surprised to see him when he came out. He decided that she knew he was an addict. No great shock, really. He had left her alone in his paraphernalia-strewn motel, after all. He thought that maybe the surprise on her face wasn't about seeing him so soon, but about seeing him as he was then, shaking, sickly, and sweating. She half-smiled at him as he approached.

"Hey, can you do me a huge favor?" he asked as he approached.

"What is it?"

He told her.

# Twenty-Seven

HECTOR'S MEN HAD TAKEN a trek through the desert to cross the border. They had followed behind a group of four men transporting heroin, cocaine, and meth, leaving a cushion of space in case they were spotted.

The drug mules were under orders to surrender to the border patrol in order to let Tomas and Rico get away, if it came to that. Of course, all the better if they could all get across with no incidents, as they had done so many times. There were spotters and supply caches along the route. Hector's organization always had men in the desert, keeping those south of the border apprised of border patrol and mercenary movements.

Tomas and Rico had both started as mules many years previously, so the journey was an easy one for them. Neither of them particularly missed their old jobs, but crossing endless miles of desert wasn't the hardship it would've been for others. Working on Hector's security crew was rewarding and fulfilling in many ways, not the least of which was a generous salary.

They made it to the outskirts of Tucson thirsty, hungry, and tired, but otherwise in good shape. There was a car waiting for them in a Wal-Mart parking lot. The tank was full of gas, the trunk full of water, food, and other provisions. From here, it was a thirteen-hour drive to Denver. Rico drove first while Tomas slept. Then they switched. They made it to Diego's house in good time.

Diego introduced them to his right-hand man, Tim, and three other men who were there. Then Diego, Tim, Tomas, and Rico headed to a sitting room to discuss their problem. Diego, for his turn, reiterated what he had already told Hector over the phone. From the very beginning. Tomas and Rico insisted. Both men spoke English very well, even if they only did so when absolutely necessary.

They listened intently as Diego explained about the dispensary that was under their "protection" getting robbed and the owner's—Lori, he said her name was—subsequent inability to pay. He explained about how her courier was robbed and killed in the street by members of the Jiménez cartel. There, Rico interjected.

"Was this courier one of your men, or one that Lori hired?"

Diego grew defensive. "He was one of Lori's, but what difference does that make? If she gets robbed, we don't get paid, right?"

"Continue," Rico said after a long moment of studying Diego's face.

Diego continued. When he got to the part about hitting one of the opposition's couriers as payback, Tim took over. He described robbing and killing Cowboy and the woman passerby.

Then he went on to describe the debacle at the Mexican restaurant. When he finished, Tomas looked confused.

"Why did you go after this man? The biker?"

"We—I thought he would be valuable," Diego said. "The other side wanted him. Word was all over the street that he killed one of theirs. I thought that if we got him, we could set a meet and then ambush them. Finally be done with them once and for all."

"But instead of getting him, two of your men got killed, yes?" Tomas asked. "And you have no idea where he is, correct?"

"We know where his girlfriend lives," Tim said, holding up a Colorado driver's license he pulled out of his pocket.

"Yes? And have you seen her? Has she been home?"

"No. She hasn't been," Tim said, looking mournfully at the license.

"Tomas," Rico said, standing up and walking into the hallway. Tomas followed.

They weren't gone long. When they came back inside, Tomas told Diego to gather his other men. "We've got a plan," he said.

Less than a minute later, the three other men shuffled into the room and stood behind the couch on which Tim and Diego sat. Tomas and Rico remained standing.

"That's everyone?" Tomas asked.

"Yes. Everyone that matters, anyway," Diego replied.

"Good."

Tomas and Rico pulled their guns out smoothly, like it was the most natural thing in the world to do at that moment. There was no rush, no jerking, no hesitation. Tomas shot Diego in the face while, at the same moment, Rico shot Tim in the throat. Rico was slightly faster after the first shot, and so he killed two of the no-names while Tomas got one. They put another round in each of the men before walking back outside, getting in their car, and beginning the long drive back to Mexico. Getting back across the border wouldn't be a problem.

It never was.

# Twenty-Eight

Trina stayed with Trouble for a full week, through the worst of it. They used the money that Murke had left at the Blue Room Inn to get another motel room on the other side of town. They paid extra to get the room without putting a name down.

Trouble had thought the money might have been a setup, but was beyond caring by the time they got there. He just wanted to lie down and sleep. Unfortunately, there wasn't much sleep in his immediate future. Not that first week, anyway. Instead, there was shaking, sweating, vomit, diarrhea, and severe depression.

During his moments of clarity, Trouble thought back to the dead security guard. He thought about looking into the ragged and bloody hole in the man's head, about seeing the man's viscera spill out from his abdomen. He thought about the nothing he had seen there. No clues, no grand vision, no *anything*. Just dead meat. But it wasn't the senselessness of death or the fragility of life that gave him strength when his withdrawal symptoms were the worst. It was the calm he'd felt when looking into that dead man's face. And in that moment, he had been able to see past the hold the drug had on him. He'd glimpsed his true self there, in the still-warm gore staring back at him.

He hadn't realized it at the time, but he saw his own weakness. Whether by desensitization or whether by his very nature, Trouble had never feared his own death. Not really. It had never scared him to look upon it as it grinned back at him, a certainty. And, along with all the other damage it had done to him, his addiction to heroin had taken that away.

And he wanted it back.

The nightmares would still haunt him, he knew. He'd been the cause of a young man's death, back in California. There was no hiding from that. He had to face it. And he couldn't face it weakened. And that's what he was on heroin. Weak.

Still, during that first week of detox, he thought about going out to get dope a lot, but he never tried it and he never said as much to Trina. Her presence there gave him the motivation he needed to get through all the times when the cloud of addiction settled on him. Not that there was anything between them. He knew she had no sort of romantic feeling for him, but still, the presence of another person helped. If she hadn't been there, he wasn't sure he would have been successful in quitting. And to her credit, she didn't shy away from it. She helped him as much as she could. She gave him water, soup, vitamins, and encouragement.

He asked her why she stayed at one point, and she shrugged and said that it was a good thing to do. And that he'd asked her to. Apparently, that was enough, but Trouble didn't understand it. He thought she needed that time to process what had happened. And although he didn't remember it when he was through the other side, she did talk to him about everything. Usually, she waited until he was dazed from exhaustion and spoke in a low, soothing voice.

So, in his small way, Trouble helped her, too.

After a week, they said their goodbyes. Trouble tried to give her a stack of cash, but she refused. He thought she might, which was why he'd slipped some into the new cheap purse she'd bought when she was out shopping for supplies. He knew she would find it, eventually.

He moved to another motel the day Trina left, as a precaution. On day nine he started working out in hopes that it would help him sleep a little bit. It did. He spent the next five days eating what he could, drinking a ton of water, and getting creative with his bodyweight workouts. He slowly started to feel like himself again. But he had some unfinished business.

# Twenty-Nine

D ETECTIVE GIBNEY KNOCKED SOFTLY on his lieutenant's open door. She looked up from the paperwork
on her tidy desk and gestured him in.

"Gibney," she said in her business-as-usual tone. "What's going on? You look tired."

"Yeah. Uh, thanks. I've got a bit of a situation, Lieutenant.
It's about Detective Bailey."

L.T. Rouche set her pen down, interlaced her fingers, and
brought her full attention to Gibney, who continued. "I got a
call this morning from a lawyer representing Katrina Parks."

"The girl from the double homicide at the restaurant. Your
case, yes?"

"Yes ma'am. Three of the suspects matched the eyewitness
descriptions given to us at the other double homicide in District
One not long ago. The one with the man in the truck and the
woman on the sidewalk."

"I remember. What did Ms. Parks's lawyer have to say?"

"Well, she wanted to meet. So I did. And Parks was there, with
her lawyer. Anyway, she had a story to tell about Bailey. Said

that she kidnapped her—Bailey kidnapped Parks, that is. And brought her to that house where all hell broke loose a week ago. Where we found her unconscious, upstairs."

The look on Rouche's face wasn't a happy one. Gibney moved uncomfortably in his seat before speaking again. "Has she said anything yet?"

"No," Rouche replied. "Bailey hasn't said anything to anyone. Not even her union rep, so far as I know."

"We still have her under wraps?" Gibney asked.

"Yes. In fact, she insisted that she be kept here at the station. She's scared of something, but we're not sure what."

"Well, Parks said that Bailey brought her to the house the same day the restaurant thing happened. Apparently, Parks called her and told her she wanted to give up the biker. But Bailey, for whatever reason, brought her to that house and kept her there for two days. Parks admitted to assaulting Bailey and running away during the chaos. Said she didn't come forward earlier because, well, the whole thing kind of soured her on cops."

"If it's true, I don't blame her. What the hell was she planning on doing with the girl? The only valuable information she had was on the biker, right?"

Gibney nodded. "Far as I can tell."

"And the Parks girl didn't know what Bailey was after?"

"No. Her guess is the same. She thinks it was about the biker. Terrence Rubble. People call him Trouble, I guess. He had some little trou—uh, problem—back in California about a year ago.

But he was only held for a month by the feds and then let go. No official charges filed. Otherwise, he has some petty crimes on his record. Mostly from when he was a minor."

"Word on the street was that everyone was looking for him, right? All the new players in town wanted to get at him? Maybe Bailey had something on the side. I hate to think it, but it wouldn't be unheard of," Rouche said, leaning back in her chair. "Shit. What a mess."

Gibney nodded.

"Why did she come to you? The Parks girl. She say?"

"Because I'm new to Denver. Her lawyer helped her with that. I'm the newest detective, so I guess I haven't had time to get into dirt and form alliances here. Only she put it more delicately than that."

"And why did she go to Bailey in the first place? That seems a little strange."

"Parks's boyfriend got killed during a robbery. Bailey worked the case. Had contact with the girl. She said that's why she was with the biker at the restaurant that day, too. She'd met him that morning. He was apparently looking for information on her boyfriend's murder. All this shit—uh, stuff—comes together somehow, I'm just not sure how."

"Was her boyfriend's case solved? She have any useful information on where the biker might be?"

"No to both. Said the biker was at the house that day, though. Which matches with the neighbors' statements that they heard a motorcycle. Parks said she saw him ride off as she was hauling ass out of there."

Rouche sighed. "Okay. I gotta take this up high. They'll probably put I.A. on the Bailey thing. Where's Parks now?"

"Staying with a friend. She gave me an address. Her lawyer assured me she wouldn't be going anywhere. I don't know why she would. Poor girl has been through hell, but she's willing to testify about the whole thing."

"Good. We've gotta find that biker. See what you and Wane can do about that. He ties to your murders—all of them. Find him and we find answers." She sighed again. "What a mess."

Gibney nodded.

# Thirty

"She's been arrested?" Tomas asked his boss. Hector nodded gravely.

Ruiz sat back in his chair at the table, as if wondering what this meant. But he knew what it meant. He knew what would have to be done. That didn't mean he had to like it. Rita had been like a daughter to him. Maybe even more so than she had been to her own father. Hector sat across from Ruiz, the look on his face one of shock fading to resignation. Tomas sat on Ruiz's left, and Rico on his right at the table.

"How?" Tomas asked.

"She was after the same man that idiot Diego was after. The one who killed Mr. G. For the same reasons. She thought he would be valuable," Hector explained, looking much older than his years. "She sent me a message about it through the usual channels. She was asking my advice, but I didn't get it in time. It's such a terrible way to communicate, *dammit.*" Hector slammed his fist on the table.

"We had to be careful, boss. It was your idea. No electronic communication with her while she was there, remember?" This was Rico, saying the wrong things.

*Just let him be angry*, Ruiz thought.

"Yes, of course I remember," Hector yelled. "She's my fucking daughter, isn't she?"

"Yes, sir," Rico said quickly.

Hector took a few deep breaths to calm down. He looked on the verge of tears.

"What can be done, boss?" Tomas asked.

"They don't know who she is yet, but they'll find out. When they do, we'll all be in danger. They don't take this kind of thing lightly." Hector said. "We have to... take care of this."

"We'll take care of it, boss," Tomas said. "Don't worry about it."

"The things we give to this business," Hector said. "She was so valuable to us there. So valuable. All that work. All those years. For nothing."

But Ruiz knew it wasn't nothing. She'd given them information that saved them millions of dollars, easily. But she had never liked it. He knew that much. She'd never liked being Sharon Bailey. She was there to make a difference for her family. That was all. And it had to end this way... Such a shame.

"All for some loser on a motorcycle," Hector continued. "I'd like to find this man. I'd like to shake his hand for killing Mr. G and then watch his face as I slowly gut him. I want him found. He owes me a life."

The three other men nodded. It wouldn't be hard. After they took care of Rita, they would find the biker.

# Thirty-One

T ROUBLE WAS IN PRISON.

It made him nervous, but not nervous enough to turn around and leave. He could leave. That was the whole point of the visit. Or some of it, at least. He sat at the visitation window for five minutes before a man walked up on the other side. Trouble looked up at the man in the blue jumpsuit and smiled.

Mason didn't smile back.

Trouble gestured at the phone, a serene look on his face. Mason stood and stared on the other side of the sturdy, floor-to-ceiling partition, mute fury on his face. For a moment, Trouble thought he would simply walk away. That would have been too bad, but it wouldn't have changed anything, ultimately.

Mason didn't walk away. Curiosity clearly got the better of him as he sat down and picked up the phone. Trouble picked up the one on his side.

"Hey there, Mason," Trouble said, trying to sound like a free man sounds. It wasn't hard. He *was* free, after all.

"I still have friends on the outside, you stupid fucking junkie. I make one call and you'll be dead by week's end."

"If that was true, you would have done it already. But it's not true, is it? Or maybe it is, but they can't find me. Hell, you had a hard enough time getting to me yourself. No, I don't think so. I think you're full of shit."

"Wait and see, Terrence," Mason sneered, smiling. Like knowing Trouble's real name was some sort of threat. Trouble couldn't help but laugh.

"Listen," the biker said, finally. "I'm only here to give you some news. You remember Sam, right? You raped and killed his wife before murdering him with his own heroin? Remember?"

Mason was silent, staring through the thick and scuffed plastic.

"Sure you do. It wasn't that long ago, was it? A month? No, more like three weeks. Anyway, I wanted to let you know that he was kind of a big deal before he retired. He spent a lot of time making friends and earning respect. But real respect. Something you wouldn't know about. Not with the crowd you run with."

"Get to the fucking point already. The fuck do I care what that asshole did?"

"I'm getting there. For a guy in prison, you sure are impatient. Anyway, it turns out that some of his friends are in this very facility."

Mason tried to hide it, but his eyes betrayed him. He was looking worried. Trouble continued. "When you are the former president of a notorious biker gang, like Sam was, you tend to have friends in all sorts of prisons. That's just the nature of the game. And those friends? Well, they were very curious to learn about you. They were upset at the way Sam died. And I gotta tell you, Mason, they're angry about it. I feel for these guys, you know? So, I did what I could to ease their suffering. Once I got done telling them about you—in detail—they seemed to calm down a little." Trouble sat up straight and looked Mason in the eye, looking for any humanity there. He found none.

"That's all I wanted to tell you. Watch your back in there, Mason."

The prisoner's mouth hung open, and the blood had drained from his face.

Trouble hung up the phone and sat there, watching, as Mason came to a terrible realization. He looked through the dirty partition, tears in his eyes, and gestured at the phone. He pantomimed, begging Trouble to pick up the phone again. He put his hands together as if he were praying—praying to Trouble—and began speaking. Trouble didn't have to hear him to know what that he was saying "Please," over and over again.

Trouble sat there in the hard plastic seat and remembered Mason calling him a little fucking bitch just before they left for the bank-house. And he had been right. Trouble had been a little bitch. But at least he had heroin to blame. What was Mason's excuse?

A rather large man with a long beard and hands the size of Christmas hams stepped up behind Mason. He had tied the top of his blue jumpsuit around his waist, revealing a white undershirt that was struggling to contain the man's bulk. Mason looked up at the man, then back at Trouble, tears spilling down his cheeks.

The big man nodded at Trouble, and Trouble nodded back. The big man leaned down and grabbed Mason under the armpits, bringing him to his feet. Trouble watched as the two of them made their way out of the visiting area, past a guard who had surely been paid to look the other way.

Trouble stood up and walked out of the visitor's area and then out of the prison. He stepped outside into the summer sun. After two weeks of hell, he was finally feeling better. His wit and humor and energy were coming back to him after a year of daily opioid use. He smelled the fresh Colorado air and thought about where to go. He had a shitload of cash on him, and he wasn't about to spend it on dope for a change. He knew the police were after him, but what else was new? They could get in line. He'd leave Colorado, no question, but where to?

He reached into his jacket pocket and fingered a sheet of paper. He pulled it out and read it for the tenth time. *Am I crazy to be considering this?* He asked himself. The paper held instructions on how to contact Murke. Trouble folded the paper, smiled, and walked toward his motorcycle. With the instructions securely in his pocket, Trouble started his bike and rode away from the prison, feeling better than he had in a long, long time.

# Epilogue

"L Legislation legalizing marijuana has been shot down in three states," the man said with a crooked smile. He was old and white and sitting with two other old, white men in large leather chairs, enjoying an evening drink. They all had the sickly look of people who spent too much time inside.

"I suppose it's no coincidence that the recent news out of Denver gave those state legislators a bad taste?" one of the other men said, sipping his expensive scotch and slouching into the large wing-backed chair.

"What do you think?" the first man said, smiling his reptilian smile.

"You're just delaying the inevitable, Winthrop," the third man said, eyes half closed.

Winthrop looked momentarily confused. "I seem to recall you agreeing with me, Franklin. Hell, the operation wouldn't have been possible at all without your say-so."

"'Operation' isn't the word I would use," Franklin said, his eyes opening fully as he looked at Winthrop. "One full-time and two part-time contractors, a few thousand dollars in expenses, and equipment that had been sitting in a warehouse. More like a blip. If it were an actual operation, I wouldn't have been able to approve it off the books. Besides, just because I approved it doesn't mean I agree with it. I wanted to see what happened. And I have."

"Was it as you expected?" Winthrop asked.

"More or less," Franklin said, letting his eyelids drop down again.

"What about you, Donovan?" Franklin asked the other man in their small circle. "What do you think?"

"I haven't been following it very closely. Something about a house exploding? A bunch of dirty ex-policemen dying. A few cartel criminals arrested. I guess I was expecting more."

"You're not seeing the big picture," Winthrop said. "The dead marijuana legislation is only part of it. The cartel scare will shut up the border for a year or so. You know, all the old lines about terrorists coming across the border."

Donovan nodded. "Still, doesn't seem like much to me. If I didn't know better, I'd think you get off on seeing your handi-work on the news."

"He does," Franklin said, without raising his eyelids.

"Well," Winthrop said, "can you blame me? Nothing beats it."

\* \* \*

Thanks for reading *Too Much Trouble*! Keep reading for a peek at the next standalone book in the series: The Death Dealers.

Please take a minute to tell me what you thought by reviewing *Too Much Trouble* wherever you got the book. Reviews truly help! Thanks in advance.

# The Death Dealers: Prologue

T HE GUN WAS HEAVY, pulling the kangaroo pocket in his hooded sweatshirt down as he walked. Although his hands were already sweaty from the heat of the night and the enormity of his task, Raymundo stuffed them in the sweatshirt pocket, holding onto the gun with both hands as he limped along the cracked sidewalk.

The pain in his leg wasn't as bad tonight — possibly because of the buildup of adrenaline in his system — but his headache was in full swing. The brace was tight around his leg, preventing him from bending it. But he had nothing so convenient to help with the awful headache. Or the terrible thoughts that kept running through his mind. He'd eaten a handful of over-the-counter painkillers before heading out into the night, wanting to have as clear a head as possible so he could operate the gun swiftly and without hesitation.

Brushing his right thumb over the safety mechanism on the Hi-Point C9 pistol made him feel more comfortable. He practiced the movements he'd have to make in his head: get close enough to verify his target, thumb the safety off, take the gun out of his pocket, point while putting his finger inside the trigger guard, and then pull the trigger. *Five steps,* he told himself. *Just five steps.* He'd already loaded a bullet into the chamber of the cheap 9mm pistol, so all he had to do was lower the safety mechanisms to make it ready to fire.

He'd spent a good chunk of his remaining money on a cab to a secluded area to test the weapon. He wanted to leave nothing to chance.

Raymundo went right at the intersection, bringing the restaurant into view. It was a taco joint — an authentic one, owned by people from Mexico. He knew the owners by name. They were immigrants, like him. It was open until twelve, another hour yet. But he knew business was slow at this time of night. That was important.

He limped up to the restaurant, seeing a Hispanic couple eating inside and two employees working. He didn't go inside. Instead, he walked over toward the edge of the parking lot where a cinder block wall separated the taco joint from the neighboring laundromat. It was dark near the wall. Neither the orange glow from the nearby streetlight nor the yellow glow from inside the restaurant penetrated the area.

He stood there, in the darkness, waiting. Saliva filled his mouth, his nerves making him want to vomit. He swallowed the spit, but his throat felt strange. Like he couldn't swallow properly. Like his body wasn't working the way it should. The pain in his leg and in his head jumbled his thoughts. He had to force himself to remember the five steps. And the reason he had to do this.

After a few long minutes, he heard the crunching of tires and the hum of a powerful engine operating nowhere near its capacity. He turned to look at the road beyond the edge of the cinder block wall and watched the front of a police cruiser come into view. The LA County Sheriff's insignia came into view as the cruiser rolled slowly past the wall. Raymundo swallowed hard, his gaze following the car as it turned into the parking lot of the taco restaurant.

He could see two people in the car — two sheriff's deputies — although it was too dark to make out details. When the driver put the cruiser in park, Raymundo stepped forward, clicking the pistol's safety off with one sweaty thumb. He was already getting ahead of himself, doing the steps out of order. But as the timbre of his heartbeat became deafening in his ears, he realized it was too late to change anything. Far too late.

The door to the restaurant was on the opposite side of the car from Raymundo, so he circled around behind as the two deputies got out of the cruiser. The driver shut his door, spotting Raymundo as he did. It was him. Although Raymundo had never seen him in person, he would never forget his face. He *could* never forget it. Not as long as he lived. Deputy Schlosser.

There was no recognition on Schlosser's broad face. Of course, there wouldn't be. Raymundo knew him — or felt like he did. But the deputy didn't know Raymundo. Schlosser's pinkish, seemingly swollen skin glistened with oil in the light from the restaurant. His short hair was thin and done up in a flat-top with some kind of gel. Raymundo was still a good fifteen feet away, but the deputy was immediately wary, resting a hand on his holstered gun.

Raymundo averted his gaze, pretending to be on his way into the restaurant. He wondered with each step whether the deputy would see him for what he was. Whether he could see what was going through Raymundo's mind. He expected the deputy to pull his gun and shoot him. Or maybe he just hoped for that.

"Hey," the other deputy called, stepping to the front of the cruiser.

Raymundo stopped and turned to look. "Yes?" he said. His mouth was now dry, his hands shaking as they gripped the gun in the kangaroo pocket.

"This place any good?" the other deputy asked.

"I'm sorry?" Raymundo said, stepping toward Schlosser as the other deputy started around the cruiser's front fender.

"You eat here much?" the deputy said. "A coworker recommended it. Said it's the best taco joint in Los Angeles."

Raymundo, now six feet away, took the pistol from his sweatshirt pocket and leveled it at Schlosser's head. The man's small eyes went wide. Raymundo gave them a brief glance before pulling the trigger. The bullet pierced Schlosser's skull just above his left eye, the angle of entry causing the upper left portion of his skull to explode outward.

Raymundo stepped up and shot Schlosser twice more when he was on the ground. The other deputy went for his gun and turned to run at once, heading for cover behind the car.

Raymundo stared at what he'd done, barely registering the screams coming from inside the restaurant. He quickly realized that it was all for nothing. He wondered how he could be so stupid. There was no saving anyone. Least of all himself.

He felt the crushing enormity of the system that would cascade onto him like an avalanche. His mind raced in a frenzy, looking for any way out of this. Looking for something that wasn't there. Deputy Schlosser's blood and brains stood out against the dirty asphalt, impossibly stark in the orange-yellow light. And all at once, there was no question as to what he had to do. It stood there in the front of his mind, seemingly inexorable. It was comforting in its dark finality.

The deputy now hiding behind the cruiser was talking on his radio, his voice high with fear. Raymundo didn't want to wait for him. He couldn't wait for him. He put the gun to his own temple, said a fast silent prayer, and pulled the trigger.

# Chapter One

SOMETHING ABOUT THE BARELY glanced motion caught Trouble's attention, awakening a deep and instinctive part of his mind. He turned his head to look down the residential side street as he rode past on his motorcycle. The glimpse he'd caught was so quick it took his mind a moment to run through the possibilities of what he'd just seen.

A man raising his arm high, something held in it, the position of his arm blocking Trouble's view of his face. Was he playing a game? Throwing a ball, maybe? Or hitting one thrown his way?

No. The angle was all wrong for that. Unless he was hitting the ball directly toward the ground. And Trouble had never heard of any game like that.

There was something about the movement that echoed violence — something Trouble was no stranger to. He thought there had been an accompanying sound for a quick moment, just barely audible over the sound of his parallel twin engine. A grunt, he thought. Or an intake of breath. Or maybe his mind was just filling in blanks, adding information to try and make a complete picture.

He played it over again quickly in his head, almost uncon-
sciously, piecing everything together in a flash even faster than
the half-second glimpse he'd gotten riding by. And it clicked.
The man was hitting down at someone, the thing in his hand
a tire iron. Maybe a wrench. And had there been other people,
off to the side, watching?

Trouble considered driving on, but the more he thought
about it, the more he realized the person on the ground — if
there in fact was one — had likely been a child.

By the time he'd traveled two city blocks past the street, he'd
decided to turn around. He checked his mirrors and pulled onto
the next street on his right, turning in a tight circle to make a left
back out onto the main road. It was nighttime in Los Angeles,
and in this part of town there wasn't a lot of traffic. At least,
in terms of Los Angeles, which meant he still had to wait for a
break in the traffic to make the left. Once he did, he gunned it,
making up the two blocks in half the time it had taken him to
traverse them the other way.

He turned onto the street in question and immediately saw
that he'd been right. Well, almost right.

He saw three men, each of them dressed in jeans and hooded
jackets and wearing black ski masks. Two jackets were black
and the third was blue. It seemed from a distance as if they all
were wearing latex gloves. All three men stopped what they were
doing and looked at Trouble when they heard the rumble of
his motorcycle turn onto the street. That was good. It meant
they were no longer beating the child on the ground — only it

wasn't a child. It was a woman. A particularly small one at that, which was why Trouble's brain, with the limited information at its disposal, had thought it was a child.

He wasn't sure whether she was alive or not, and he wasn't about to make the mistake of putting all his attention on her to find out one way or the other. Instead, he scanned quickly for weapons, computing his odds. He had a loaded Sig Sauer P220 in a pocket in his leather jacket, and another of the 45-caliber ACP pistols in one of his saddlebags. Nine rounds in each weapon.

But it didn't look like these men were armed with anything more than hand tools. At least at first glance. The only visible weapon was the black tire iron held in Blue Jacket's hand. Trouble slowed as he approached, his motorcycle engine chugging away under him. He looked at them like he was just a man passing by. But unlike a regular passerby, who would undoubtedly turn his gaze away in acquiescence to the hard stares he received, Trouble kept his eyes fixed on the men. He wanted to see what they would do. Ideally, he wanted them to run away.

But they didn't.

Their heads turned in unison as Trouble rode past, doing ten miles an hour. The street was lined with ranch-style houses built in the fifties or sixties. Many of the yards no longer had lawns, just patches of dirt with weeds growing out of them. Those that did had sickly yellow grass. There were a few cars parked on the street, and some in driveways. The three masked men and the beaten woman were in front of a brown-and-tan house, the windows all dark. They occupied a space of about twenty yards between two vehicles: a silver Chevy SUV ahead and an old Saturn sedan behind.

Trouble stopped just ahead of the SUV, parked his bike, and walked out into the middle of the street, heading back toward the scene of the assault. The three masked men stepped away from the curb and in front of the bloody woman. They took a protective stance, as if they were worried Trouble wanted to beat the woman himself. *This is our beating,* the stance said. Or maybe they just didn't want him getting a good look at her.

"The fuck do you want?" Blue Jacket said, bloody tire iron held casually by his side. The man formed the head of a shallow triangle, the two guys in black jackets standing slightly behind and to the side. And he was a big man. Wide, tall, and heavy. Trouble, who was around six-foot-two, pegged the guy at six-five or six-six. Slightly overweight, maybe, but mostly muscle. Easily three hundred pounds.

"Would you be surprised if I said I wanted you to stop beating that woman?" Trouble said, stopping about ten feet from Blue Jacket. Even with the loose jackets and jeans the other two men were wearing, he could tell they weren't small. They had some bulk under their clothing. Just not as much as their apparent leader did.

Blue Jacket *tsskd*, sucking his teeth. "Man, get the fuck outta here or we'll fuck you up." This was said with a Chicano accent, as some Los Angeles Latinos talked. The strange thing was, the first sentence didn't have this accent. It had sounded to Trouble like a regular West Coast white guy.

"What did she do, anyway?" Trouble asked, ignoring the man's command. "Or do you just not like women?"

"Did you not hear what I said, white boy? Mind your own business or get fucked." Still with the accent. The other two men glanced at each other behind their ringleader. Trouble was unnerving them. These guys weren't used to people standing up to them. They didn't seem to like it.

"I'm not leaving. And I already called the police," Trouble said, following the truth with a lie. "So you do what you need to do. I'm right here."

Blue Jacket laughed without humor and then took a step toward Trouble, who tensed up, preparing for a fight. One of the guys behind Blue Jacket reached forward and grabbed him by the shoulder with one latex-gloved hand.

The two of them whispered for a moment, and then looked down at the woman. She hadn't moved since Trouble had pulled up, and he couldn't tell from where he was whether she was still breathing or not. He thought not.

They seemed to come to a consensus, the two guys in black jackets stepping away from the woman, heading toward the SUV. Blue Jacket stood there for a second, looking down at the woman. Before Trouble could do anything, he brought the tire iron down on her head, the sound of it a sickening wet thud. "Fuckin' bitch," he said.

Trouble had his .45 out, the safety off, by the time the guy turned around. "Step the fuck away or you'll get a bullet to the chest," Trouble said. "Fucking bitch," he added, realizing with those words that he was really and truly angry. There was a quick and dirty conversation raging in his head about whether to kill this guy and take off. But for it not to come back and bite him, he'd have to kill the other two guys as well. And that was just a bridge too far for him, even though his rage thought it was the best idea in the world at the moment.

Blue Jacket raised his hands, stepping away from her just like Trouble said. The other two guys were trying to creep toward the SUV, but that wouldn't do. For all he knew, they had semi-automatic weapons in there. He changed his angle quickly so he could more easily cover all three of them. "I haven't forgotten about you two," he said. The other two put their hands in the air.

He knew he had to call the police about this, and it was tempting to hold them at gunpoint until he did so. But Trouble was wanted in at least one state, and he wasn't sure if he had any warrants out in California. He settled for his best shitty option: get them out of here, call 911, and get gone. He'd already seen that the SUV didn't have any license plates, but he had an idea about how the police could identify it.

"Here's what you're going to do," Trouble said. "You're going to—" Headlights splashing on Trouble's back broke his speech as a car turned onto the road behind him. *Fuck*. He could tell by the sound that it wasn't a police cruiser. It did not sound well cared for; the struts groaned, and components rattled as it made the turn. Trouble figured it for a sedan. And in a moment, he was proven right.

The old boxy sedan rolled slowly up, coming abreast of Trouble before the driver apparently realized what was going on. Trouble kept his head turned toward the masked men, using his peripheral vision to keep an eye on the car. The driver gunned it, taking off quickly down the road and turning right at the intersection a quarter mile away.

It wouldn't be long now until the police showed up. And Trouble needed to be gone. He'd done his part.

"Okay," he said. "Here's what's going to happen. You're going to get into your Chevy and drive away. And I'm going to keep a gun on your man here until you do. Anyone makes a move I don't like, I'll kill him and then take my chances with you. Understood?"

None of the men said anything.

"Or I can just shoot you all right here. And that's just what I'll do if I don't get an affirmative answer out of you."

"Yes, we understand," one of the black jacket guys said. There was no phony accent there. He sounded like a Californian.

The other black jacket guy said he understood next. Blue Jacket only nodded.

"Toss the tire iron down," Trouble told him.

He did.

"Okay, who's driving?"

"I am," Blue Jacket said.

"Good. You're going to get in the car first while your friends stay where I can see them. Then they can get in and you assholes can drive away. And that'll be that. Now, move — but keep your hands up."

Trouble walked sideways as Blue Jacket moved toward the Chevy, passing his two buddies as he went. Trouble changed the angle again, making sure to stay far enough away to prevent an attack but close enough for accurate shots. The guy got in the driver's seat of the SUV and put his hands on the steering wheel without being told. The front window was already down, making things easier on the biker. Gun still trained on Blue Jacket, Trouble got a little bit closer, then told the other two they could get in. Slowly.

He watched, swiftly shifting his eyes across all three of them as he made the other two get in the back seat using the driver's side back door. Once they were in, he gave Blue Jacket permission to start up the car. The keys were already in the ignition.

"You're so fucked," Blue Jacket said as he put the vehicle in drive, once again sounding like a white Californian.

"You hit my bike and I'll empty this clip into you," Trouble said, knowing his bike, parked just ahead, would be a tempting target for an asshole such as the one hiding behind the ski mask.

The SUV pulled away from the curb, and Trouble walked with it a few steps, keeping the barrel of the gun pointed at the guy's head. Then, when the back of the cargo area of the SUV was directly across from him, Trouble shifted and fired three quick shots into the panel just below the back window. The vehicle tore off down the road, just as Trouble hoped it would.

Once the taillights had disappeared around the corner, Trouble ran over to the woman and leaned down, putting two fingers on her neck to feel for a pulse. There was one, but it was faint. Her face was so swollen and lacerated that he had a hard time imagining what she looked like before. He knew she was small, Black, and close to death. It looked like her right forearm had been broken — no doubt a defensive wound — and her skull was likely fractured in a couple of different places.

Trouble pulled his phone out with his left hand; he didn't want to set the pistol down. He was about to dial 911 when she moved, turning her head. One glazed eye peered out between two swollen eyelids.

"I'm gonna get you help," Trouble said. "I'm calling an ambulance. Just don't move."

Her eye rolled around, then came back to settle on him. Her lips moved. She was saying something. Trouble leaned down, putting his ear close to her mouth. She spoke one word, twice over. Trouble nodded. "Okay," he said. "But I don't know what that means."

The sound of a revving engine caught Trouble's attention, and he quickly hooked the woman under her arms and dragged her toward the nearby Saturn. Shots rang out just as he pulled her behind the cover of the car. He heard five quick shots, three of which *thunked* as they hit the car. He still had his phone in his left hand, and his pistol in his right. The silver SUV, lights off, kept driving. Trouble stood up and leveled his gun, but he didn't fire. He didn't want to risk a stray bullet hitting one of these houses or a car on the cross street. He watched the SUV disappear around the corner.

He went back and knelt next to the woman, hoping he hadn't made things worse by moving her. He breathed a sigh of relief after checking her for bullet wounds and finding none.

He sat next to her for several long moments, watching the street in case they came back.

The woman's eyes were no longer open. He wondered what she was trying to tell him with that one word. He had no idea.

***

Grab your copy of The Death Dealers now on Amazon to keep reading!

# Also by Matthew Doggett

## The Death Dealers

WHEN HE PREVENTS A murder, one drifter is thrown into a twisted conspiracy that points to the most dangerous gang in Los Angeles.

## Trouble

When Trouble stands up for what's right, he finds himself in the crosshairs of an insane small-town sheriff with one goal: kill Trouble.

# Undead Annihilation (Undead Trilogy Book 1)

A zombie apocalypse. An unspeakable evil. Can one detective team up with a mysterious vampire to save his city from total destruction?

# Undead Assimilation (Undead Trilogy Book 2)

Weller and Diirek unwittingly unravel the mystery of the apocalypse, unearthing a whole new world of monsters while they're at it.

# Undead Extermination (Undead Trilogy Book 3)

In this brutal conclusion to the Undead Trilogy, Weller, Diirek, and a few old friends must go to war with an army of the undead to save the human race from total enslavement.

# About the Author

MATTHEW IS A FREELANCE writer and author. He writes in the thriller, horror, and science fiction genres. He's a regular writer on the SCP Experience podcast and the Dr. NoSleep podcast. His nonfiction writing appears all over the internet. He's currently traveling the globe looking for the next great place to spend a few months. Follow him on social media or visit his website to stay in touch.

https://matthewdoggettauthor.com

https://patreon.com/matthewdoggettauthor

https://www.facebook.com/MatthewDoggettAuthor

https://open.spotify.com/show/3ELCNltCdM1QDCjlS9 WZ6T?si=2be19d1901964e49

https://matthewdoggettauthor.com/trouble

Printed in Great Britain
by Amazon

28805252R00169